FADAR

FADAR

R. Campbell-Butler, CPH CHyp

JANUS PUBLISHING COMPANY
London, England

First published in Great Britain 1995
by Janus Publishing Company
Edinburgh House, 19 Nassau Street
London W1N 7RE

British Library Cataloguing-in-Publication Data.
A catalogue record for this book is available
from the British Library

ISBN 1 85756 173 2

Jacket design Harold King

Printed & bound in England by
Antony Rowe Ltd.,
Chippenham, Wiltshire

The characters and situations in this book
are entirely imaginary and bear no relation
to any real person or actual happening.

Contents

Dedication

To my Mother and Father who gave me life.
To my Wife who gave me encouragement to write this book.
To my children who give me love and pride.
To my grandchildren who have given me a future.

RCB.

In memory Died 15–11–94.

MY MARGO.

Oh ma wee Sister
   that very special spark in my life,
The déjà vu that blended our souls, . . . our souls
Will carry on unchecked by death, or time,
What goes around comes around
In the never ending circle of our lives.
Do not cry, for we will hold each other's hands again
And share once more that bond, . . . that special bond
That is rare amongst the animals called mankind .
You were one of God's brightest rainbows
Whose radiance filled every corner of my mind
An unselfish being with an open giving heart
And all who knew you loved you
As I did always, right from the very start.
Your love will always warm me
And soon chase away this grieving dark.
We will meet again my love, my love
And rekindle once more that bright spark
That was you, . . . my Sister, . . . My MARGO.

YOUR RONNIE.

Meet you in the Um-bra.

Prologue

The year is AD 3052 and the world is in its dying throes. The thick, yellow, polluted air can no longer sustain life as we know it. Apart from a few domed cities, starvation and disease have allowed only grotesque mutants to roam earth's putrid surface. Now those remaining in the protected cities are also in great danger.

In a last desperate bid to save the expiring planet, a scientist, a general, a soldier and a young girl set off on an incredible journey. Drawn mysteriously off course, they find themselves under a long-dead sea where they meet the three-hundred-million-year-old Hydra. As keeper of the world, he alone holds the key to the future, but needs help if he is to complete his great quest on earth.

Here is a compromise that the author found for himself that can also help others to pacify their *id*. The existence of a greater being is not challenged but confirmed. The one step beyond can easily be digested. The other side is closer than you imagine and lays easy on the mind. Beneath this unusual and compelling story lie the great controversial issues of religion and science, faith and non-faith, which the author explores in imaginative and telling detail. Once glimpsed, however, this is a vision of the end of the world that few will be able to forget.

1

The Reasoning

The world was on the brink of madness on this the 20th day of January AD 3052. The planet earth was crying out for a miracle that couldn't happen, for man the living legend had surpassed himself. He had dragged himself from the prehistoric slime through the dark ages into the golden years. He now takes the longest retrograde step of all into almost oblivion. Poor mother earth had yielded all she could; excavated at such a driving rate she had become a ball of useless garbage. Over-populated to its extreme, the atmosphere would have been deadly to a man born 200 years before. They had utilised the seas, both poles, the highest mountain. They had built upwards, downwards into space, the moon colony, a natural tree was a phenomenon. This cannot be allowed to carry on something will have. . . .

Malise gently stroked the retention button on the arm of his favourite chair and his daily paper faded away. He sat for a moment his eyes closed, letting his mind wander, answers, answers, with his experience and insight he should do more, but what the hell. He turned his thoughts to himself, 42-year-old research scientist a doctor of philosophy, of parents English–American, not that nationality mattered any more, they all spoke a common language. He moved his recliner to a steeper angle as if to help him remember. He flicked his eyes open for a second: the room was full of his own bric-à-brac he hated modern plastics. Flicking the light defuser to green he shut his eyes once more. Slowly, very, very slowly she came back to him, he lay quite still feeling her with the depth of his mind. It was still painful for a journey taken a thousand times. She had been so beautiful and so very young: he had been twenty and she eighteen. Ula, she had been his whole life. Her most striking feature had been her eyes, pools of deep brown, her pupils the blue of a beetle's back. Slim and athletic with the sexual appetite of youth her face had been framed with long auburn hair.

The high church had seen fit to bless their marriage, Malise had always had reservations about the church: he had never been convinced it had the ability to solve any problem and very definitely not his. They had spent seven glorious days in the huge underwater leisure centre, making love, eating and drinking wine till their honeymoon was over. He smiled to himself. They had been very contented but . . . very sore. The monoroad was straight and level all the way to their flight point. He had put the car into automatic and they had fallen asleep in each other's arms.

He could still taste the anaesthetic even after twenty-two years, his pelvis had been broken, two fingers of his left hand had been torn off but had been replaced by electro surgery leaving hardly a scar. He never did find his wedding ring and Ula, his lovely vibrant Ula, was dead. He had gone to the morgue to see her. She lay there still and white and so beautiful her flaming hair framing her face. There was not a single mark on her, he had looked at the tag on her toe, cause of death unknown. He remembered sitting by the long metal drawer talking to her as if she was still alive, holding her ice cold hand and willing the life back into her slender figure. That's how they had found him, his broad face awash with tears of grief his throat gasping words of disbelief. They atomized her body after a short service, the Hospital Cleric chanting about a better place and God. At that moment he lost whatever faith he had in the Father, Son and bloody Holy Ghost. He had promised to lose himself in his work and leave religion to others – he had no time for their God. Anything that could kill something as pure and beautiful as Ula and had taken her so young a life away . . . had to be evil, such a love he had thought then could only come once. He had framed the letter from the Monocar Hire Firm to remind him of reality. Sorry to hear from our depot re your accident regret any inconvenience . . . hope you will use us again thirty per cent deducted from your next hiring.

His wrist communicator brought him back to the living the soft voice sounded louder than usual.

'Time 07.55 hours five minutes to work schedule hour, be punctual we are working for the common good.'

He was ready and joined the mêlée of bodies like so many ants all knowing where to go and what to do.

'Malise . . . Malise . . . bloody hell man come alive.' Malise looked around apologetically he had walked past his office he shook his head knowing what was coming.

'All our yesterdays again . . . yeh?' Chesterfield Kincade was of medium height and slight in build. His bright ginger hair was his most outstanding feature, besides his dry wit. They both fought the inner council for more and more material for their projects, Malise knew behind his verbal crap Chez was a true friend who would never let him down.

'Chez, yer froggy crap, double portion.' Malise laughed. Chez bent his head in mock rebuke.

'Only on my mother's side, my father was an American bastard like you.' Another day had started. The outer office was clinically cold but the laboratory was like an Aladdin's cave harbouring every sort of experimental instrument they could beg, borrow or steal. The Holy World Institute was pretty good in their way, the technicians helped all they could but the church always had the last word, to Malise's disgust.

'Drink?' Malise nodded. The so-called coffee was hot but almost tasteless. He had tasted the real thing years ago when he was at school: the whole class had clubbed together to buy a small flask, he had never forgotten the strong bitter taste. Like everything good it had long gone.

'It's no good their expecting too much, there's just too many people and not enough land and clean air. Dr Henderson was saying the other day the earth population outside the domes has been estimated at increasing ten fold in ten years. It's our own bloody fault, what do you expect when you tamper with nature. We should have realised that death at any age was a safety valve for the population but we knew better – the great and mighty human race, idiots!'

3

The communicator bracelet buzzed angrily on Malise's wrist. The small screen burst into life. The bright face of Father Selby smiled at him his white collar stood out against his black cassock.

'Morning Malise.' He looked down at the directive on his tidy desk.

'Chez and yourself are required at the council meeting at eleven, be prompt if you please, and Malise.'

'Yes, Father I'll do my best not to abuse the cardinal, but as I told her at our last encounter, she needs me I don't need her, I'm . . .' The priest coughed loudly.

'Malise please, as a favour to me?' The pleading look on the young priest's face made Malise smile.

'OK, Father, just for you, see you soon.' The screen went blank and he was gone Malise loved to aggravate him. The next few hours flew by as the duo collated the latest figures drawings and photographs. They both knew it was futile. If they didn't make a major breakthrough soon the flood gates would open and there would be wholesale chaos that could never be reversed.

The watery Sun tried its best to penetrate the crystal clear travel tube, the whole complex was like a huge spider. The body sixty miles long with eight legs branching off each ten miles in length they in turn had appendages, housing laboratories and other living quarters. Malise looked down at the fast-moving ground. It was difficult to comprehend that below them was the Australian Simpson desert: it was green as far as the eye could see. It looked cool and lush but he knew better: it was an electro-charged carpet floating one foot above the sea of sand, its purpose to keep man and animal well clear of the complex. The yellow acceptance bar glowed brightly as they entered the main body of the complex and they glided silently to a halt. Although Malise was inherently anti-social, the main building never failed to impress him. The artificial sun beat down on the milling bodies socialising in every crevice, relating their every thought hoping their partner cared enough to listen. Almost every nationality was represented in its sculptures and building design. The centre was dominated by a two-mile square hundreds of shops, entertainment of all kinds and the most beautiful gardens surrounded by decorative walls, grassy fields and flowers of every known variety all artificial of course but they smelt like the real thing.

4

As the evening drew in, the vast astrodome would spew its moon and stars onto the passing crowds. It was indistinguishable from the real thing but it kept one's psyche in relevant contentment. Malise liked the strong feeling of freedom: the sheer size banished the claustrophobia of the laboratory. The height of the ceiling was over 2,000 feet constantly changing in moods and colours, the clouds looked like great sailing ships of yesteryear battling against the angry winds, in this case always winning, unreal but convincing to the eye.

'Malise . . . over here.' They turned and saw the plump figure of Father Selby waving them to their next transport. The journey took just under sixteen minutes, most of it done in silence, young Selby still not sure of Malise, he had been given the task of curbing his tongue and he knew he had little hope. The Central Council building was strangely plain on the outside but the main debating hall was ornate to the ridiculous. The large cross above the president's chair shone dark and rich, every grain reflecting a partial change in shade. The Christ figure hung as if the 3052 years of sin was breaking his back. The representational signs of the major religions were evident around the walls; great wooden benches swung in a half circle showing no favouritism to its members. The presidential office was re-elected every five years. He or she was always a church member, the present office being held by Cardinal Terinda. Her Eminence was a hard, cold woman whose opinions did not match reality. Her skin was black as ebony and clashed with her scarlet robes, her rosary was one of the most beautiful things Malise had ever seen. The stones on her cross were said to have come from the crown of King Solomon, about 500 years ago it would be worth a fortune but money as they knew it no longer existed. The first four benches were filled by senior councillors and mixed church persons. They settled well to the front of the cardinal, all well over a hundred years old, the women looking far the younger. Malise watched the cardinal closely. She showed no sign of emotion, her heavy 160 years sat on her well. Her voice was strong and steady; when she spoke all would listen or be rebuked.

'Councillors we are gathered here today to consider any advice Dr Malise can give us. I am under great pressure from the collective church councils in Rome, I can delay them no longer. May the Lord protect us in all we do.' She lifted her eyes to the great cross before continuing.

'Dr Malise please instruct us on your findings.'

Malise turned and nodded to Chez, who in turn switched on the large video screen, as the lights dimmed it hung translucent like a page waiting to be turned. It was now Malise wished he had faith instead of raw nerve. He looked around the room. 'Dr Kincade and I have exhausted every avenue for a real solution. Our conclusions and our consciences cannot be questioned, church or no church!' Malise stood next to the screen his pointer ready.

'Firstly, let's take the world as it is today. Every square mile is over-populated except the domed areas or complexes, either here, in space or on moonbase. As we are aware we were chosen for our IQ not our sexual ability, the latter being the cause of this problem, and we have extended life beyond all expectations. Over 500 years ago when the mass population exploded we did nothing. We had it all. This was the Utopia the world had waited for. The blacks have the top rating in population numbers. Well just look at ourselves, there is no real white skin left, it's either black or brown.'

Malise looked the cardinal full in the face for any rebuke. He felt sure he saw a slight smile of satisfaction flicker for a micro-second, her eyes were like brown marble. Malise turned back to the screen.

'I don't wish to transgress but we all know the world council in 2054 made it a law that couples have but one child and, if lost for whatever reason, could not be replaced, in other words population control, and it would have worked. Our coloured brothers' revolt followed soon after. The Asian countries were in small states who eventually united. Their unity was for a common cause as soon was to be realised, conquer and spread their race. For the first time since the mad man Adolf Hitler tried to conquer the world for his own Aryan race. Racialism: the antagonism of man against man purely for the colour of his skin, the basic breeding being ignored. Consequently the Caucasians, due to this mass explosion of numbers, became a minority race.'

'In this chamber and indeed in all the protected areas we have multi-racial populations interbreeding but keeping to the law and it works, it works well. I'm not here to justify ourselves. It's the billions upon billions hunting in packs and breeding like flies. Women being violated and left to fend for themselves to bring up mutant children. We have returned to the Dark Ages. The old diseases are back multifold and some we have never experienced before. The surface of the planet is suppurating with human filth, our atmosphere is unbreathable to the normal human.'

'Is there a solution Malise . . . that is why we are here.'

'Those in protected areas with advanced drugs and a recycled air supply in theory have an unlimited life span.' He went on for a further hour answering questions from all over the chamber giving them undisputed facts to digest. He switched off his pointer and neutralised the screen, the silence in the chamber was deafening. He walked within a few feet of the cardinal. Her face was drawn, he had laid the world's agony on her shoulders, he spoke to her softly.

'Your Eminence . . . there is only one answer, just one.'

He looked up at the Christ figure and remembered Ula. 'Mass annihilation of the outside population and a full sterilisation of the planet's surface, there is no other way or eventually we all die, it's in your hands.' She sat for a moment speaking softly to the cross in her hands.

'My people Malise . . . my people.' Her voice was thick with emotion, she looked into Malise's eyes for reassurance; he shook his head and looked away, he could give her nothing.

'Malise, I know I am but a barren island but they have anointed me with their children and their children's children they have planted in me their trust and needs. For I am them and they are me . . . can I abandon them now . . . can I?' An emotion he had not felt for a long time raced through his computer brain and was thrown to his tongue.

'You love more than I hate!' The absurdity of his remark caught him by surprise, she looked away. The chamber rose as young Selby helped the cardinal from the great ornate chair. She stood tall and proud, as she passed, she laid her hand on Malise's shoulder her fingers were long and lean.

'I thank you my son for myself and the council, the decision is not mine to make.' He touched her hand and felt her pain.

2

The Presumption

For two weeks the scientists carried on with their research waiting for a decision, any decision. When it did come they were totally unprepared for it.

'The decision is no, Malise . . . and it will not be revoked.'

The cardinal's voice was low and heavy she looked tired. Malise felt his blood rise he hadn't bargained for this.

'It's crazy your Eminence . . . unless something is done soon we won't have a choice . . . it's bloody suicide . . . crazy!'

'The Church will not condone mass murder, Malise, not now or ever. We cannot kill billions out of hand, not the Church.'

'So what are you all going to do? Kneel and pray for a miracle?' Malise threw a sheet of figures in front of her. 'You can't miracle your way out of that, that is reality.'

The cardinal looked at the figures and shook her head.

'Reality, your Eminence, in just under six months there will be no more air for them to breathe. The poor bastards will die anyway, if you do it my way we might save something.'

'Malise, it's out of my hands, are you sure of your figures?' She looked up into his face and he nodded, she knew he was. She lent forward and passed her hand over the inter-video screen. Young Selby appeared at her command looking very nervous.

'Send in Dr Ashley, Father, and some refreshments . . . now!'

The cardinal rose to greet the young doctor. Malise gave her ten out of ten for impression, she could certainly make an entrance. She was tall and slim with jet black hair, her all in one silver suit accentuated her ample bust. It was her eyes that were her most striking feature, the irises were red. Malise had only seen it once before, she had been an albino. He could contain his curiosity no longer. He looked at the girl.

'Your Eminence, with all due respect . . . Dr Ashley?'

'Please call me Amy, Dr Malise.' She looked like the cat that had just swallowed the cream; he nodded across to her.

'Please call me Dr Malise, all right!' Her smile vanished.

'Well, your Eminence, explanation . . . please?'

The cardinal walked across the room to a large global reproduction of the moon and spun it slowly.

'Moon base Copernicus, 46 miles across surrounded by mountains at least 12,000 feet high . . . really beautiful.'

'Your Eminence, we all know that, we have been there.'

'I do beg your pardon Malise, I was thinking out loud, Dr Ashley has come to us from there . . . this morning.'

'Why?' The irritation was unmistakable in Malise's voice.

'To help Malise . . . to help, be patient.'

'Your Eminence, there is only one way . . . I've told you.'

'No, Malise, there has to be another, at least try, please. Take Dr Ashley to your area and discuss her ideas or at least listen to them, let yourselves out come in here Selby, now.' The journey back was an awkward one, Chez went on like a broken record as he explained the surroundings to the young doctor. She in turn kept glancing over her shoulder at Malise, who remained distant and foreboding. On docking Chez took her to reception where a suite was allocated to her. Malise made straight for the lab, till now an all-male dominated fortress. He didn't like the way things were working out, not at all.

She entered the lab with a self-assurance that sounded an alarm in Malise's head . . . this was no ordinary woman. Chez followed behind, like a lap dog. She sat opposite Malise and opened a large file spreading the papers across his desk and looked him straight in the eye, she was ready, if he wasn't.

'I care, whatever you think, I care, desperately I care. Who the hell wants to live in a dead world. I'm young and want a life, I want to love and be loved not to rot like a decaying vegetable. I am not playing a game, Dr Malise, I think I can help.' She stood up as if to make her point hands on hips. 'My name is Amy Ashley, Amy to my friends . . . *right!*' The atmosphere in the room was electric. Chez coughed and looked away. He had never seen Malise backed into a corner. Malise walked purposely to a large cabinet and brought an ornate decanter to his desktop filled three glasses and handed them round.

'Dr Kincade, may I introduce you to Dr Amy Ashley, Amy to her friends so I am told . . . mind you I could be wrong.' The fusion was made, female laughter had never been heard inside those chauvinistic walls. The day slipped away and the evening was softened by the still flowing brandy.

Chez excused himself with a slurred goodnight, his attempt at the hand identification lock was a near miss. He coughed, stood erect and tried again. The door silently opened and with one last flourish he was gone in both respects.

'Malise, Malise I think it's time.' Her voice was a whisper. He sat for a moment digesting her comment, the smell of her was overpowering. It had been a long time he tried to gather his thoughts. The scientist in him said negative, his memory threw two naked bodies writhing in animal pleasure. The man in him ached deep in his gut . . . he fought to control it.

'Take me home Malise . . . please.' Her hair fell like a black fan across her shoulders. She turned to look at him. The arms of the chair held him like a vice he was going nowhere fast, 'Amy.' He closed his eyes to stop the room's antics. She rose and knelt between his knees, her thumbs stroked his temples softly, her elbows laid lightly in his groin.

'Malise . . . oh Malise, you tried so hard but yours is not the way, believe me tomorrow not tonight . . . tomorrow.' She bent her head and was asleep. The inert figure spun back the years. Her head was laid squarely in his lap, her red eyes half open as if looking at him through contented slits. Her zip had slipped to her belly and there was the strong smell of a woman. His erection was strong, so strong that it slightly lifted her head, he laid back in the large chair and was content. At least he was sure of one thing, he was still sexually alive and the feeling was

10

good . . . so good. The morning crept into the complex with its daily problems especially for Lab 13. Chez woke Malise with a hard shake. His head was laid to one side at an odd angle.

'Christ.' He sat up and looked around 'My bloody head, I feel awful I think I've died, my tongue, yek!' Chez poured what passed for coffee and handed one to Malise. He smiled.

'I don't feel very clever either, what time did Amy leave?' Chez's simple question set up a slight panic in Malise. He was damned if he could remember. In fact the latter part of the evening was a complete blank, he remembered Chez leaving and that was about it. What the hell did he get up to? He threw the remainder of his coffee down the sink.

'I'll be back soon Chez I'm just going for a shave and a shower and a change of clothes wouldn't go amiss.' Amy was there when he returned. He was still shaking, never again.

She looked round and smiled. She asked him if he was all right. he lied and said yes, even though he felt like the pits.

'Are you sure you're all right Malise, you look awful.' She stood looking up into his eyes, he pushed her gently away.

'Amy don't do that, if you really want to know I feel bloody awful . . . satisfied? What about this brilliant idea?'

'Well, if you two physical wrecks sit down I'll go through it.' She spread her papers once more and took to the large blackboard, an antique she was not used to using.

'The chalk is in the drawer.' Malise smiled with an effort.

'Thank you, I think you got this lot from the ark, I would like you to give me a chance to state my case however mad or irrational it may be . . . fair?' The two men nodded.

'I was stationed on Moonbase Copernicus for two years as a pathologist, interesting work. As it was I found myself with time on my hands. I loved to spend my free time outside the base. The silence is unbelievable, I used to make my way towards Bulliadus, the crater next to Copernicus. The first few times out I really didn't notice anything. As you know our planet, even as it is now, looks beautiful from Luna. I never tired of watching it just hang there in space. I used to get so homesick and tired of looking at the same old faces day after day. In answer to your question Malise, no, I didn't, my love life was quite dormant . . . satisfied?' Malise was visibly embarrassed.

'I didn't say a word.' He looked at Chez for confirmation.

'Think about it, Malise, please don't feel uncomfortable. I should have told you I am a psychic and a telepath.' Malise stood up and pushed the chair across the room. He spun on his heels his face dark with anger.

'You are all we need, you've come to save the world with thought transference, holy shit I don't believe this, *wow!*' She didn't bat an eyelid she waited for him to calm down.

'Malise, you said you would listen to me, I insist on being heard, or don't you ever keep your word?'

'It's crap Amy, one hundred per cent crap, you can't expect us to swallow this.' Now she was angry, her eyes were pulsing red danger signals, she had cornered him again and he certainly didn't like it.

'What's the matter Malise is it me . . . or your guilty conscience, you asked the question . . . *yes?*'

He replaced his chair and smiled wryly his temper had gone. 'Go on Amy . . . you really did catch me off guard, sorry.'

She nodded her appreciation but still made her point. 'The gifts that I have I was born with, but my doctor's degree I had to work for and work bloody hard. I am good at what I do . . . truce?' He lifted his hands in mock surrender.

'Anyway, it was on my third or fourth time out on my last month that I felt a presence, only slightly at first, then stronger every time I left the base. The lunar silence is like nothing else I have ever experienced, that particular night I felt it calling and I knew just where to stop. I got out of the buggy and I knew I had to kneel in the dust not just anywhere but a certain spot, the feeling of urgency was overpowering. I shut my eyes and laid my mind open to whatever it was, the first time it wasn't clear, then it got louder in my mind, Omega Fadar, Omega Fadar, Omega Fadar. I sat in the dust for three hours and heard the same thing over and over again. It didn't take me long to work it out: Omega is Greek for the end; Fadar is ancient Maya for father so combined, 'The End Father', it was being repeated over and over again and coming from our planet. I got moonbase to try and pick it up but nothing. I could hear it plainly but for them nothing, it's on no known frequency.' She put down the chalk and sat on the edge of the bench.

'Well what do you think?' Chez threw in a feeble smile and interestingly, he shuffled his feet in appreciation.

'Malise what about you . . . anything?' He shrugged.

'Amy, what do you really expect us to say, be fair, this is right out of the blue. You tell us what you want to do, I'm willing to try anything, it's got to be better than nothing.'

'Right then.' She had the bit between her teeth she had their curiosity if not their faith, that was something.

'I think we should try and find the source, if it's not a radio beacon what the hell is it, there is a powerful energy somewhere sending out that signal, let's find it.'

'I agree with you, Amy, it's certainly strange, very strange.' Malise sat for a moment digesting the facts on the blackboard scant as they may be.

'Is it possible for a concentrated thought to travel quarter a million miles and obviously beyond?' Malise tried to keep any doubt from his mind.

'I was thinking the same thing.' Chez wasn't so lucky. 'Because it isn't laid down in black and white it can't work, is that it Chez? Thought transference and the occult have been in evidence for thousands of years. If mankind had taken another genetic avenue we probably wouldn't have vocal chords at all. We only use a third of our brain, and some of us not that, do they Chez?' The abrasive remark sliced through the already tense atmosphere, Malise broke the pregnant silence that followed.

'Right let's open your Pandora's box Amy, can you honestly believe that all you have told us is possible?'

'Yes, and another thing . . .' He stopped her short.

'Please, Amy, just answer my questions . . . please.' He seated her down gently.

'Have you ever come across this sort of thing before?'

'Yes . . . well, not so strong, or over such a large distance.'

Malise walked up and down the lab keeping his questions short and to the point.

13

'In your opinion is it human, from a human source I mean?'

'Yes . . . I think.' He cut her short again.

'You think, marvellous . . . bloody marvellous, don't you know?' Amy's voice snatched back its confidence.

'Yes, I'm sure, because of the tone of the voice, the feeling it was a plea for help not a statement of fact.'

'Finally, do you know where the signal or whatever you like to call it, came from?' Malise's voice had a tone of tired tolerance. Amy looked at the floor before answering.

'Yes . . . yes, I do.' She saw the doubt on both their faces.

'Amy?'

'Malise, I do possibly, not the exact spot but the general area. I made a grid just enough to cover the globe. I spent hours concentrating on each square till I traced the strongest signal. It took a long time and a lot of patience. I tracked it down to the North Temperate Zone. As you know the earth's atmosphere is all but destroyed, you can't see the surface from that distance any more.' Malise was still not quite convinced although now deeply interested: if she had found the source she had one hell of a gift.

'You're telling me you scanned 197 million square miles of a planet and came up with an believable answer purely by using thought transfer and reception . . . amazing, quite amazing.'

She smiled and allowed his admiration to flow over her. 'Remember, Malise, two-thirds of the surface is water.'

'Is the North Temperate Zone as near as you can get, that's still a hell of a lot of land to cover.' Malise switched on the video screen. The schematic diagram of the earth seemed to hang in mid-air, a perfect hologram. Amy thought for a moment and stuck her neck out with an educated guess.

'I think we would be looking for latitude between thirty to thirty-five degrees north, longitude approximately thirty to forty degrees west.' Malise followed her instructions.

'That's approximately between the Azores and Turkey.' He turned back to the screen and juggled some new figures.

'That's about 9,000 kilometres from where we are now. If your figures are even close it will be a miracle. And you worked that out

14

from a quarter of a million miles away . . . Jesus.' Malise was convinced she had a hell of a brain . . . and body.

'Let me check one thing, Amy, was Omega Fadar the full extent of the message you heard, anything no matter how small?'

She looked through her notes that had scattered themselves from the desk to the floor. She picked up a crumpled piece of paper and straightened it out.

'There's this, but I only heard it once; the word is Kypros. It means copper. To be honest I am not all convinced I heard it, I was very tired at the time . . . but it could have been.'

'Hmmmm, it doesn't mean anything to me. Chez make me an appointment with the cardinal for tomorrow morning, leave the answer on my videophone, I'll catch it later. Right, young lady, you and I are going to the main complex for dinner. It's five now and we haven't had a meal all day. I'll meet you at eight; by then I might be half civilised, or at least in a better temper . . . OK?' She cleared the desk and smiled.

'Yeh . . . fine.' As he disappeared through the maze of corridors, she realised how hungry she really was.

The time for the meeting came and went. She was her beautiful self, the journey to the main complex seemed to take seconds, whittled away by small talk. Malise had reserved a private booth at the Black Scorpion, his favourite restaurant. The cuisine was excellent, the surroundings luxurious to the extreme. He always had that nagging guilt at the back of his mind; there were starving billions out there, except for pure luck he could have been one of them . . . god forbid.

Amy slid her long slender hands across the table and encased his large knuckles. He could feel the warmth of her seeping through his skin.

'We are trying hard to help them Malise.' He pulled his hands away. Involuntarily his voice had a tint of anger.

'I wish you would stop that . . . keep out of my mind.' She threw her head back and laughed, deep and throaty which aggravated the situation even more.

'Sorry . . . I really am . . . forgive me . . . please?' She really was a beautiful creature. Her dress was a glistening pink with dark red garnets that matched her extraordinary eyes, her skin was faultless cream, he

15

knew one thing for sure, she had one hell of a disturbing effect on his system.

'Can you read a mind, I mean any mind, whenever you want to?'

'No not always, it really depends on the person.'

'I don't understand.' She retook his hands in hers.

'It's the brain pattern, Malise, when you feel something strong enough like love, hate, suspicion, desire anything that will cause your adrenalin to flow. Your brain is like a radio transmitter. People like me have the ability to receive. It's actually not that uncommon, it's just that most people don't take any notice. I have honed my gift to a razor sharp edge. By the way, human sex drive gives off the highest signal of all.' Malise smiled; he felt his colour rise slowly.

'You must be nearly deafened most of the time.' She bowed her head in mock embarrassment but her sparkling eyes flashed a challenge – there was no embarrassment there, none.

'Thank you, sir, she said . . . it doesn't really work that way I have to concentrate on the subject. The signal on the moon was so strong it eventually filled my mind, that's why I hesitated when you asked me if it was human.'

The dinner came and went, the wine sweet and strong, Malise plied her with a thousand questions which she answered with patience. She had never been married, which he found very hard to believe. She had had a relationship for a short while but he had been killed on the outside, his whole expedition had been wiped out. The hovership had reported that they had literally been torn to pieces and eaten as they were non-diseased.

'What about you, Malise, what I know of you is you're a loner, an atheist, you have been married but your wife was killed. Why do you insist on Malise . . . you must have another name?'

He lent forward and drew her to him; she was soft and yielding, her young hard breasts pushed urgently against the back of his hands with open pleasure, she smelt unbelievable.

'Amy I know this must sound so corny but would you mind if we went back. I've got plenty of drink at my place . . . and we could talk. I'm not really a public person, do you mind?' He adjusted the light defuser to a gentle pink. Her eyes haunted him they changed with the shadows. The logs on the video fire looked real as they sent their flickers to every corner of the room, as if searching for some hidden secret. He swallowed his large brandy as his door warner sounded, Amy's voice slid gently through the com.

'Special delivery . . . this offer is unrepeatable, collect now.' He smiled and hid his brandy glass empty but for the stem behind a large pile of books. It had warmed him well. She glided into his apartment and settled herself on a large white rug, her eyes were wide and contented. She stretched her long legs as if to claim her territory for the remainder of the evening. Malise felt the heat rise in him.

'Drink?' He wasn't quite sure if her robe was wearing her or she it, whichever it was, there wasn't a great deal of it.

'Thank you, you promised Malise, you're not getting out of it.'

'What?' His forehead creased in remembrance, the brandy and the wine plus the night before were really getting to him. He hoped to god he wasn't going to make a fool of himself.

'Your proper name.' She lent forward the large brandy glass warming in her hands. Malise tried hard to focus. He settled himself next to her. He had never felt so relaxed for years – maybe too relaxed. He felt his barriers slip away, he couldn't bring himself to look her in the eye . . . not yet.

'It goes back a long way Amy.' He looked into the soothing flickering fire trying to winkle out the dulled memories he had tried so hard to forget. Did he really want the pain to return again? His deep intake of breath and deep sigh was his sign of unconditional surrender.

'I have been hurt twice in my life. The second time was Ula, my wife. Her death killed what little faith I had left. The first time was thirty years ago. They were just finishing this complex at the time. My father was a construction engineer. He had built it from the ground up and was guaranteed a place in the complex as were his family, that was my mother and I. She was such a tiny person Amy, she was beautiful, that kind of inner beauty that some people have. She never complained . . . never.' He held out his large hand and let the flickering flames run through his fingers the glaze of remembrance cloaked his eyes.

'You know I never saw her without a smile . . . not once isn't that

17

amazing.' His throat was getting thick and sore. 'Dad was like me, tall and broad. I remember he used to look at me and say, we're built like brick shit houses boy, only the Lord can knock us down. Big as he was he was full of love and a devout Christian. So they called me Simeon Malise which means obedient servant of the God which I was for twelve years of my life. The complex was finished. 10,000 were chosen to stay, allowing for a further 10,000, this would be eventually taken up over a long period by births. Medicals were called for, it was mandatory, that beautiful tiny uncomplaining angel was riddled with cancer, she must have been in agony for years and never said a word. She had shielded her torture with a smile, she knew what the complex meant to my father and the future it held for me. They wouldn't allow her to stay, sorry this is the future of mankind you have to be one hundred per cent. The doctor had held her tiny hands in his and told her that she was the complex, that she was the very courage it took to build it but he was sorry she had to go, would she forgive him. My father explained it all to me the night they sealed the complex, his large hands gently stroked my wet cheeks. You are our future son, remember what I told you about the Lord, there's only one left to blow down, make him work for it, son. She had looked up into his eyes with such gratitude. She kissed me as only a mother can and was gone. I watched them go down the ramp to the sand trackers with hundreds of others. They waved to me as the electro carpet started to creep towards them making a return to the complex quite impossible. I saw them mouth a 'God bless you" over and over again. Then I saw my mother encircle their hands with her rosary. They shouted and waved to me once more, father bent and kissed her then they both walked into the electro carpet, their loss of life was indicated by two small sparks.' Amy cradled his sobbing head to help the pain escape.

'I'll be nobody's servant ever again, Simeon can go to hell.'

18

3

General Aaron Zerta

'I don't agree. What you are considering is suicide, you know nothing of the outside.' The angry voice belonged to General Zerta, overall chief of security, all military personnel came under his command. His purple uniform was festooned with decorations. He was tall and slim his premature greying hair made him look older than he was. Well known for his bravery, he had made more contact with the outsiders than any man alive. His disregard for the church was almost treasonable. Malise liked him.

'Malise.'

'General.' The general turned to the cardinal.

'I take it I have the floor.' She nodded there was little or no love lost between them. She looked tired and older than Malise had ever seen her.

'Only got your report two days ago Malise. It is extreme to say the least but practical. It is the only long-term solution to protect the people. As you remarked at the time, I believe it's only a matter of time before the poor bastards die anyway, I wouldn't leave an animal to die in those conditions.' He directed his comment to the church benches.

'The outside world is finished through lack of nutritious food and clean air. There is disease upon disease; we have harvested a population of mutants. There are parts of the world in which they in no way resemble human beings. Morality is a long forgotten word. Years ago I used to go amongst these forgotten people, they got to know me and trust me to a degree. I used to try and give them messages of hope but no more. There is no way we can help them . . . none.' He pressed a sensor on his metallic left wrist. His whole left hand was made up of brightly shining metal, he had lost his hand in a skirmish patrol on the outside years before. No one really knew the whole story, like him it had become part of his legend. He systematically flicked through a calendar of moving slides taken all over the world. Most of the hideous reproductions held little resemblance to safe people.

What flesh that was left hung in loose folds that in turn was covered with suppurating scabs; there was no evidence of hair. One family had waved to the camera, their rotting teeth a black message to the world. The child, a twisted dwarf with a large lopsided head, had no indication of eyes. His bleeding mouth searched for the yellow nipples of his mother's breast, she had nothing to give but her own pain.

'Bloody hell.' Malise's outburst was uncontrolled as he turned his eyes from the screen, his disgust was evident. 'How long would that poor little bastard live for?' As a reply the general threw another slide to the screen. It was a large pit that was crawling with some sort of life form. Amy had moved closer to Malise and was clutching his hand. He could feel her nails piercing his skin, she heard herself speak her thoughts. What the hell is that? Her stomach heaved inside her, she could almost smell the decay. The general turned with a cynical smile.

'You ask how long the children of these creatures live for, a day, a week, a month, that is all they are living for now. That's a pit about twenty-five metres deep by about forty metres wide, where they throw their dead, the movement,' he shrugged his shoulders, 'the not quite dead. Gas builds up, millions of maggots trying to fight their way to the top.' He turned to face the cardinal, his face was hard.

'Eminence, that may give you some idea of life outside, there is not a hope in hell of saving those poor bastards, they must, not maybe, they must be destroyed . . . now!' The cardinal smashed her frail hand down on the ornate ancient Bible, her eyes flashed with hatred and frustration.

'My and the Church's word is still and will be . . . NO!'

General Zerta took three paces backwards and pointed to the painful figure of Jesus. 'If you believe your mumbo jumbo, his father had the

20

right idea and dealt with it as he saw it, no ifs no buts. Genesis, the earth was corrupt in God's sight and filled with violence and despair. He sent rain for forty days and forty nights, and water prevailed upon the earth for one hundred and fifty days. Killing all that had offended him but saving a handful of seed to start again, for man was made in his image. So what makes now any different, the situation is exactly the same. Or is it that you and your bloody church are too frightened to take the role of God?'

The chamber wrapped itself in electrifying silence, the cardinal slowly lifted her head and expounded her deliberation.

'You surprise me, General, on your knowledge of the Bible but I have the feeling that you read only the passages that were conducive to your theory. I am sure I am right. If you had read on, Genesis once more. The Lord, said I will never again curse the ground because of man. For the imagination of man's heart is evil from his youth, neither will I ever again destroy every living creature.' The general bent his head in mock reverence aggravating the cardinal further.

'Touché your Eminence . . . you are a worthy opponent indeed. Malise, help me off with this junk yard.' His metal arm split the well tailored sleeve. 'Shit!' The general's face went red with exasperation. 'Here take this.' He threw his tunic at the cardinal's feet. She lifted her hand slightly. Young Selby appeared and removed the offending garment. The cardinal was utterly confused by the seemingly violent outburst. The security guards drew their lasers and all but one pointed their weapons at the cardinal.

'No!' The general's voice cracked like a whip.

'Holster your arms . . . now.' The young guard still knelt at the foot of the cardinal's chair with his weapon pointing at the general, his forefinger taking up the first pressure on the trigger. Malise had never witnessed such cold courage. The general crouched down in front of the young trooper allowing the muzzle of the weapon to brush his shirt. There was no trace of fear, only bewilderment. He spoke quietly to him.

'I'm your general, boy, what's your name . . . come on.'

'Campbell, sir.' The general looked down at the laser levelled at his chest.

21

'Why then Campbell?' His voice was soft but deliberate. 'Talk boy don't be afraid, we're both men both soldiers.'

'Firstly, sir, I am not afraid, you are my general but she represents my God.' The general shook his head and stood up as if the weapon did not exist. He smiled at Campbell.

'All right, boy, you have made your point. Eminence, you have a follower.' The tension was broken, the relief was felt all round the chamber. The cardinal cleared her throat and pointed to the general's tunic to make her point.

'General, I am purely an intermediary. I have no power except faith, I am like your tunic, a shining pseud given for the services rendered.' The general knew she was right.

'Quite, your Eminence, that is the point I was trying to make. It is not time for medals or even faith, it is time for action.' He turned back to Amy and Malise.

'I am probably the only man alive that can take you among the outsiders and, most important, bring you back. I put myself at your disposal.' He looked over his shoulder at the young trooper.

'And young Campbell here, you're coming with us, I want you where I can see you . . . right Campbell.' The young guard's face remained impassive but his self assurance and arrogance shone like a lamp. 'Aye sir.' Was the only indication of acknowledgement.

The general smiled and whispered to Malise. 'That young bastard reminds me so much of myself when I was his age, he's in for some pain, sure as hell he is.'

The week that followed was the most physically exhausting Malise had ever endured. The general had almost gutted the search ship, having it refitted to his own specifications. All Malise could get as a reply was 'You'll see, just fit them properly and learn to use them and I mean use them all.' He had attached a transparent blip to the belly of the craft so Amy could be well away from any electrical interference. She lay there for hours at a time meditating or learning to use the directional and communication system. Chez was his usual self and when told he would have to stay behind he made no complaint. Young Campbell worked around the clock with his general as he called him, he was never directly disobedient or insubordinate but he always had a droll answer. Out of earshot the general called him his Scots terrier because he would not back down from any task he gave him. It was zero minus fourteen hours and thirty-five minutes to departure time. Amy and Malise stood looking at the gleaming ship that was to take them to god knows where or what. It was a cold, awesome sight Amy shivered with anticipation rather than lack of warmth. Malise pulled her closer, she responded and tried to melt herself into his contours, giving a long and heavy sigh.

'What's the matter, Amy cold feet, you started this.'

'No I haven't got cold feet exactly.'

'What then?' He looked down at her pale face. Her high cheekbones seemed to cast shadows under her eyes, she looked tired and very vulnerable.

'Would you say there's a chance we might not come back from this, a chance no matter how small . . . truth?'

'Yes . . . but.' She stood on her toes and kissed him hard.

'You are frightened.' He stroked her long black hair, it shone reflecting the hangar lights. Her groin pressed hard against the outside of his leg. He could feel her body trembling, her large red eyes were moist and searching.

'Oh, Malise we've only just found each other . . . I don't want to lose you.' She wrenched herself from his grasp and clung to him, her strength was such his ribs ached, she buried her face in his chest.

'Malise, can you hear me?' Her voice was coming in low deep sobs.

'Make love to me . . . now, tonight, so we have something to remember . . . please!' He bent and picked her up, her arms encircled his neck. He felt the wetness of her tears run down his neck. He turned his head and whispered through her hair. 'Your place this time?' She nodded her consent.

She lay naked and inviting, the air in the room was rich in perfume, the lights defused and the music low. The water bed vibrated gently causing small ripples under the red satin sheet. His impatient arms encircled her body – it was firm and lithe. The tips of her breasts stood hard and proud willing his mouth to engulf them. His tongue ran from her knee to the flat of her belly, pausing for a brief moment to drink from her womanhood. Her back arched in spontaneous delight, her throat growling a further invitation that was readily accepted. The flood

23

gates of conformity were smashed aside by animal wanting. She rode him like a great stallion but knowing just when to stop, she withdrew allowing the tide to subside before a further onslaught of fire. They changed places over and over again. They were like two young wrestlers each enjoying the other's move. Her taut smooth bottom pushing, always pushing, her fingers coaxing and ensuring perfect entrance. She lay on her back, her arms flung wide in ultimate submission, her straining legs wide apart. He sat astride her, his penis lay throbbing in the valley between her hard breasts. They both glistened with pearls of sweat that poured from their tiring bodies and lubricated the folds. He bent and kissed her, her tongue engulfed his teeth darting with the speed of passion. Her eyes opened wide clashing with their full redness, she threw her head back and sobbed her words of want.

'Now Malise . . . NOW!' She pushed hard on his hips half guiding half forcing him into place. His penis slid wetly down her belly she thrust him into her, her whole body was quivering. As their climax erupted, their bodies stiffened to catch every atom of pleasure. The adrenaline had met its match, the two spent bodies entangled themselves in sleep, as always Morpheus had won the battle of the night.

Malise and Amy made their way to the departure area, the greyness of the morning did little to cheer the situation. They huddled together for warmth, their limbs consciously touching, trying not to lose the memories of the night. The rotating light around the ship made shadows dance on the hangar walls.

'Looks as if we are the first to arrive!' Malise's questionable conclusion was thrown to the darkness.

'I'm afraid not, sir.' Young Campbell appeared out of the shadows that hugged the belly of the ship, his laser was resting in the crook of his arm.

'Sorry if I startled you, sir.' His eyes were cold but alert. Malise had seen that expression before somewhere.

'We don't have to be formal Campbell, I'm Malise. For my own reasons it would take too long to explain, this is Amy, we will be locked in that ship for god knows how long so formality would be pointless.' The young Scot seemed to relax slightly. He holstered his laser and pushed back his cap. 'Thanks for your concern Malise, Amy, but if you

24

don't mind Campbell will be near enough, for MY own reasons. Let's check the ship before the general arrives.' They checked and rechecked for over an hour. They were so absorbed that the two men failed to notice the arrival of the general. The intercom burst into life. Amy's voice from the blip sounded slightly distorted, Campbell adjusted the damping.

'Say again Amy . . . repeat Amy please.' The crackle died away her voice came through crisp and clear.

'The general has arrived with his entourage . . . have a look.' The transporter spewed its cargo onto the hangar floor, the general's white flight suit stood apart from the dowdy habits of the clergy. The cardinal's long black cape made her almost invisible in the dim lights of the hangar. The general had insisted the crew wore different coloured flight suits, Malise blue, Amy red, Campbell black at his own request. As he said it would be much easier to recognize each other in an emergency. The lasers had very fine triggers, a mistake in identification could be fatal. All three men could fly the machine and Amy said she could if she had to as it was very similar to the ones she had used on moonbase. She just hoped she would never be put to the test. They watched through the blip as the general made his parting promises. The cardinal majestically had her cape removed, her red vestments were caught by the rotating lights. She stood with her head high and blessed the ship and its crew. It was obvious the general was not impressed, the outer hatch hissed closed with a resolute clang. The look on the general's face indicated it was to keep the clergy out and them in, his gruff voice filtered through the control room.

'Thank god for that . . . Campbell?'

'General.'

'Put this hunk of junk into phase one, don't wait for them to get clear.' Campbell's proficient hands darted among the controls, the general's remark had brought a rare smile to his lips. The engines started their slowly climbing whine.

'Phase one in sink, sir, ship ready for take off, sir!'

The party below scattered and made an undignified retreat to the transporters. Only the cardinal remained as she was looking upwards, daring the general to destroy her.

25

'You've got to admire the bitch!' the general's remark was not for his crew, he and she had quiet admiration.

'Hold her there, Campbell, steady.' The anti-gravity motors held their low growl, the cardinal turned on her heel and was gone, the large steel doors clanged behind her.

'All round surveillance, negative resistance, activate both hangar air-locks.' The large iris smoothly opened its fans. The polluted air came rolling in like a yellow mist.

'Phase two, lift ninety degrees, forward slowly.' The ship hovered for a moment then slipped into the pollution that was man. Amy watched the complex cover its face with the yellow mist. She was still bemused at the speed at which everything had happened. She could shut her eyes and see the snug quarters that had been hers on moonbase. The earth had looked so different from there, gone was the beautiful blue that it once was but the yellow planet looked very much alive. The heavens with their eternal backcloth studded with billions upon billions of blinking stars and planets seemed to look on at the stupidity that was man, knowing it had all been done before and probably would be again.

'Who wants to see the sun, clearly that is, without this muck?' The general's question hung in the air, it sounded like a father's promise to a child. They each had their own momentary vision of it as it should be. The agreement was unanimous. The computer was fed, the ship angled and increased speed. The great Australian continent shrank beneath them, possibly for the last time.

The search craft was built for stability rather than speed. Amy lay in her clear cradle listening to the cross references of the crew.

'Phase three engaged electro testing airlocks and pressure points. Height six miles and passing through troposphere, holding flight angle, speed mark one.' Malise's voice gave Amy warmth, she drove her hands deep into her pockets and felt the pulsing of her body, she rubbed the flatness of her belly and wanted him close.

'Height thirty miles and climbing, stratosphere entered, it should be a smoother ride now we have left the convection behind, what's it like outside Amy?' Her voice was strained.

'It's getting brighter now the mist is thinning.' She re-angled her couch so that she was lying on her back.

'It's thinning fast now . . . it's gone . . . my god, it's gone.'

There was a pregnant silence. 'Look at that sun!' Amy's voice held an awe that radiated throughout the ship.

'Level off, stabilise at sixty miles, reduce speed, changing to auto pilot . . . now.' The general's voice was just audible. The sun's rays flooded the control room, all lights were extinguished to get the full effect. The ports seemed to be on fire. They stayed in the sunlight for nearly an hour as they allowed the sun to play on their bodies. They retreated into their own private thoughts, the general most of all.

His memories shed the years to his newly appointed captaincy. He had worked damn hard for it, he hadn't taken a leave for two years, but now was the time. He was to spend his two weeks at the underwater holiday resort dug deep into the North Sea just off the most northerly tip of Scotland. Twenty-five years ago, he smiled to himself, where the hell does the time go, how many times had he said that to himself. He could still see her face, he had always thought it odd that it had never faded. In fact, it seemed to come back to him more and more just of late. They had bumped into each other in the large restaurant. The walls and ceilings were transparent and there were hundreds of specially bred fish swimming everywhere even in the table tops. He remembered it was such an odd feeling, it was as if you were in a goldfish bowl. The instant attraction had put him off at first, he was forty and never had the time for women. His career had been all he had needed, till then. They met, fell in love and loved like an intense flame – the more it was fed, the hotter it burned. She was fifteen years his junior. They spent two weeks blissfully happy giving themselves to each other with no reservations. The day before his leave ended he presented her with twin gold pendants, one for her, the other for him, promising like all lovers never to remove them, he never had. They planned to meet the following day to go to the complex on the mainland to meet her parents. He never saw her again. That night he was escorted under guard back to complex five. From there straight to moonbase with no explanation. There he spent three long years. As hard as he had tried over the years, he could find no trace of her, it was as if she had never existed. He unconsciously rubbed the pendant – she had been real enough to him.

'General . . . general . . . are you all right?' He looked up to find

27

Malise shaking him. His concerned tone broke him free from his aching memories.

'Yes, fine, just relaxing and enjoying the sun, it's been a long time.' He stretched, breathing deeply to express the stale air from his lungs, it was time to make a move.

'Right, let's get out of this orbit and try our luck below, secure all stations, may make sure you're comfortable before we descend. Where exactly are we, Malise, do you know?'

'We've drifted quite a way, I'll have the exact position in a moment, I don't quite understand this.' The cabin was alive with memory banks selecting their own colours, dancing to the tune of intelligence, the darting asking fingers were unyielding in their questions, but blindly accepting the answers out of hand as was man. The machine was invincible because man's knowledge had told it so. The sunlight slipped away as the ship descended, the yellow haze quickly returned.

'That's it, level off at thirty thousand. Campbell, take the first watch, wake Malise in two hours then me there's a good way to go yet. Amy, get some sleep you'll have enough to do later.' Time passed slowly as they approached what they estimated was the Azores. Going to the first sweep, their nerves were taut with anticipation. They started their criss-cross search pattern 500 kilometres west of Lisbon, bringing the ship down to fifteen thousand feet. Amy concentrated with every fibre of her being but could feel nothing or hear anything. The very monotony of the task planted a seed of doubt. Had all this been born due to her psychic experiences? Had she really heard anything at all. She was tireder than she had ever known. She felt virtually numb but for a tingling sensation that ran through her body and her scalp felt as if it was on fire. She felt detached from the small craft as if in astral projection, Malise's voice seemed to be coming from a long way off. There was also a deeper voice a calm voice telling her not to be afraid all would be well . . . just relax.

'Amy, for god's sake . . . Amy!' The three men knelt looking at the blip in total bewilderment. Malise was shouting at the top of his voice trying to make Amy respond. She was floating about two feet above her well padded couch, cocooned in a white glittering cloud, the strands of her hair pointing in all directions emitting spasmodic flashes.

'We're going down . . . look.' Campbell's voice held a tone of disbelief. They were indeed going down although all controls were normal. The general shouted to the men to get back to the controls and increase power output. The impulse engines screamed at full power but still the ship kept falling. Nothing they did would make her recover.

'We're going into the drink, General, we're miles from the nearest land. What a lousy bloody end, shit.' Malise had just time to get a glimpse of Amy before the Atlantic ocean swallowed them sucking them down to its lowest depth, the small craft sank like a stone. The general looked at Malise. They both knew the craft would never stand the pressure of the deep ocean. As Malise said, what a bloody way to go.

4

In the Beginning

The ship came to a sudden halt and stood on an even keel. The cabin was flooded with a warm bright light. Malise unclipped Amy and laid her head gently on his lap. The general and young Campbell were coming round, he hadn't passed out like the others. The craft had taken about ten minutes to come to rest. Half-way down the light had appeared and got brighter the deeper they descended.

'What's that noise . . . listen?' The general raised his hand in command, the silence was broken by a steady humming. The surprised look on Campbell's face in another situation would have been laughable.

'It's the engines, they're still running, I don't believe it.'

'They can't be!' Malise spun round to the consol. The computer ran a service check. They all looked on unable to believe their eyes.

'All systems A1, General, no structural or mechanical damage at all, we're still functioning perfectly, don't ask me!'

'It's impossible, Malise, we're thousands of feet below the Atlantic Ocean . . . it's just not possible.'

'Look at this.' Amy's voice was high with excitement.

'We're on dry land and the Sun, there's no yellow fog the air is crystal clear . . . I'm opening the hatch.' Before Malise could stop her the loud hiss of the hydraulics vented themselves to the outside atmosphere. The fresh clear air filled the cabin, the ozone from the ocean played on their nostrils. Her unsteady voice spoke for all of them.

'Where the hell are we for Christ's sake?'

'Cut the engines, Malise, and we'll have a look.' The general pressed the extension gantry and was first to set foot on the gleaming white sand. After a preliminary check on the outside of the craft the general split them into two parties to meet back at the ship in one hour. Each took a flare to mark their positions in case of trouble, the wrist communicators had a range of about ten miles, fifteen at a stretch, he doubted if they would need the distance.

Malise and Amy followed the shore line. The animals and the sea life were amazingly tame. Amy held out her hand and two sulphur-crested cockatoos landed and ran up her arm rubbing their heads on her neck and cheek.

'Am I dead Malise . . . or dreaming? Is this a page from Genesis, are you Adam and I Eve? This is crazy we fall into the Atlantic Ocean and find this.' Malise held her tight. The strange feeling was unbelievable, if this indeed was death why had he waited so long in joining it.

'You are not dead, you are hallucinating due to rich oxygen mixture . . . it will be compensated, you are in no danger, I repeat you are in no danger!'

Malise and Amy never heard a word, their flight suits lay as they fell on the sand, their naked bodies thrashed like children in the clear blue sea. Shoals of fish clung to their legs as if trying to communicate, two dolphins were their constant companions, nearly following them onto the beach, their sonic chatter almost deafening. They lay a long time absorbing the warm rays that filtered down from above. They felt very much alive, enjoying each other's body. Their racking chests deflating to normal pattern as the atmospheric mixture adjusted to their needs. They dressed and made their way inland. The incredible beauty unfolded before them, the island or whatever it was, seemed to be built in steps and there were millions upon millions of plants and trees of every kind. They all seemed to be in miniature, grown to a predetermined size then arrested, everything looked as if it was waiting for further orders, as if suspended in time for some reason. The narrow path zigzagged up the steep incline unfolding the land below them, the rich colours looking like a large prism. The colours not blending but kept deliberately apart,

31

man's hand had had to be in this somewhere, this was beyond nature's capability.

Amy kept moving her head from side to side as if looking for something she knew should be there, something was missing but she didn't know what. The central steps they found were cut deep into the side of whatever they were climbing, the top was still out of view. The higher they ascended the more beautiful became the carpet laid out before them. The intermingling smells of the millions of plants made the air heavy, their nostrils flaring in open acceptance, this was real . . . or were they dreaming?

Amy seemed determined to reach the plateau that towered above them first, she was on all fours clawing at the smooth steps in a fit of desperation. He had never seen her like this. She was at least twenty feet above him, her back black with sweat from her labours. She was almost frantic in her efforts as the muscles in her buttocks rippled as if trying to break free from the wet encumbrance of her flight suit. He stood for a moment watching her youthful enthusiasm generated by god knows what. He called her several times but her inner drive ignored all, it kept her going till she cleared the top and was gone from his sight. Malise laughed aloud. He wasn't in that much of a hurry. He sat down and rested twenty-five steps from the top. He recounted his trodden way sixty-six, plus twenty-five, ninety-one in all. An odd number like the situation they found themselves in, yet a number that stirred in the back of his brain shouting to be remembered. Where would they or indeed how would they go from here? He sat and looked at the scene below. The pure white sand edged the clearest blue sea he had ever seen, the shoals of swimming creatures seemed to be on top of the water rather than below. He stood in utter surprise, his voice high with disbelief at the sight that caught his eye.

'My god it's from the history computers.' He felt his mind succumb to the scene as if it was a natural sight. The beauty of a large Spanish galleon lying on her side, shimmering through the water. Even her sails were still intact; he could see them clearly moving gently to match the underwater currents. Her cannons still breaching her gun ports as if in anticipation of a surprise. His eyes moved across the bay to yet another shape which also lay on its side. He couldn't make it out clearly at first as a large shoal of fish hazed the outline. He sat for a moment mentally urging them on. They seemed incommunicative then, as a harmonious gesture, they slowly dispersed. It didn't sink for a moment then the number painted on the grey superstructure turned his brain back in time, U12 his voice hissed through his teeth in disbelief. 'It can't be . . . not after all this time?' He shut his eyes tightly and shook his head, but it was still there.

'A submarine . . . well, I'll be damned, an old U boat.' The grey seawolf had a large hole in her hull – it was so clear he could see the torn metal. How many men had died in her metal casing and how many had she brought to grief before meeting her match. She and the galleon should have been covered in silt and barnacled out of all recognition but they were as clear as the day they were sunk. It didn't make any sense, he turned and looked up the steps.

'Amy . . . AMY, where the hell are you . . . AMY?' His only reply came from the wild life. They screeched their concern remaining climb took what was left of his energy reserve. He stood on the lip of the plateau and contemplated his new surroundings; he must be at least five hundred feet above the sandy beach. He moved forward shouting her name, she had to be here, there was nowhere else. Then he saw her. She was on her knees, her hands touching the walls of the long squat building that ran the length of the wide plateau. Her head was back as if she was searching for something. Her long black hair touched her waist. He ran to her thankful at her safety and lent forward to gather her in his arms. She turned her red eyes flashing in anger. She pulled her hands roughly from his, her face contorted in a mask half-hate, half-frustration. She knelt, shutting her eyes in deep concentration, her palms pushed hard against the rock, her knuckles white with pressure.

'What the hell are you up to Amy . . . Amy come on.' As Malise looked around for anything that moved, he felt the hair stand on the nape of his neck.

'I don't like this Amy, there's something very strange here. There's no sense in any of this, come on, let's make a move.' He lent forward and touched her. She didn't respond. She hissed through her clenched teeth:

'Will you shut up Malise!' She shrugged his hands from her shoulders and closed her eyes once more.

'JUST LEAVE ME ALONE . . . please . . . let me try.' Her voice came between deep sobs. Her fingers stroked the ancient rocks as if feeling for any form of communication, her breasts started to rise and fall in a strange, almost convulsive, movement. Her body rose and fell, pivoted at the knees, sweat ran freely from her forehead, gathering under her chin. Malise watched the undulating body for a few moments and realised she was emulating the human sex act; it was as if she was making love to an imaginary lover.

Her breath rasped as she pushed her groin hard against an outcrop. Her frenzy peaked and with a long deep gasp that could have come from her very soul, she slid slowly onto her back. Her legs splayed wide, arched at the knees, the crutch of her clothing saturated as if she had given in to multiple orgasms as she was satisfied by some invisible force. He stood over her not quite believing what he had seen. Her eyes flickered open, the anger had gone. Her face was soft and relaxed, she smiled a faraway smile and was gone. She had dematerialised before his eyes. He filled his lungs and shouted. 'Amy . . . AMY . . . Ameeeeeee!'

'Malise . . . Malise for god's sake, man over here.' Young Campbell's voice held no patience his face was full of anger, his chest rose and fell with exertion of climbing.

'Where the hell have you been, where's Amy. It's been three bloody hours, more, remember after an hour . . . a flare?' He took a deep breath and got his second wind.

'We've been calling you for over two hours, not a bloody peep, it's no fun climbing this thing, it nearly killed the general . . . now look Malise.'

'Hang on Campbell . . . now just hang on.' Malise grabbed Campbell's wrist to stop the prodding finger. The next thing he knew he was flat on his back, Campbell sitting on his chest with his laser pressing the underside of his throat. Campbell's eyes were like steel.

'Never do that again Malise, you might have the strength and weight but I have the speed . . . ok . . . OK?'

'Get off his chest Campbell . . . NOW!' The general's voice sounded tired but firm. Campbell stood up, pulling Malise to his feet.

'If you two have finished?' The general stood, rubbing his left forearm, trying to pacify his gleaming metal hand. His ghost fingers still twitched with pain when fatigue laid its hand on his shoulder.

'Where is Amy, Malise?' He sat heavily on a low wall. 'Well?'

Malise sat next to him and shook his head.

'God knows . . . she was with me till five minutes ago, then she just vanished, dematerialised in front of my eyes. I know it sounds crazy but that's what I saw. I just don't know.' Malise waited for the characteristic disbelief. He couldn't blame them but it didn't come, the general hadn't taken his eyes from the ground.

'Strange, very strange, but not entirely unexpected.'

Young Campbell had walked off to explore the long, oblong building. There had to be an opening somewhere in its structure.

'What do you mean not unexpected?' Malise's voice was full of reproach. The general looked at him as if he had committed a gross misdemeanour.

'What the hell have you two been doing the last three hours, have you no appreciation of our predicament?' Malise realised he and Amy had been too full of each other. The scientist in him had been pushed to the back of his mind, which was not like him.

'Campbell and I went back to the ship to recheck the course figures, we are miles off course, too much to be a mistake.'

Malise shook his head trying to clear his clogged brain, he had never felt so disorientated in his life.

'Bottom line, what you are saying, General, we've been brought here . . . yes?' The general shrugged his shoulders.

'Malise . . . general, here . . . over here!' Campbell's voice broke through their assumptions, both men turned to see him pointing to something on the wall curiosity wouldn't allow him to be ignored. 'Malise.'

'Yes General?'

'Give me a hand . . . careful, I don't want Campbell to see.' Malise pulled him gently to his feet; a deep flash of pain crossed his worn face but was quickly covered by a smile.

'It's my age Malise . . . don't worry about me.' Malise knew damn well it wasn't his age but now wasn't the time.

Campbell was scraping at the wall with a deep-bladed knife, the smile

35

and look of disbelief was comical to see. As they approached he sank to his knees and dug frantically through the top soil.

'I knew it . . . I bloody knew it!' His excitement was contagious. Both men ran the last twenty yards and knelt down beside him. 'Well?' The general was gasping for breath; he sat on his haunches till composure returned.

'Come on Campbell . . . What?' He regained control and fixed Campbell with a cold stare.

'You'll never believe it, sir . . . you'll never believe it!'

'Campbell . . . what for Christ's sake?'

His young face was almost childlike, as he bubbled over with enthusiasm.

'God, General, gold, the whole bloody mountain of whatever it is, is solid bloody gold, five hundred feet of solid gold. Malise joined the general sitting on the floor and prodding at it with his knife, paring away the surface soil till there was a dull clunk. A deeper scrape and there it was, gold gleaming back at them.

'Jesus . . . Jesus!' The general smiled.

'You could say that, Malise.' Young Campbell was lying prostrate laughing quietly to himself and muttering some inaudible comment, something about being too bloody late. The general sat for a long time, looking at the bright gash between his feet.

'Another time, another place, and we could have had the world at our feet, it still holds that charisma that men died for.'

Malise cast his eye over the long structure for the first time. He was at such an angle he could see over onto the top. His eyes were tired and burning but he could see the two objects quite clearly. Two large egg-shaped structures stood firmly on steel legs. He estimated they must be at least fifty feet across. Each had a cross firmly embedded on the top. One had the cross lying on its side while the other was upright.

'Strange . . . very strange.' Malise voiced his thoughts.

'What?' Both men answered simultaneously they stood back and followed his gaze. There was a long silence eventually broken by the general.

'They look like some sort of machine, some sort of vehicle, the one on the left looks old, no, not so much old as used.'

36

'Yes, I see what you mean.' The scientist had returned to Malise's brain. Look at the two metals. You can see the difference from here. The one on the left is duller and pitted, the effect you get when metal has been exposed to the elements for a prolonged period of time, especially wet or damp atmosphere. The other looks as if it has a transparent shield around it, there's not a mark on it. Look at the way it gleams, it looks almost alive.'

'What do you make of this Malise, I think its some sort of hiero-glyphics, it's not like anything I've ever come across.'

The general's metal hand made short work of the fungus that covered the golden walls. The effigy that appeared stood proud arms out-stretched, holding an open book, each page covered with deep-cut figures. The book had a four-dimensional effect, when the full light hit it, it seemed to come alive, silently turning the pages all different. All three realised it was trying to communicate with the written word, each had a buzzing in his brain as the pages turned. Small fragments of memories either conscious or subconscious laid themselves on the indi-vidual, they were a collective receiver given a question to answer. As suddenly as it began, it stopped, lying flat against the wall once more.

'What did you make of that, Malise?' Both men looked at him for some form of reassurance. Malise shrugged and put his hands on the large golden book, it was warm to the touch and the pages turned easily although there were no apparent hinges. He vaguely heard a voice above his buzzing brain. 'Easter Island . . . Mayan . . . Cuneiform.' He continued to turn the pages, the voice getting clearer.

'Roman . . . Runes . . . Ancient Egyptian . . . Rosetta . . . Aztec . . . Babylonian.' He touched each golden page in turn and marvelled at the intricacy of the inscriptions laid out on the bright golden surfaces. As if from far away he heard his companions asking him how he knew, indeed how did he know? He had no knowledge of ancient scripts of any kind. His head spun; he filled his large chest with air for hopeful relief, then felt the black pit of unconsciousness reaching out to give him rest.

'Malise . . . Malise, listen, concentrate, concentrate, please . . . please my love.' The last two words settled gently on his brain.

'It's Amy, Malise . . . I'm safe . . . in no danger, I'll be with you soon . . . in no danger . . . soon my love . . . soon.'

'Malise . . . come on, man.' The slap was loud and penetrating, his head snapped back against his collar. He opened his eyes slowly. They both stood over him, their eyes shouting for an explanation. He pushed his back against the wall and shook his head demanding clarity, Campbell helped him to his feet.

'It's Amy . . . god knows where she is . . . she read the scripts not me, she said she was safe . . . she.' He got no further.

'Go to the centre of the terrace to the point below the AZIMUTHAL and wait . . . go now!'

'Did you hear that?' Malise looked at his two companions – both men nodded.

'Thank god for that, I thought it was in my head again.'

Campbell spoke over his shoulder, 'What's an Azimuthal?'

It brought a smile to Malise's face.

'It's an equidistant projection of the earth's surface taken from a specific point, or in other words a map of the world on one side of the globe . . . OK?' Campbell winced.

'Thanks . . . thanks a lot.' He was none the wiser.

'Come on you two, down this way.' The general kicked the divot over the gold scar and made his way down the terrace till he found the map on the wall. It stood out clearly against its background. The land masses were green and brown, whereas the oceans were bright blue. It was about twenty feet across, the details were intricate to the extreme. All three gazed in admiration at such fine workmanship.

'Look at the map, Malise, can you see something strange about it.' Malise stood looking at it for a moment, at first missing the obvious. It was a few moments before the general's perception struck home.

'Now that has to be a mistake, there's no way I can accept that, it's impossible. If that map is right we could be in a lot of trouble.'

'What . . . what is it?' Campbell once more had his laser held firmly in his hand. He was on one knee, his head almost on a swivel, the general turned on him.

'Put that damn thing away, Campbell, we're not in any danger are we Malise?'

'No, I don't think so, General, if whatever it is wanted to do us any harm, it would have done so long before now. Out of curiosity, fire that thing at the wall, go on Campbell.' The trigger clicked as he pointed and discharged the weapon but there was nothing, no bright shaft of light, no black burned sterile hole . . . nothing. Malise smiled as he watched Campbell holster the weapon, the look of resignation painfully rested on his face twinned by a wry smile.

'Well, come on, Malise, make your point.' He looked at him hopefully for some mistake that would cover his own embarrassment. Malise pointed to the map above him.

'It's the continents, Campbell . . . they're only just beginning to separate. This map shows the earth as it would have been millions and millions of years ago. Long before man as we know him ever existed . . . long before.'

The look on Campbell's face was of disbelief. He was no scientist but this had to be wrong. A map millions of years old was crazy, the three men stood silently beneath the Azimuthal.

Amy's voice was warm and clear when it came.

'Come ahead slowly, there will be no resistance . . . walk into the wall . . . come, have faith in me, don't be afraid.'

The three men exchanged glances, their eyes following the voice's direction but there was no entrance, only solid wall.

'Just walk forward, have faith, walk forward . . . now!'

Her soothing voice drew them forward, the wall seemed to wrap itself around them, there was no solidness, no sudden stop. The golden molecules parted as mercury to a probing hand, then they were through. The sudden darkness took them by surprise, they stood quite still trying not to breathe, the blood pumping loudly in their ears. The blue-blackness stroked their bodies exploring every crevice for any evading light. They could feel it playing on their skin trying to recognise each in turn, their brain cavities tingled as if a charge was running through their cells. A second voice cut through the darkness. It sounded cold and detached.

'Do not be afraid. I have no need for a light source, you are being scanned for your requirements. Be patient.' The light defused at first, slowly adjusted to their need. They found themselves in a large empty

39

chamber, at least empty to their eyes. Malise sought the source that lit the capacious space but was unable to pin it down. The general seemed to have shed years, his eyes were alert and searching for any sign of movement. This was his type of game and Campbell was his shadow. Malise stood silent, his heart pounding. He felt the blood surge pushing against the back of his eyes. It wasn't fear more excitement and a paralysing lack of understanding. His ears ached, the very drums extended to the full, trying to catch any sound foreign or congenial. He felt his body being encircled once again as some sort of force field danced around him. He capitulated, it wasn't an unpleasant sensation. His probed memory threw his thoughts back to his mother's arms, a memory of gentleness. This was unique and enduring, he had forgotten the warmth of the feeling.

'I mean you no harm, Malise . . . there is nothing to be gained in you resisting me with body or mind . . . accept that I am, for our sake.' There was no struggle in his mind, as a man he now felt fear, as a scientist he glowed with curiosity. What was this force that treated him so gently?

'I am the Keeper, the constant companion of tomorrow and the dispatcher of yesterday, I am here to wait, to observe, to serve you and your kind, when the time was and is right.'

'Where are you?' Malise could see no sign of anything, no movement. The voice seemed to be coming from inside his head, the colour flashes in his brain only added to the confusion.

'I have no physical form at this time, I am purely energy.'

As if too prove a point a brightness flashed and struck the back of his brain.

'Open your eyes and come to me, Malise. Walk forward, you will know how.' The voice had grown stronger.

'Open your mind, Malise!' Without hesitation Malise strove out, his surroundings became brighter and his confidence grew. The entity halted his advance and spun him around. The sight that met his eyes was incomprehensible.

Campbell crouching like a cat with his familiar laser, as if an extension of his pointed limb. He stood like a silhouette, his black flights suit contrasting with the sudden brightness. His right arm extended across the general's chest held as a slim but impregnable shield of loyalty. The general's face gave nothing away only his large metallic hand showed any sign of life, reflecting a beam of light to the third figure. Malise stopped and looked again. 'What third figure?' His throat felt dry, there had only been three of them he looked closely at the third figure. He was the third figure, he was observing himself. The three stood like granite, not a movement, not a flicker of the eye. He looked down at his body, there was nothing there, then panic took over.

'For Christ's sake . . . there's nothing there . . . how?'

'Take one step at a time, Malise, you are in no danger nor are you in the realm of fantasy. Everything that is to happen here was destined long before even my seed was struck. In that you are older than I.'

Malise felt the heat expand in him. 'What the hell does that load of crap mean, what does age or time mean to you whatever you are . . . go to hell!'

The entity hung about ten feet from the ground, a blinding white centre, the corona seemingly composed of multi-coloured flares extending in all directions pulsing like sensors. He felt the fingers touch his mind.

'Three hundred million years ago, the earth was as the Azimuthal shows. The continents of this world were breaking up and drifting apart. We colonised a large island that was to be called Australia. There were five thousand of us and equal amounts of animals from our own planet for husbandry purposes. We were to propagate, told to spread throughout the globe, our technology was even more advanced than yours is now, but different as you will see. We were given nothing but tools and our animals to make a future, I was the only one allowed to keep the memory of our past.' Malise's hollow laugh did nothing to defuse the situation.

'I don't believe a word of this . . . three hundred million years ago, from another planet . . . for god's sake.'

'Open your mind, Malise, you are a scientist, you know what is possible, we need each other's help.' Malise felt confused.

'What help can I give something like you, I'm not even sure you exist or if I am dreaming all this.'

Amy's voice broke into the silence.

41

'You can help, Malise my love, be patient. Hydra will explain and answer all you ask of him.'

'Amy, where are you?' Malise mentally turned full circle in search of her, she moved from the shadows into the living brightness that was him. Her eyes seemed to glow, her hair shone blue, he reached out for her, but felt nothing.

'Amy, for god's sake, help me, explain?'

She turned to the entity, her hands outstretched, her voice was warm.

'Oh Hydra . . . Hydra, my love, my Lord, my life . . . this is only a man, who thinks and feels like a man. He is but a child in your hands, a primitive of little knowledge.'

A light flashed from the entity to Amy, surrounding her with a pulsing aurora, the yellow light revealing her as naked. Her body arched and moved as if caressed by invisible hands. Malise had never witnessed such total surrender and exotic beauty, then there was silence. A silence of such extremity it could almost be heard. It was followed by a heavy sigh.

'The fault is mine, Malise.' The light seemed to dim.

'Shla is of course right, you may be the primitive but I am the fool. I have limited powers but far beyond your present understanding or reasoning. I have searched your psyche and feel your frustration. We will start with your fears, then deal with your curiosity. I have forgotten the feel of flesh or the need for a body. The disorientation of the spirit can be devastating, it took me.' There was a silence that spoke of eternity.

'Malise, it has been a great length of time since I felt as you, to feel an object and have an equal and opposite reaction . . . come, follow me.' The light moved further into the chamber, after a backward glance at the three figures he followed. On passing through a large ornate door, a colonnade appeared supporting entablature of great beauty. Behind the great columns, the walls appeared to be of gold and silver. The designs were strange to Malise, he had never seen their like before not even in the history computers, they seemed to be almost alive. A large golden planet hung in mid-air, slowly revolving on its surface was mostly water much more than on earth, three silvery moons followed in silent reverence.

'Cura Malise . . . my home planet in the Nebula of Hydra.'

42

'Your name.' Malise spoke without thinking.

'Yes, Malise, I was named after a Nebula, two thousand million light years from earth, a distance you will find hard to relate to. Has the change made you feel safer in yourself?' He had confused Malise again till he suddenly realised he could see his reflection. His hand was touching the gleaming gold, he looked down and he was there, all of him.

'It is not what it seems, Malise, but you have what your brain requires for solace.' Malise stood for a moment before turning to meet the entity. He felt the hair on the nape of his neck stand proud, maybe all wasn't as it seemed but he was scared as hell.

'Are you there Hydra . . . as I am?'

'Yes, Malise . . . I am as you want me . . . for now.' Malise's voice was soft and restrained, his feet seemed to be stuck to the floor, his muscles locked.

'Amy, are you there . . . Amy?'

'Yes, Malise Shla is here . . . for both of us. Turn, my friend, for now we are three.' Malise turned slowly, allowing his eyes to follow the contours of the walls, his brain afraid to keep up with the screaming of his imagination. He stopped involuntarily as a movement stirred in the corner of his eye, he had never felt such fear, this was alien to him in more ways than one.

'Malise . . . come Malise,' the voice, though reassuring, held no con-viction. The last few degrees of his full turn seemed to take an eternity . . . but now he could see.

Amy stood tall and proud, more beautiful than he had ever seen her if that was possible, the long white dress threw out the colour of her eyes. The contrast of her hair served as a frame to her milk-coloured shoulders, her smile was warm as always, yet there was a difference. He or it stood by her side. For a few seconds, it seemed to change shape and colour. Malise concentrated and from the apparition appeared a perfect male form. He stood tall and straight, taller than Malise, his slightness was almost painful, his irises were vivid blue, unlike Amy's. He too was in white but his clothing was tight, it was almost indistinguishable from his pale complexion, so this was Hydra the Keeper. They came forward and took Malise's hands in theirs. They felt solid and warm. Whatever fears he had began to abate, if this wasn't reality it was nearer sanity.

The two men walked side by side along the high wide passage. Amy followed, slightly to the rear, Malise could feel her subservience. Then he remembered, Shla not Amy, the name seems to fit her well, it also answered a lot. The passage at last opened out into a large empty chamber again devoid of any contents. He looked at Hydra for an explanation, he in turn smiled and nodded.

'This room will answer most of your immediate questions, it has information from the beginning of time . . . as I know it. Remember all you see and hear . . . has been . . . it cannot be altered not by a fraction of a second. We can explore time, any part of yesterday, observe and relate but not change, you cannot change the choice of yesterday.'

The room slowly hazed and transformed before his eyes, the metamorphosis was to be complete. Banks of flickering light sources dressed the walls, rows upon rows of translucent cases filled with artifacts of all shapes and sizes followed the contours of the changing surrounds. A large stellated crystal emerged from the centre of the highly glazed floor. Malise was neither surprised nor afraid. He wondered if Hydra was patronising his lack of ability to handle the paranormal. On trying to displace the tops of the sparkling cases he could find no opening of any kind. He walked slowly from one to another, allowing his brain to absorb the wonders of the contents and digest the familiarity of others. Hydra and Shla watched him with practised patience, he left no corner of the chamber ungleaned. He returned to them with a million questions, Hydra beckoned him to sit down opposite.

'Do you think it's important, important to you I mean?' Malise creased his forehead in reply.

'What important, I don't understand . . . what?' Shla smiled.

'The general, Malise, and his kind, you have been thinking of them constantly, they can see what you see and feel.'

'That may be but the general has a right to be here, more than I, he has.' Hydra stopped him.

'All right, Malise, but there are no rights here . . . here there is only my choosing . . . at least for now!' Malise felt a distinct heat as Hydra's

44

voice rose, then there was stillness. Hydra was visibly moved, but by what, Malise had no way of knowing.

'Very well.' Once again the tolerance was in his voice. The general sat dignified and relaxed. He smiled faintly at Malise, thanking him for his concern. Campbell, as usual, looked confused. Shla rose and gently brushed the general's forehead with her hand and was gone once more. Even though Hydra had materialised he still seemed to be outlined by a glow of energy.

'How long have we been here, my watch has stopped?' Malise looked sideways at the general and shook his head.

'Mine too.' They both turned to Hydra for an explanation.

'Time as you know it is of no consequence.' Before any questions could be asked, Hydra turned and fixed his gaze on the large crystal. A brilliant blue light shot from the centre till all points joined as one, the living screen pulsed like a giant monitor awaiting a question.

Hydra relaxed, he closed his eyes as if trying to remember. Malise had never seen a man so pale. His large hands lay flat by his side, it was only then that Malise realised he had no nails. He looked closely at Hydra's skin, what he could see of it was smooth and oily in appearance. Then it clicked, he had no hair, none at all, he had been so in awe of the man he hadn't noticed, Hydra raised his hand for silence.

'Gentlemen, I hope you will be indulgent with my memories, the retrospection I think you will find interesting. It has been a long time since I have held a conversation. You may find it slightly one sided I hope you will be considerate in you attention . . . and allow me to finish.'

'Your planet consolidated approximately four thousand five hundred and fifty million years ago, it lay in the darkness of space, erupting and billowing sulphurous fumes at the heavens, who in turn blinked indifference for four thousand million years. It cooled and began to have and hold water, the mother of life, but little life forms algae, xenusion, sea pen. Then came your Cambrian period which lasted seventy million years, evolving new creatures, sponge, worm, jelly fish, and the greatest of its period, the trolobite, a thinking creature well armed for its protection, making it the most dominant of its time. All this, of course, being monitored as the planet's evolutionary cycle took place. The Palaeozoic

Era, which lasted at least three hundred and forty five million years, decided the main factor of the planet, as it is now two-thirds water. In the following Triassic period, animals and creatures of all kinds readily evolved.'

Malise kept trying to speak to ask one of a dozen questions that sat on his mind, his throat felt restricted in some way stopping his thoughts being spoken. His conclusion was Hydra was not ready to answer questions . . . yet.

The great crystal had shown them their world from the beginning of time and its agony to give birth to very unwilling life. The large screen flickered and changed colour for a moment catching their attention. The general sat calmly as if it was an everyday occurrence, Malise never failed to be amazed by the man. Hydra once more raised his hand for their attention.

'This is a visual record of my planet taken approximately five hundred million years ago, that is in your concept of time, primitive as it may be.' His voice had softened but still demanded obedience. His captured audience had no option but to obey his courteous demands.

The screen burst into life projecting a planet very similar to earth but green instead of blue in appearance. As it turned slowly on its axis, one thing was evident, nine-tenths of the planet's surface was water. The land that did exist was covered in what looked like canals. The deep cuts criss-crossed in all directions as if something was trying to break up the remaining land and drag it under the sea, like reclamation in reverse.

There was still life on the land you can see, full evolution would take a few million years.'

The sea came rushing towards them, without a ripple they were under, the water was so clear and the colours amazingly irradiant. The angle of descent was slight though fairly rapid. Malise could almost feel the pressure of the water on his body. The quadra-vision illusion was most effective, whichever way he turned, his head was surrounded by watery walls and he found himself trying to hold his breath. The sea life was abundant, strange creatures of all shapes and sizes, their fear seemed non-existent, they had to be pushed aside as they rushed to greet the recorder. As they dove deeper, the light did not defuse as one might expect but seemed to be the same at all depths. The ocean floor was bright gold in colour as it reflected the bright sunlight back to the surface. In whatever shade there was, fluorescent corals threw their colours to the sky, giant sea urchins bounced about in comic fashion. Malise noticed that each species seemed to be allotted its own territory, in this they seemed to stay except for right of way. It was only at the shore line or rocky outcrops that they seemed to mix but here they were much smaller and not fully developed. This could have been their laboratory of evolution. The creatures he had seen had little in the way of a mouth, the complete lack of plankton was also strange.

Malise felt his throat relax and his head clear, the general coughed loudly and bent over for relief, Malise patted him on the back, realising he had been experiencing the same discomfort.

'Thanks.' The general smiled and straightened up. He squeezed Malise's arm as if to prove he was really there.

'You have a question Malise?' Malise knew Hydra could read his mind but he seemed to want him to make the effort.

'Yes I have . . . you general?' He ignored Campbell.

'No Malise, I don't understand any of this . . . yet.'

'I can't see what you are getting at, Hydra, our evolution is similar to yours. All this proves to us is that you are an alien, what else can it prove?'

'Alien . . . Alien, oh Malise.' Hollow cold laughter electrified the air.

'I have been alone too long, too long without my own kind, the interbreeding of the stars must have some effect.' The crystal dimmed as Hydra walked from the brightness, he had a look of frustration carved heavily on his gaunt face.

'I will tell you from the beginning, show you my people as they were, before they came to this planet. You, Malise, are as much an alien as I, you will see.' The general and Campbell looked at Malise for an answer but he shrugged his shoulders in reply.

'When my people arrived on this planet, they were all adult homo sapiens transferred back to a body we had rejected millions of years previously through lack of efficiency.'

The crystal again glowed with life revealing the clear waters of the planet, a planet probably long dead.

Malise felt a wave of serenity sweep over him, the feeling of utter

47

peace etched itself on his brain as he watched the creatures twist and turn. They swam in pairs curving their scaleless bodies to catch the sun. They swam so close they might have been one creature, their graceful dances were mesmerising. Malise felt as if he could reach out and touch them, he closed his eyes to digest the moment.

'Look at that . . . beautiful!' Malise snapped quickly back to reality. The recorder zoomed in to reveal some sort of city, carved rather than built, of what looked like sandstone. The sun was the main feature that blazed the pediments of the buildings, which looked very Greek or Roman in design. The once deep-sculptured rock had been well weathered by the movement of the sea. It was still a very impressive sight, the buildings forming a large square with avenues branching off at all angles. Sleek fish glided majestically between the lavish pillars, Hydra's voice was heard above their thoughts.

'We are approaching my family's area, my parents are about to come into view.' The three men strained their eyes past the large fish but could see nothing, there was no form of life they could recognise. Malise shouted into the brightness.

'Where Hydra . . . We can't see a thing.'

'They are filling the screen now.' His voice was soft and thick as he relived the memory.

The men looked at the screen in stunned silence. The general was first to speak, then just above a whisper.

'Good god . . . they're dolphins . . . Jesus, this is too much for me.'

'Yes, the dolphins, as you call them, were my people, they were not spawned upon this planet they came from my world. Gentle, loving creatures, chosen from billions of galaxies. The only ones left are under my protection. Your kind managed to almost kill them off with your pollution and barbarous slaughter. As all of your history relates, kill what you fear or do not understand.'

Malise remembered the beach and how the beautiful creatures had nearly followed them onto the sand. Of course it was Amy . . . Shla, they had been after her, they knew her. The crystal died and the brightness had gone.

Malise stood and tried to get some reaction from his body but felt nothing, neither tiredness or energy.

In the Beginning

'So you are telling us we are descended from dolphins. We had a split evolution, some took to the sea and some to the land. That doesn't sound that impossible.'

Hydra smiled and placed his hand on Malise's shoulder.

'No, my friend, this is not what I am telling you, for that is not the way of things, please sit.' Malise succumbed to his request but he was now more confused than ever. The general sat looking at Hydra, then shook his head in confusion.

'You ask too much of us, I can honestly say that I have never really been afraid in all my life, at least not for myself. But you Hydra, or whatever you are . . . scare the shit out of me . . . and I don't like it!' The general rose and walked the floor his head lowered to help him bring his thoughts together and to keep his gaze from Hydra's eyes.

'Recap . . . you tell us you were brought from another galaxy, you have lived millions of years. We find you under the sea with Amy's help.' Hydra interrupted.

'Shla, general . . . Shla.' The voice was calm and irritating. The general coughed away his embarrassment.

'All right . . . Shla!' His face was red with exasperation.

'Then you tell us she belongs to you and is equally as old. We have seen animals here that have been extinct for thousands of years and a sea free from pollution. Plants, trees, shrubs of every size and shape that no longer exist in the rotting world above. A beautiful island crowned by what looks like an Aztec or Mayan temple and, of course, made of solid gold, three-hundred-million-year-old maps that could only have been taken from a satellite. An entity that can change shape at will, and let's not forget our new-found ability to walk through solid walls. Oh yes . . . the crème-de-la-crème, two great steel ships topping your domain, adorned with the cross of Christ, the most revered symbol of faith on this planet . . . on an alien ship?'

The general was clearly shaken by his outburst. He wiped his dry lips with the back of his hand before continuing. 'Are you the God we have revered all these centuries, are you . . . are you? Or are you the Christ the Son of God waiting to come again as you promised . . . well, are you?'

There was an electrifying silence, the general stood almost touching

49

Hydra, Malise felt a sudden danger for him. 'For all that's holy Hydra . . . tell us.' The key that had waited over three thousand years to be turned pressed heavy on its tumbers. The general raised his hand to touch Hydra but didn't quite make it. A hand shot from the shadows and gripped his wrist with such force the knuckles shone white.

Shla smiled gently, led him back and sat him down speaking quietly in his ear. 'Neither a hand nor a breath shall be laid upon the keeper for he is not of your flesh. Be patient, General, for even I am not of the complete understanding, I am but a buffer for his despair and an ear for his sorrow.'

Hydra stood like a Greek god, his fine features catching the glancing light making every angle sharp. Agitation radiated from him as a pulsing sound, he looked at the cold crystal for inspiration then turned and confronted the three men.

'I am not your God . . . I am not anyone's God, longevity was placed on my shoulders by misdeeds of me and mine.' He raised his hands in despair.

'How do I tell children the story of the Universe . . . how?'

'From the beginning.' Malise's voice was strong with conviction. 'And leave room for questions, our questions.' Hydra smiled and lowered his hands in mock submission.

'Maybe not so stupid children, for we are sons of Fadar.'

'The Fadar?' Malise looked at his companions and back to Hydra. 'What the hell's, the Fadar?'

'The Fadar, Malise . . . the creator of all things and places, all time past, future and now. The tender of billions upon billions of galaxies, the sewer and reaper of the cosmos to his liking, the bender of time and place, and for your speck of dust . . . your God. A silent spirit burning in your brains that brings you fear and love you don't know why or even want to control. Your theories on cosmogony are pathetic even at this late stage.

'The general retaliated: 'What about our solar system? Never mind the others, we have tried to get in touch. Is there any life at all out there?'

Hydra glanced at the crystal. It burst into life and produced a hologram of the solar system: the nine planets in their varying sizes and distances from the mother Sun who in turn spat luminous gases at her revolving children.

'There is your weed garden with its only flower a wilting blossom it maybe, but still as yet alive . . . just.'

Malise marvelled at the detail of the system, the great Jupiter with its twelve satellites, their shadows racing across the vast surface of the planet with its many swirling coloured bands; Saturn, the show piece of the solar system with her multi glowing rings; Pluto, the outer guardian with its two-hundred-and-forty-eight-year orbit and a frozen surface. Then there was Mars the Red Planet of hope or had been, Earth's sister planet in space where the over-populated surface of earth was to spill. It was always left too late, no one would take the responsibility or the cost, it had been defeated by ifs and maybes. The earth, which had been bright blue, was now a yellow pall filtering the sun from its surface. Hydra walked into the hologram and out the other side to make some obscure point that no one caught.

'They are all void of life, but some have been briefly touched over the ages, but the only glowing residue that is left is this speck of dust. This is the only planet in this system that Fadar gave his most precious and volatile gift.

The general turned his head and looked at Malise, his eyes showed his annoyance and disbelief. He had been immobile too long, his strong voice had an edge.

'What gift Hydra . . . if there is a greater being why has he allowed this special planet to deteriorate to this? I know it's an old, tired question and, as usual, you won't have the answer.' He stood up and pointed an accusing finger at the hologram.

'This is nothing new. I have yet to see anything that cannot be explained, you're a fake Hydra . . . just a very clever fake!'

'Exactly, General, as you say, nothing is impossible, nothing.' He looked at Malise, who shrugged his shoulders. Campbell looked at the floor in ignorant submission.

'Shla . . . come.' His voice was soft yet penetrating. She was there, a vision in gold that reflected his aurora in all directions. He took her hands in his and turned her to face him, their eyes seemed to pulse in unison. Hydra pointed at the general.

Fadar

'There was a man such as you that I observed a tick in time ago. He too was not satisfied with the word. His only grave consolation was plunging his eyes into the nail-torn hands and touching the bleeding flesh of his beloved friend and teacher, are you the resurrection of the doubter?'

Malise tried to catch the general's expression but he slowly went out of focus. His stomach heaved and his head began to spin; blackness crept across his consciousness. Hydra's voice seemed to get farther and farther away.

'A lesson in acceptance, concentrate, concentrate, now open your eyes for this is no dream . . . or illusion.'

Malise found his eyes heavy and slow to respond, the blackness he found himself in was dotted with piercing, flickering specks, some brighter than others. He moved his head to try and get his bearings; Campbell and the general were directly in front of him. They were looking over his shoulder. Both men wore expressions of utter disbelief. He tried to turn but his feet would not grip. His two companions reached out and slowly spun him around, there was no way he could have been ready for the sight that presented itself.

The earth stood high in space, the moon smaller but equally awesome. They seemed to be suspended halfway between the two. His brain rejected the spectacle more from fear than intelligent reasoning. He was sure he could feel the pull between the two opposing bodies: he felt as if he was being torn apart. His brain was near bursting point when he realised he could hear voices; he looked across at his companions. Both their hands were over their ears. They seemed to be screaming, their heads were thrown back but no sound could be heard. The voices got louder and louder: Thousands all screaming at once as if trying to attract his attention – the noise filled every corner of his brain. He thought he heard his name called: he tried to concentrate on that one.

'Simeon . . . Simeon . . . SIMEoooooon!' Then it was gone. Hydra's voice at last penetrated the fog of nausea. Malise grasped it in desperation, as a drowning man would a log. He held on tight till full consciousness returned.

'Is there still any question in your mind, General?' The general sat looking at the floor, perspiration dripping from his chin; he slowly met Hydra's gaze.

'Real . . . or fantasy Hydra?' Hydra smiled back at him.

'Come now, General . . . you know the answer to that.' Young Campbell looked at Hydra with renewed respect.

'The voices, there were so many of them, like millions of souls crying for help . . . I heard my mother's voice.' He turned and grasped Malise's wrist, his eyes were wild.

'I heard her Malise, I know I did, she said the same thing to me as she said the night she died; it was about my father. You have his beginning and his end, he was your beginning and his end will be as yours. I still don't know what she meant. I've never known my father. Could it be possible, Malise?' He was well and truly shaken by the ordeal. Gone was the combat security guard, left was a confused young man whose Achilles heel had well and truly been found. Malise unclasped his hand and sat him down.

'You have amazing powers, Hydra, that wasn't in our minds. We really were there . . . standing in space, I mean?' Hydra smiled his reply, there was no need for an answer.

Malise walked across to the huge crystal and ran his hands over the faultless gem it felt the cold of the ages.

'I heard voices too Hydra, there was panic in their cries, I heard one special voice!' Hydra nodded.

'Yes, I know Malise . . . you all did . . . you, too General?'

The general acknowledged without looking up.

'What are they Hydra, they sounded afraid and trapped.'

'They have been . . . and they are. I weary Malise, I am not used to this form.' His head bowed slightly and for the first time he looked vulnerable, Malise felt an overpowering feeling of pity for this lonely being.

'Go now, with Shla Malise, she will answer your questions. Go where you will and ask what you will, for you will have need of the knowledge.' It was there again that inference that Malise was connected in some way with the underwater mystery.

'Come with me, Malise, we will be alone.' She stood with her hands extended, he took them in his. They were warm.

'You have a lot to answer for young lady.' He wasn't so sure about the young any more. He looked over his shoulder at his companions. Shla answered his question.

'They are deep in their own world of thought, let them be content in their remembering.'

The water was warm and clear. He shut his eyes and let the tension slip away even if it was for a brief moment. She had led him straight to the pool. It lay cocooned in a natural rock surrounded by sweet-smelling plants. He had never seen their like before. They were real, not some scented imitation, this would be his heaven for now. She had disrobed them with no hint of an apology; he felt it was not the time for questions. They swam and played like children, made love and slept in each others arms like any other lovers. But one thing was clear to him – this woman with the yielding body and the familiar feel was Shla, Amy Ashley no longer existed.

He woke refreshed and ready for what was to come; just knowing that she still cared had revitalised him. She stood watching him stretch life back into his limbs; he arched his back like a large cat as if trying to undo the tired knots. His muscles rippled like snakes following the contour of his back. It gave her an inner ache and a wanting for this man who had entered her maze of existence.

The entrance was guarded by a great monolith as high and as far as the eye could see; the distance they had come was of no consequence, his brain had succumbed to the mysteries of his surroundings. He was satisfied to drink in their reflections. There was no point in trying to distinguish or categorise, to enjoy was enough. As they ascended the ornate steps, a warm light filled the immense chamber but he wasn't ready for its contents.

He recognised full-size ships cradled to hold them upright; all were undamaged, each sported a name and a date. Beautiful preserved galleons of centuries ago, strange-sounding names, mostly Spanish, he could smell the pitch that had kept the sea at bay. The larger and more modern caught his eye. USN warship *Wasp*, 1814, Captain Johnson Blackley – the name stirred a germ in his brain. He wandered between the ships digesting the names and dates and trying to remember. *Cyclops* 1918, *Porta Noca* 1926, *Aneta* 1973, *Sandra* 1950, all freighters. *Scorpio* 1968, good god its a nuclear submarine, it's the same name as the one in the bay. *The Spray*, a sloop 1909, *Revonoc* yacht 1958, *Enchantress* 1964, *Witchcraft* 1967, and dozens more dated up to 2095, the last time a boat was used for transport. As he stood looking at the beautifully shaped bow, a long shadow caught his eye. The giant *Superfortress* gleamed under the bright lights. 1962 was her date, then five Avenger Torpedo bombers 1945, two SBD Dauntless 1945. The two large airliners looked like sisterships – *Star Tiger* 1948 and *Star Ariel* 1949, a beautiful DC3, a giant US Air Tanker 1962, and many smaller planes all in perfect condition.

Malise's brain had had more than enough to be going on with: in the back of his mind some of the names rang a bell, it was like looking at a live history book. There was something missing. He stood thinking for a while then it dawned: 'missing', that was the key word, each and every one had been reported missing on the dates shown, either sailing or flying over the Atlantic, even the crews had never been heard of again. His memory still ticked over, Atlantic . . . Bermuda Triangle then Ogwanaland. As the Greek Plato had said, the great Island West of the Pillars of Hercules adorned with every beauty a man could want, this surely was it, above or below the sea.

He laid his head on the metal undercarriage of the large tanker; the cold metal helped him gather his thoughts:

'The people, Shla, what happened to the crew, are they dead or preserved like these long-forgotten memorials?' She came forward and wiped the sweat from his forehead. She took his large hands and laid them on her breasts. Her heart beat strongly between his thumbs, she pushed herself hard against him. 'I'm alive Malise . . . am I?' Her sharp groin cut into his leg; he felt himself stir as any man would, she ran her pink tongue down his sweating neck and buried her teeth in his shoulder. He felt her nails puncture the surface of his skin. 'Am I alive, Malise?'

He pushed her away in frustration, she laughed and fanned her hair across her shoulders, her eyes flashing a challenge.

'Are you sure Malise . . . are you really sure?'

He wasn't sure of anything any more.

'The crews Shla . . . all the people . . . where?'

'Everything will be made clear, everything has a sequence but first come.' The stairway curled in a wide spiral, as they climbed higher they entered a sweet-smelling mist, then finally, a large transparent dome. The island lay spread out below them, the pure clear air blended the colours together like a giant patchwork quilt.

'Malise . . . Malise, my love.' He turned slowly unwilling to take his eyes from the kaleidoscope of colour and raw beauty. She stood like an ancient priestess, both arms raised to shoulder height, each pointing in different directions, her head was back and her eyes closed. He followed one long slender arm. His eyes sprung from the pointed finger, through the dome to a large metal sphere. A once bright surface was dull and pitted, the cross lay on its side bent and twisted but still clinging to the rusting metal. It was the only object Malise had seen that showed any sign of age, its companion seemed to glow resentment at his observations, it seemed to vibrate with life. Shla looked at him in answer.

'They are the past . . . and the future, a second chance for this tired world of yours.' The blockage was there again in his brain, half-explanations, half-truths, they did nothing but service his frustration.

'I don't understand . . . what are they . . . what past, there is no future. This planet is a suppurating ball of death.'

'Hydra started to tell you, he and his people landed on this planet as it was emerging from its infancy. That was approximately three hundred million years ago and, as he said, the continents were beginning to break up. The ships were dismantled and a settlement established, as he already explained, a metamorphosis took place in the seeds of his people during the long trip from Cura. They were the first *homo sapiens* to set foot on the plush young planet, they, like the Israelites long after them, were given their covenants to keep. They were commanded to procreate and spread numbers across the land, they cultivated the ground and domesticated the animals. They bred them with their own with some strange results. They set order and built under their own judgement a new and advancing civilisation which, in the beginning, showed promise. Hydra, the chosen leader of the community, was given the gift of longevity. He was to live till the task was completed. Then, after one hundred and fifty million years, with drastic results. They had not moved from their original sight and the population had hardly increased in relation to the years. The Fadar, seeing his covenants had been ignored, called Hydra to him. He related that all but he would be returned to the sea in their original form never again to walk the earth. He also said that all land would be covered by water to cleanse it of their seed. He left in a place chosen for Hydra two orbs, or arks, surmounted by his cross, each to be released at a time designated by him alone. He put in the arks seeds of all plants and animals that were to take their place in the new world. He omitted such as dinosaurs, a hybrid of no future purpose. He also placed within the ark the seeds of his new people: fighters, this time gathered from galaxies from such immense distances the mind cannot conceive, not one but a mixture of cultures. Zerma the white seed, Panta the yellow, Krana the brown, Hano the red. It would be their right, when planted, to hold their lands and create their customs but honour him always by whatever name they chose . . . for this time he would not be forgotten. The planet was cleansed and Hydra banished beneath the sea, the keeper of the new world.

'Sixty million years passed before the water receded to its final course. Seed was planted at every stage of recession, animals and plants flourished. Yet another eighty-nine million years passed before the first seed of man was planted upon the earth. The animal evolution was ripe for his introduction but this time he had to learn for himself, a blank page that only he could write. He was given a brain that was hungry to learn. He would never be allowed to know all, that mistake had been made, the ark returned to Hydra where it stands now.'

Malise looked once again at the toppled dented cross, the sights it must have seen as it painted its new world and the sounds it must have heard as it sailed through the milleniums. . . .

'And you, Shla, where do you fit into all this?' She walked passed him and looked down at the picture of life below, her head rested gently on her cupped hands. She had a melancholy look on her beautiful face.

'Why did you have to kill such a beautiful planet, and in such a very short time? It took you a million years to destroy a paradise that took hundreds of millions of years to grow.' Tears fell freely from her eyes. They echoed the pain of the hundreds of millions that had died in torturous hunger and disease. He felt ashamed of the human race.

'You still haven't answered my question Shla.'

She wiped away the free-falling tears and smiled at him. 'I'm sorry for my weakness Malise, my makeup is not the same as Hydra's. I feel for

57

this speck of dust, this planet is my home. He made me Malise. I am not of one race but of many. He made me from the debris of seeds left in the ark and of part of himself, not as you see him but from his physical body. He has kept it all these years. Hydra's own body has a gash in the chest where a rib was removed for the making of me. I must confuse you, Malise.'

She wiped away the remaining tears and smiled at him. 'I confuse myself sometimes, I assure you I am not the same as Hydra, not the same makeup at all. I haven't his powers or his memories. I can only do what he lets me. My body is the same as yours and just as vulnerable.'

Malise felt even more confused. 'I don't understand. Hydra said you were as old as himself!'

Shla interrupted him. 'No, Malise, think back. The general said that it was his conclusion. As I have said, I am made from many seeds and part of Hydra's cadaver. He has not used his physical body for millions of years. It rests in the crystal, I am almost as you, Malise. But older.'

He smiled at her and reached out to hold her. She moved away from him. He knew his remark had touched a nerve. He moved towards her but stopped just out of arms' reach. 'I'm sorry, Shla, I can't seem to grasp time in millions at this moment. I'm having trouble with days, never mind years.'

She didn't turn round. Her gaze was fixed on the blue of the sea. 'You will.' Her voice was very positive. 'As Hydra said to you, time is irrelevant here. This is the only place on earth that it virtually stands still. If you think of events rather than time, you will find it easier to comprehend, it's only a matter of adjusting; yesterday, today and tomorrow run into one.'

They returned a different way. The scenery was breathtakingly beautiful. Malise had never seen so many live creatures running free, they seemed to have no fear of the human form at all. He watched them explore and look at him with friendly curiosity.

Shla called over her shoulder. 'There Malise!' She pointed to a glass building about a hundred feet below them. 'That should feed your incessant curiosity.' The building was much smaller than he had visualised from above.

As they approached, the walls and roof looked like clear glass but, on entering, they changed – there was no way they could see out. Malise reached forward and felt the opaque wall; he turned to Shla for an explanation. 'Well?' She in turn walked past him and raised her slender hand. Artifacts of various shapes and sizes filled the room. She changed them at will, Malise watched her in fascination. A smile played in the corner of her mouth, he knew she was playing with him to see how far she could push him. She loved to watch his temper flare.

Hydra could not be goaded by her: she was always careful in his presence, for his power when aroused was a terrible thing to witness. She had seen it only three times in her memory, each time many thousands of people had died, innocent and guilty alike.

'Well?' Malise's voice held an edge.

'It's just a storeroom connected to the crystal, that's all.'

'Of what Shla, to the point, come on, I am still practising with the millions . . . a storeroom for what?'

She turned and looked up at the gentle glowing ceiling. She coughed to clear her throat. 'They are banks of live souls, persons that have lived, incarnation of a special kind of soul. They have been used upon the planet over and over again to accelerate the advance of mankind as you know it.' Malise shook his head.

'Shla, for god's sake . . . what?'

She stopped him in his tracks, looking him straight in the eyes. 'Yes, Malise, for god's sake, for that is what *you* call him. Leave your old ways of thinking behind learn and take in now, don't try and evaluate your knowledge and memories against ours. Accept and learn or you are no good to Hydra, open your mind to what you think is the impossible . . . absorb.'

Malise felt utterly trapped. She seemed to know his thoughts as they accumulated in his brain; she seemed to be able to foretell his every movement, his wishes and desires. She was almost part of him; maybe that was the way it was meant to be, he didn't know . . . yet. He walked backwards and forwards running his large hands across the seemingly smooth surface of the walls. As he did so, jumbled pictures flashed in his brain none making any sense. Battles, places, people, music, plush lands with bright green fields, blue clear sea and bright vivid skies, fashions of every kind. He spread his arms wide – he wanted more.

59

He removed both hands from the wall and stood for a moment he could hear his heart beating loudly in his chest the pressure points behind his ears pulsed in tune. He could just see Shla out of the corner of his eye: she was watching his reactions, he felt like a child with a new toy. He moved closer to the wall and closed his eyes then gently placed his right index finger firmly on the tiled surface. The reaction was immediate. He found himself watching the launching of a giant rocket: the words *Saturn 11* were blazed along its length. The roar was deafening, he could almost feel the heat as the mighty rockets motors spat their flames at the scorched launching pad. It slowly pulled itself from the ground ice and flame mingling as one. The whiplash parting of the lines as it clawed its way into the sky, a great roaring yellowness spitting its contempt at the gravity that tried to pin it to the ground. He seemed to be enveloped in flame and noise, he pulled his finger away and it was gone. He felt the sweat drip from his hair run down his face and gather under his chin. He wiped the wetness away and looked at his hands, they visibly shook. He drove them into his pockets and turned to Shla: 'History lessons?'

Shla smiled. 'In a way, you just recalled events that those special souls were involved in. The wall if you look closely is made up of tiny segments each one a recording of an event that changed history even in the smallest way. They are similar to your computers but these are actual events not suppositions. You have the turning points of the world at your fingertips.'

Shla's hand made a slight movement and a large ornate bench appeared. She motioned him to sit down. This he did with a feeling of great relief, he put his head in his hands and sat for a moment. Shla ran her fingers through his tousled hair. 'It will come my love . . . just don't be afraid of it, you have been given a chance that no other will ever have.'

Again that insinuation that he had been singled out, why him and for what? He looked once more at the wall and was amazed at its texture. He could almost feel its living presence. He shook his head in acceptance. 'You have the turning points of the world at your fingertips, Malise, you can if you wish, walk back in time to witness the events, but not take part. You can observe at will, but you can change nothing here.' She turned and pointed at the opaque door. 'Your turn will come up there. If you concentrate on any one event you can transport yourself there in mind if not in body. Others will not see you but you will in all intents and purposes be there: you will feel and hear everything around you.'

Malise looked closely at the small segments: each was centred with a minute black dot. He passed his hand slowly over the surface, being careful not to touch the protrusion. 'You're telling me that each dot is a person's soul?'

'No, only an event, a moment in time, there are few souls harboured here. The rest lie in the umbra of the moon.'

'How?' Malise's attitude had changed: he was ready for anything, he felt that there was nothing that could surprise him any more and he was willing to learn.

'They are held in time unable to return.'

'I really don't understand . . . return?' Malise waited for her explanation.

'Hydra will tell you of those, for he is the keeper not I, but anything else.'

Malise turned back to the wall and spoke out loud more to himself rather than to Shla. 'There must have been millions of souls used to make up this visual library . . . millions.'

Shla put her arm gently on his shoulder. 'No, my love, only twelve, each one of these segments below represents a record of the time they spent on the surface of the world as Hydra's envoys, after their reincarnation, if you like.'

'You know of these twelve, Shla?'

She turned and smiled at Malise. 'Yes, I have watched them grow, for I on occasions have been part of them. This is their twenty-fifth millennium. Their seeds were planted to help the planet prosper. Without them it would be likened to a child without learning, it would stagnate in its own stupidity. The twelve were gathered together only once since their existence and you have read about that, it is in your recorded history.'

'How often?'

Shla answered him before his words were formed.

61

'When Hydra thought they were needed . . . he would not allow stagnation . . . he made that mistake.' She looked at him with an exasperated expression. 'He is the keeper Malise . . . he has the power.'

Malise returned the expression. 'OK . . . ok, what about Fadar, what power does he have help me with that one, I am trying, Shla, honest to god I really am trying!'

'Malise, try and understand this is not an Aladdin's cave full of magic, what you see and what you hear *is*, even though it is hard for you to comprehend. You are a link and eventually you will understand; you are an important link but the choice will be yours, as it has been since the beginning . . . Fadar is all!'

Malise wanted to follow her line of retrospection but for some reason he felt it wasn't the time. She rose and extended her hand to him, without any further discussion, they left behind the glistening crystals and their recorded memories. Their time span was the hardest to conceive. Time, what did time matter here? He hadn't realised he no longer possessed a watch, in fact this had been the first occasion he had thought of time since they had dived beneath the sea. He couldn't imagine what had happened to his watch or could he recall the last time he had seen it. For them, Shla had said, time was of no consequence but what of the surface? Time was for them very much a consequence, a life or death consequence.

'What do you make of this, Campbell?' The general sat comfortably watching the rotating crystal. Hydra had been gone for a very long time. Like Malise, he had realised that he was no longer in possession of a watch. The spectrum of the crystal reflected from the blackness of his eyes; the greyness of fatigue had gone from his lean face, and Campbell knew he had resolved himself to the situation. He knew even the general couldn't tackle this, at least not head on.

'I don't really know, General, but a point you did make was we are here for a reason . . . Hydra's reason. Another time, another place, I could give you dozens of reasons but not now not here.'

The general elbowed his way to an new position facing the young trooper.' What do you mean son, clarify.'

The non-military son caught Campbell offguard, he had never heard

62

this kind of softness in the general's voice before. His hesitation brought the sharpness back.

'Come on boy . . . let's hear your version of this insanity.'

Campbell ran his hand down the slowly revolving crystal. He took his eyes from the base and cast them into the darkness that was the roof. It didn't make a sound, just revolved at the same leisurely pace. He turned and looked the general full in the face. 'I know this sounds mad but I think he brought us here to use physical bodies as tools of some kind, to do something for him that he can't do for himself. He is a powerful man and if we are to believe everything he says a wise one.'

The general was shaking his head and smiling.' What could we possibly do for him, he has more power in his little finger than they have in whole of the domed city or in fact all of the remaining cities rolled into one.'

'Granted, General, he has powerful energy to move energy, but without the aid of Amy, or Shla whatever you like to call her, can he move the physical. Can he move a being or an inanimate object from point A to point B.'

The smile had gone from the general's face. Campbell could see he was digesting his conclusions, he had now got his full attention. 'Go on boy!'

'Not only that, sir, why send Amy?'

'Shla.'

'Yes, sir, shla, why, why send her to us to bring us here for whatever else she is, she is physically solid, an ordinary human form, her age is irrelevant.'

The general nodded in reply.' She is certainly human and for sure solid, a very beautiful solid.'

Campbell ignored the general's observations, a soldier he may be but that didn't mean he was lacking in either feelings or insight, anyway she seemed to have claimed Malise as her own.

'I am not quite sure of all of it, sir, but let me run it past you.' Campbell stood up and walked backwards and forwards for a few seconds before carrying on. He always thought better on his feet, he could also avoid the General's piercing eyes.

'Shla came to us, as did you, when it was proven without a doubt

63

that life outside the domed cities were doomed. How long the cities would last was a matter of speculation. Outside, the atmosphere had broken down, the sea had been barren for the last hundred years. It is most unlikely that any life exists on the outside at all, the air would be too toxic even for the millions of mutants. There wouldn't be enough of them left to eat, so with their food source gone death would follow . . . yes?'

The general nodded.

'Shla came to us claiming she was a psychic and a lunar base had picked up a signal, she even gave the coordinates, which, General are not of this place. That is the main point, General, the coordinates are not of where we are now, wherever that is, but Shla is and she knew of this place.

'I don't know what the other location is but it must be important. Another thing, why Malise, why single him out, Hydra gave some indication that all this was something to do with him. His past or future . . . why didn't he confide in us? He could have said something . . . but not a word.'

'Because he didn't know Campbell . . . and in fact he still doesn't!' They both turned at the sound of Malise's voice. Campbell felt uncomfortable, as if he had betrayed Malise in some way talking about him when he wasn't there to defend himself.' Did you hear all that.'

Malise nodded. He could see the young trooper was uneasy.' Most of it I hadn't the heart to interrupt.'

'*Well?*' There was more frustration than anger in Campbell's voice. Malise moved forward and touched Campbell's arm in appeasement. Shla stood quietly in the shadow of the crystal.

'Now, look, you must believe one thing. I knew nothing about this place before we came, not a lot even now. I have come to more or less the same conclusions as yourselves . . . with no great help from others may I add.' He looked accusingly at Shla. 'But one thing, I have seen a lot more of it than you and what I have seen was very hard to digest.'

'How?'

Campbell was stopped dead by the general's raised hand.

'Where are we, Malise, do you know that?' The general's voice was

64

hard. There would be no give from him.' Where, an educated guess . . .
please!' Sarcasm lay heavy on the general's tongue.

'OK, ok, General, an educated guess. I caught the last coordinates,
we drifted a hell of a long way off course. I reckon we are just off the
southern coast of North America . . . that was. Could be around Cuba,
Haiti, Puerto Rico, there are three hundred coral islands in that part of
the Atlantic, only twenty were ever inhabited. They were known as the
devil islands, or a popular name for that area was the Bermuda Triangle,
and what I have seen around this place I am sure I am right, you should
see their museum, you would never believe it.'

'How the hell did we get that far off course?' Campbell's voice was
of disbelief. He shook his head and looked away.

'You answered your own question, Campbell, we were brought here
and, as you, so rightly said, for a purpose. We will learn that when
Hydra's ready.'

'How many times are we going to hear that Malise? I'm sick to death
of all this mystery. I would rather have stayed behind and taken my
chances with all the rest. At least we knew the situation, if not how
long.'

Shla watched the three men banter their thoughts and opinions from
one to another, sometimes heated then falling into an awkward silence.
They were trying to keep their 'now' in a realm of feasibility where the
norm had no place. Campbell, as usual, came off worst. Malise felt anger
rise in him.

'I think you're pathetic, Campbell. If the world had been led by
people like you we would have never got out of the Dark Ages.'

Campbell's usual reaction when challenged was to reach for his now
non-existent laser.

Malise shook his head. 'Typical!' Campbell's over reaction was shown
on his face – his neck was scarlet.

'This is getting us nowhere, gentlemen, Hydra is probably being
amused by our irrational display of ignorance right now.' The general
smiled. As he lifted his head to look at Malise, his eyes softened.
'Campbell is not altogether wrong Malise, these are the Dark Ages. You
are the one with the brains, we are the soldiers. Can anything be done
for now?'

'Yes, it can and we four can do it.' Shla stood next to the crystal allowing her hands to brush the facets as they slowly turned.

'All the answers to your questions are here and with my help you can absorb, all you have to do is ask the past, it's all here. The future will come to you in time but this I can tell you, you and all the people of the world, past and present, will be part of it. You have nothing to fear except fear itself. You may see and go where you wish time is irrelevant.'

Malise moved closer to her, watching the large crystal catch the light and throw it back to him. 'You're talking about the fourth dimension, time travel, Einstein's theory that was never proved to work, well in theory it was, but never in practice.'

Shla moved out from the darkness. She was wearing her flight suit, gone was the sensuous attire, her clothing was more fitting for the mood.' Einstein was near but not pure time travel, his theory was that the traveller did not move, that time changed around him. When refined, in theory and practice, there are no bounds. He can travel at will and observe firsthand, for he will in all intents and purposes be there. Remember what you see will be as it was not as scholars wrote, for reality and the pen were never good companions. No language will be closed to you, you will understand everything, whatever the race or creed.'

'How does one manage to induce this miracle of hypnosis?'

Shla looked long at the young cynical face of Campbell, smiled and walked past him and held out her hands to Malise. 'These are our return tickets, as you might say. She held out two crystals about the size of pigeons' eggs. She placed one in each of his hands.' Clasp your hands, Malise, and try to let your mind go blank.' She gently stroked his forehead.' You will find it easier if you close your eyes.'

He took a glancing look at his companions and did as he was bid. The crystals felt warm to the touch. The longer he held them, the softer they seemed to become. They felt almost alive, colours of all shades and mixtures flooded the back of his eyes.

'That will be enough.' She held a slender hand towards him and took one of the crystals. She placed it about her neck, it was attached to a thin golden chain. The other crystal was still warm as Malise laid it on his chest. The chain looked fragile and yet Malise knew it was quite the reverse.

They stood for a moment, looking into each other's eyes. Malise had tried to place the feeling he felt for her; it wasn't the same as Ula. He had been young with Ula, in love with love, all he could see then was every day at a time blinded by the obsessions of youth. They both had a good start, the future would take care of itself. That kind of feeling had been burned out of him a long time ago, this was different. Passion was a certainty, familiarity had been bonded in a very short time, the feeling of having known her before was overpowering; above all else the feeling of permanency was well and truly encamped. Are these the crystals that were embedded at the top of the panel we were looking at? Malise stopped for a second and realised he could not put a time to it . . . earlier. You said there was only twelve crystals but I noticed thirteen. He also noticed that the crystals they wore about their necks were two halves of one crystal.

'You should also remember that I said I joined them on occasions. We each have our own vehicle. On no account must either of us be parted from our half of the crystal. If this were to happen one of us would not return . . . it has happened before.'

Malise was about to ask but she put her hand over his mouth. 'The time is now Malise . . . please!'

'I expect we are being left behind again while you two zot off to god knows where.' Campbell's voice held an air of acceptance, it was obvious to himself and the general that Malise was the centre of their adventure, they were just there to be used when the time was right and not until.

Shla turned and looked at the two men. 'I presumed that you would want to accompany us.' Her matter-of-fact answer caught young Campbell off guard. He had resigned himself to his fate as the rearguard. 'Just touch our hands when we are ready to go or return. The crystal joined will carry all four of us with no effort. But remember, Malise, retain the crystal or you do not return till it is in your possession . . . understood?'

'Yes, I think so.' Malise fondled the stone and looked at the one around Shla's neck. 'They are the same as the others we saw?'

The other two heard the doubt in his voice.

67

'Yes, exactly the same. Have you chosen your time, Malise?'

'Yes.'

Shla moved closer to him directing the two men where to put their hands. Malise stood pulling himself to his full height, opening both hands to encase the others. He could vaguely hear Campbell's voice asking where the hell they were going, then came the cascade of brilliant changing lights and mingled unfamiliar sounds invaded his brain, then a blackness darker than he had ever known, then they were there.

The crystal glinted and threw his reflection back at him. He was glad of it, it proved that he was still there. He could have gone but for what, they would tell him when they returned. He wanted a face-to-face confrontation, not a four-sided debate, especially with Malise holding all the cards. He always believed in the Roman way: meet your enemy head on. He had *his* thoughts, *his* questions, *his* feelings, he didn't have to guess what they were. He walked not so much with curiosity of his surroundings but to feel the movement of his limbs. If his present body was all in the mind, then his mind's legs had become very stiff. It was like when he had lost his hand. Even to this moment he could feel the ghost fingers moving in protest. Before he realised where he was, he had passed through the wall of the chamber yet again.

Campbell never hesitated, he just walked straight at it, not giving it a second thought; he knew, he could feel Hydras' presence. As Malise and Shla were bonded, he had felt an affinity for this strange creature growing inside him, god knows why, maybe they were reflected in their loneliness. He turned and looked above him, expecting something to have changed, but it hadn't. The azimuthal, the book; he took a few steps backwards. The orbs were still fascinating. He would love to know what they were, they were so different. One with its pitted surface, it looked as if it had survived a thousand storms. Its cross bent crazily to the side as if in utter capitulation, the sights it must have seen. The other so new so shiny, he could almost feel the power radiate from its glistening shell, both had a feeling of great majesty. The parapet wall was warm to the touch, he kicked away the green moss with his heel. The glistening gold smiled back at him. He tried to calculate how many tons the place would weigh but gave up.

'You are either a very brave or a very foolish man, General.' He

68

smiled to himself. He knew Hydra would come to him, he felt he wouldn't leave him alone to wander about. They walked in silence for what seemed like an eternity, the general finally giving in. He sat on the low wall of the temple and looked down at the shimmering blue of the sea. The air was heavy, the ozone cast his mind back to his youth. The waters of Queensland's domed city had smelt the same with the same clear blue, till the full force of the contamination killed off everything.

'Why did you not go, General?' Hydra's voice cut through his pleasant thoughts. He looked downward and followed the water's edge. Their ship lay shimmering in the white sand. He thought how small it looked. 'You weren't thinking clearly at the time . . . or were you just afraid . . . was that it, General?'

'No . . . I was not afraid as you put it . . . what would be the point of being afraid? You brought us here. You could stop us leaving or destroy us, you can do whatever you wish. That much I have learned, and I have never abandoned my responsibilities.'

'Never?' The tone in Hydra's voice was full of recrimination. 'Never, are you sure, General?'

'No never!' His voice was high with indignation. 'Not knowingly.'

'Never, not knowingly . . . convenient, General, well I know of one and you will have the opportunity to resolve it quite soon.'

'What the hell do you want of me, Hydra?' A second of guilt struck him but he didn't know why.

'You are the one who wants, General . . . you are the one full of questions and burning curiosity . . . are you not?'

The general raised his hands in mock capitulation.

'May I ask you something, Hydra?'

Hydra nodded. The general stood a moment choosing his words carefully.

'Were you always such a martyr . . . and such an unmitigated bastard as you are now, or have you worked at it over your millions of years? God forbid living for eternity, if you're the result, humanity personified, Christ.'

There was a long pregnant pause. The general watched Hydra intently. He knew through his temper, he had put his life in his hands. With a

69

flick of a finger he was dead but he felt they were two of a kind. He watched as Hydra's aurora rose to a bright red. The anger flew in all directions then slowly subsided to a pale yellow and was gone. He stood grey, with an almost transparent outline, all anger had gone. The general heard him laugh for the first time very quietly but it was there.

'I suppose I must be!' He laughed a little louder. 'You know, General, I have never thought of myself for such a long time. I have never had the occasion to . . . you get tired of your own company. You forget who you are or, in my case who you were, you forget the hurt and compassion of other beings. I have never known friendship for thousands of years, it has been a luxury I have had to do without.'

'What about Shla? The words rolled through the general's brain but did not pass his lips, the time was not now. He walked towards Hydra and stood within a metre of the entity, he held his hand palm upwards as was the international sign of friendship.

'My name is Aaron Zerta, general of the world security force, which is possibly now non-existent.' Hydra hesitated for a moment.

'Aaron, a good name for one so forceful . . . Egyptian in origin.' He laid his hand on the general's, an act of compassion on both sides. Hydra felt warm to the touch.

'Well, Aaron, your companions will be gone for a while, their choice, may I add. You have my undivided attention. It is easier for me to deal with one face to face. I will answer your questions in the simplest possible way. If you do not understand, we will compromise . . . make yourself comfortable.'

The general sat on the step of the apron to the temple. He could see shoals of fish lazily changing their direction in the clear blue water far below. It took him back to Scotland, another lifetime that lived in his subconscious and was forever green. Margo was never very far from his thoughts, more so now, if his life was to end the last word on his lips would be her name. It was the only real emotion that he had ever felt and it hurt like a mortal wound.

'When you transported us.' He pointed his finger upwards. 'We did really go didn't we?'

Hydra nodded casually.

'I heard hundreds, maybe thousands, of voices, but saw nothing, except the bloody moon that scared the shit out of me. And, of course, the very yellow-covered earth that looked like a suppurating ball of matter. I also heard a very special voice, my Margo's a voice I could never forget. In fact we all heard a voice that was special to each one of us.'

Hydra once more nodded in return.

'Well what are they damn it?'

'In your terminology, spirits, souls, the energy released from a dead cadaver. There weren't thousands, there are millions upon millions, an unthinkable number held in the Umbra and the Perumbra of the moon. For the time being they will stay there for there is no release for them.'

'Margo is amongst them?'

'Seemingly.' Hydra's matter-of-fact reply made the hair rise on the back of his neck.

'You're an aggravating bastard, Hydra.' Aaron looked for the slightest sign of irritation, there was none.

'I can't see any point in that statement.' His very drollness made Aaron smile.

'Where are they?'

'Where can they go?'

'For Christ's sake, Hydra, don't answer a question with a question, please tell me. I don't want to know out of idle curiosity what you have told us and by our own observations none of us have much time to contemplate a navel.'

'Aaron, Aaron, time means a different sphere here. The legendary four score and ten don't apply. We are like the ones you heard, awaiting our release.'

'But why are they there in their millions?'

It was in the fore of Hydra's mind to repeat himself but refrained. He told Aaron from the beginning of his failing, his banishment, the orbs, Shla and his kingdom, such as it was. 'So you see Aaron each and every life form has a force, an energy that cannot die. The vehicle that carries it will die but not the force, you cannot destroy that energy. When the body dies the force returns to the Umbra or the Penumbra, or if you like the place of rest to recharge itself. When this is done, it is then used again by another vehicle for its lifespan. In the beginning there

71

were more animals than humans but over the millions of centuries they died off for one reason or another. In the last century, man has slaughtered out of hand; turning from animals to humans, he has all but destroyed himself, total genocide, that is just about to happen. So there you have it, the souls or energy have no vehicles to return to, so they are trapped, watching their world wither away and die. Millions of them, such as your Margo, have fresh memories as they are in the early stages of recharging, that is why she would still know you.'

The general sat for a long time looking at the shimmering water and, remembering her face, he finally stirred.

'How can I get to her, Hydra, she knew I was there.'

'Easily, Aaron . . . just die!' His answer was blunt and to the point.

'How the hell can I die, you've got my bloody body; I can't even make that decision.' He felt a great pain in his throat; he had never wanted anybody or anything so much in his life. Life was such a little thing to lose to have her back, in fact, the transition would be welcome, now he knew life didn't stop at death. He felt Hydra's hand touch his arm, he had never thought him capable of feeling, at least for others.

'I need you, Aaron, have patience, your Margo will still be there when it is done, I promise you.'

5

A Friendship Made By
Time

'I have your word, Hydra?' The general looked long and hard at the
pale shining face.

'You have my word, Aaron Zerta . . . as a friend. Do you think I
could be a friend again after all these years. The general smiled and
nodded his head. 'Of course . . . it will just take time.'

'Enough of this moroseness, if you wish to know more just ask Aaron.'
The general felt at ease with himself but there were so many questions
he could never ask them all. In fact did they really matter, now they
had Hydra to protect them?

'You told me of the orbs, fascinating.' He pointed upwards to the dull
and dented one. 'Quite a story, the laying of the seeds, white, brown,
yellow and red and the flood etcetera.' He felt Hydra look at him. 'No,
Hydra I doubt nothing . . . just a question . . . the blacks?'

'The blacks, what of the blacks, Aaron?' He felt as if he had touched
a raw nerve.

'If the seeds laid by you were white, red, yellow, and brown, were
the blacks an offshoot from them through population explosion and
interbreeding?

'Hydra shook his head his eyes seemed to glaze for a moment. 'No,
they are of this planet, they could have been so strong, such great people,

but they tried to span thousands of years, in one step, impossible for any race. They eventually realised they could not dominate other races by intellect, so they tried to dominate them by pure force of numbers. This they did until your earth could no longer cope with their mass. Then, as you know, you fractionised, made your domed cities where only the intellectuals were housed, you even turned the workers who built them out to die, Malise's family was one correct?' The general nodded.

'The first black, as you call him, took his first step 500,000 years ago. They came from the mating of a *homo sapien* with a *homo erectus* in that joining all future species would be *homo sapiens*. They were not the first, man but the first really *thinking* man born of this planet.'

The general sat for a moment, trying to digest Hydra's statement. History bore out most of it, but not all.

'I know this is of no relevance to you but I always thought that *homo sapiens* didn't come on the scene till 35,000 years and Neanderthal man followed *homo erectus*, even though they died out.'

'You still question me, Aaron.' Hydra shook his head and once more touched his hand. 'Oh ye of little faith. As I told you, I had a helper like you.' He stopped for a moment in thought, just over three thousand years ago he too had to be shown before he would believe even his closest and beloved friend. 'Well, Aaron, here are my wounds for you to touch.'

The blue water blurred before his eyes. The general could feel the acid vomit surge from his stomach and burn the back of his throat, he shut his eyes and hoped for a reprieve. His first realisation of any sort of recovery was a feeling of great warmth and of a bright light trying to force its way into his befuddled brain. He slowly opened his eyes, shading the light with his hands. Surrounding him was grass taller than a man in places, the land was green as far as the eye could see. The sun's heat was unbearable, the humidity gave off suffocating smells he had never encountered before, the ground was soft and spongy.

'Where the hell are we, Hydra? Hydra?' He was shouting hysterically. 'Hydra!'

'I am here Aaron . . . be calm, I am here . . . behind you.'

A large flock of strange birds took to the air causing yet more noise.

74

Animals of various sizes and shapes broke cover, took a brief stock of the strangers, then disappeared into the plush greenery; all was quiet again. The general could hear his heart beating frantically in his ears; fear penetrated every cell of his body, his voice sounded like a croak.

'Where the hell have you taken me now, for Christ's sake?'

Hydra's laugh was warm, it sounded human for the first time. He turned to face the voice, he looked human, he looked for the lack of a better word . . . warm. His skin was light brown, no longer pale and dead looking. His hair was dark, in fact black, it had a bluish sheen, like the old raven's wing; he stood as tall as himself. He had a striking face, almost Greek-like, fine boned. His eyes were large and brown, his smile was the most amazing thing about him – it seemed to light up his whole face, and he wore a flight suit just like his own. Gone was the aurora, he was a whole man.

'Don't be surprised, Aaron, this is the body I used then.'

'Then . . . when was then, for god's sake don't speak in riddles, Hydra.'

Hydra took no notice of him. He stood, taking in deep breaths of air, filling his lungs to capacity. He had a large stupid smile on his face. To the general's surprise, he started jumping up and down, flattening the grass around him and sniffing the air; he grabbed a large handful of greenery and started to chew it cocking his head to one side to catch a far-off sound.

'I had forgotten what it was like to have the five senses. I feel so alive.' He laughed and waded his way through the high grass to the general's side, grasping his arm.

'The smells, Aaron, the smells.'

The general smiled thinly. All they were doing to him was making his stomach heave, the nausea was almost painful. Hydra marched off carving a trail through the long grass; he had no option but to follow. They were rising all the time. It was hard work trying to keep up with the flaying figure in front of him. There seemed to be no tiring the man. Then suddenly they were out of the savanna. The trees were less green and the ground was firm, a cool breeze ran passed their bodies and they could breathe normally again.

The general lay prostrate on a large flat rock, his heart threatening to pound its way through his chest. He turned his head and saw Hydra looking upwards at something and smiling, he stretched his neck to see but a large tree with its branches trailing the ground was in the way. He laid his head back on the cool stone.

'Why is it so hot, Hydra?'

Hydra didn't turn round but spoke over his shoulder. 'The Equator!'

So matter of fact, so bloody irritating, the general stood up and walked over to where Hydra stood, leaning against a small tree laden with fruit of some sort.

'Where on the Equator . . . if it's not too much bother.'

'It's no bother, anything for you . . . my friend.'

The general was finding it hard to cope with the new Hydra. He felt it was probably him. So much had happened in such a short space of time, he had to give it a chance.

'It's a beautiful place, a place that just before your time was called Kenya . . . look Aaron.'

The sky was turning to red as the sun began to sink, he watched in fascination as it slowly spread across the blue like a forest fire, but this one no one could put out.

'No, there Aaron.'

He followed Hydra's extended arm. The great mountain Kilimanjaro rose in such majesty, the snow lay clear against the blackness of the rocks, the reddening sky made it an awesome sight. He had never seen such raw beauty. It just didn't exist in his time; you cannot compare artificial with the real.

'Such beauty, Hydra . . . did our world once look like this? We were such fools, can they ever forgive us?' The general sounded as if he was in prayer, not a thing he did easily.

'Yes, my friend, I know.' Hydra had seen it so many times before but searched for a comparison in his own far-off memories, a thought reflected from his own seed. Vague memories of undersea ridges of colour, of golden warmth filtering through to the depth, the inflection was the same, they both had their own beginnings, that would never change. The night's quietness settled around them, the stars were strikingly bright, the large moon looked near enough to touch. He could see every crater. Two thousand one hundred and sixty miles in diameter of shining white. He could see the rainy sea, the shallow crater Archi-

76

medes, and above the crater, Plato. Copernicus stood out bolder than any, forty-six miles across, ringed by mountains twelve thousand feet high, it was hard to believe that one day in the future moonbase would settle in the middle of the vast crater. He lay on his back for a long time just drinking in its beauty, Hydra's fire flickering in the corner of his eye.

'What time are we in Hydra . . . that I will understand.'

The voice that came from the darkness was full of concern for his companion and reflected he had not asked a great deal. 'Approximately five hundred thousand years back from your calendar, a long time ago for you, my friend.'

The general lay quietly, allowing the words to play on his mind, a long time ago, my friend, along time ago. His brain seemed to be turning in slow circles as if falling down a well, in slow motion he could see the sides slowly revolving, slowly going deeper, and deeper, and deeper. He reached for the sides, as he slowly went down and down and down, slowly relaxing as the warmth of relaxation took over his body, as his brain relaxed and gave up its tension, he carried on down and down turning, slowly feeling every muscle give way. Hydra for the first time had thought of his companion and not of himself, Hydra's voice seemed to guide him into a valley of utter contentment.

'Relax, my friend, and feel free and safe for I am here, let your thoughts wander to a peaceful place as you sink deeper and deeper. That's it, you are going down and down, gently and warmly relaxing into safety and contentment, that's it, believe in me, my friend, and let go as you spin deeper and deeper and deeper, down and down into a soft and relaxing state.' Then oblivion.

The morning came quickly, he stretched and felt good, better than he had in years. He had never slept so well since . . . god knows, and he felt young again and ready to tackle anything and go anywhere. He lay on his back and took stock of the sky, it was so blue and so clear, the sun was low, just coming out from behind the great mountain. It was brilliant orange, its fiery fingers searching into every crevice to breathe life into the planet once again, nothing was spared its curiosity. For one who had never seen such brilliance, there were no words only a feeling of awe at the world that had been. A lone cloud sat in the sky, a sculpture of dazzling white, it seemed to defy gravity, it was the first white cloud he had ever seen. The sky in the city was purely a projection cleverly done, as it was it had never made the hair stand up in the nape of his neck like now.

'Beautiful, isn't it?' Hydra's voice seemed so very far away. He turned his head and saw him smile. He was enjoying the general's indulgence.

'Yes, my friend it is.' He pushed himself onto his elbow.

'You must have see some sights in your time, Hydra, what stands out in your mind? Not a history lesson but something that happened to you or effected you in some way.'

Hydra sat thinking for a moment. He drew his knees under his chin and clasped them tightly to him. He reminded the general of a small boy about to tell his spellbound friends a yarn of a lifetime.

'There have been many, Aaron, this being one of them. I have been back here many times in the past to see this miracle.'

The general had no idea what he was talking about nor was he about to ask; that could come later but for now he wanted to know as much about the man as possible.

'I remember so clearly when we landed and to this day I don't know why I was chosen. I wasn't asked or told, I just knew, so I got on with it. I was the only one to awaken at that point, in fact I thought I was the only one to survive the journey but this wasn't so. All but three had survived. I buried those and got on with the task of preparing the ground for the others. I wandered this new world for ten lonely years, searching and preparing, mapping, interbreeding the animals I found in the carrier ships with those I found around me with some very strange results . . . some still survive today in spite of the great flood.'

'Where did your ships land . . . did they all land in the same area?' Hydra gave no indication that he had heard his question. He didn't turn, he just carried on.

'Remember our landing was three hundred million years ago. The planet was not as it is now. All the planet's land mass was virtually in one piece, the continents were just beginning to separate. It would take another one hundred million years before they broke away completely. Where we landed was to become known as Gondwanaland, in the southern hemisphere that incorporated in its boundaries what was to be known as South America, Africa, India, Australia and Antarctica. The ice cap then covered almost all of South America, half of Africa and the west tip of Australia. Antarctica was welded to all those continents by a great sheet of ice. The Australia we found ourselves in was much as it was up to a few hundred years ago, abounding in animal life. Then, one day, as if an alarm had gone off in their heads, they all awoke and turned to me for guidance. This I gave, still not knowing and still asking, why me. They, like me, found the new bodies hard to cope with at the beginning but soon adjusted; they quicker than I, for I was the only one with memories of our home planet and knew what I had been before. I found the new body very cumbersome and slow, the amount of effort that was required to move from point A to point B was enormous to what we had been used to. Time was on our side, it was either adjust or perish.

'We built our first settlement close to the sea. There was plenty of fresh water. I had long since found out what we could eat and what we couldn't mostly by trial and error and in the beginning being sick a lot.' He grimaced at the thought. 'The ships were dismantled and every ounce used for some useful purpose. In just over a year we had a healthy colony, each man and woman worked for the common good only. I lived apart. I made the laws and they kept them. I was never challenged for my position. They seemed to know right from the start that I was different. They treated me like a demigod and I allowed it, this being my downfall in the end. You must realise how difficult it was for me, I had no idea how old we would grow before death, I had no idea who would succeed me if or when I died. I could not let myself think of immortality. The very thought was too hideous to even consider – living on and on, as others died around me, but this was to be the case. Our lifespan was to be five hundred years. In the beginning, the idea was the more we populated, the shorter our lifespan would become. This, in fact, never happened. A woman could not have a child till she was over two hundred years old. Don't ask me why but over the years this became a fact. In the beginning I though we were never going to populate at all. I thought we would all die out one by one, but, as I have said, I had no way of knowing how long we would live. The first six hundred years were the worst. After that we had some sort of

Fadar

timescale to work to. I received instruction now and then, not written or sent in the true sense of the word. I just used to wake up and know what had to be done, and it was. There were times when I wasn't sure if it was my instructions or his. My life was being laid out for me like a well read story: you can tell what was coming on the next page . . . so I thought.

'Then came Sirchii, out of the blue. I had never thought of love. Five thousand years had gone by and I had never had a union with woman but now it had come and with a vengeance. She was the most beautiful thing I had ever seen; the same thing every man feels when he falls in love, my body ached for the wanting of her. I was completely disorientated. She was small and slim, with a pale complexion; her eyes were bright green and she had the smallest hands I have ever seen. She aroused in me feelings that up till then I had never had to cope with, remembering my origin. I knew nothing of bodily contact of this nature or passion and the hurt of it almost became unbearable to me. Sharing a life with another was completely foreign to me. To think of another before oneself after a lifetime of celibacy was a daunting task, to say the least. To me, Sirchii was all that had been missing in my life. I had spent what seemed to me then an eternity looking after others. Now there was someone to give their life to me and add to that life. Twin sons were born to us and then a daughter, they were the golden years when the quality of my life was rich beyond any realms I could have imagined. Our community grew in culture and in knowledge but not so much in numbers. Our population came almost to a stagnant halt, the deaths and births all but cancelled each other out. We were also content and did not want to move beyond our bounds.

'With the love and complete contentment came the complacency. We forgot our purpose, I in my folly had become Fadar, the words of wisdom in my brain became mine. I took or rejected them as I felt, there was no repercussion, I was the complete master. I allowed great statues of myself to be built, mountains of gold in my image. This I did knowing in my heart that a day of reckoning would come, but after thousands of years of adulation you become immune even to yourself. It is easy to cast an eye over your shoulder when the deed is done, I should have known better, but for the enormity of time. I had even

80

allowed my beautiful Sirchii and my family and their families to live alongside me in my loneliness. This too I took for granted.

'The day was like any other until about midday. It happened slowly at first, the sky becoming darker and darker blocking out the sun. I thought at first it was an eclipse. The air around us became dank and filled with an overpowering stench. Then the wind, slowly at first, building up to an unbelievable strength, picked up millions upon millions of gallons of seawater and threw it at the defenceless city, flattening every structure. Then, as the inhabitants fled to the nearest hills, they were driven back by great landslides, thousands upon thousands were killed. Then it stopped as quickly as it had begun. By this time, my family had gathered around me. Sirchii held my hand and smiled, there was no fear in her eyes. The noise was was unbelievable the cries of fear were deafening and the screams of the dying pitiful. They looked at me for a help I could not give. I had no idea what I was dealing with . . . not then. I remember looking at the sky to see if I could see any break in the clouds. Then the realisation struck me . . . it wasn't a cloud. The vast machine spread as far as the eye could see. It literally filled the whole sky from one horizon to another. It had to be thousands of miles square. That's what had blotted out the sun and no doubt caused all the other damage. Fadar, or his envoy, was here . . . as he had promised. There was no more destruction, no one else died, at least physically, for six days. They sat and awaited their fate on the seventh. They were spoken to, all were spoken to, not just Hydra. Where the voice came from I don't know not even to this day. I don't know if it was inside our heads or from the giant ship, but one thing I do know it was a voice to be obeyed. All my people were to be returned to the sea and live the rest of their lives in their original state, never to be mortal again. Any resistance mental or physical was met by disintegration.

'That day, Aaron, was the darkest day of my life, I stood and watched as my beautiful Sirchii and my whole family just walked into the sea, I never saw any of them again. I for my punishment was made the keeper of this ball of dust. I was told I had to seek a land and settle there till I was called again. This I did. It took me twelve hundred years to find the island in which the temple now stands. It was not always below the sea − it sank after the first orb had completed its task. There has been

81

many tales told of it over the centuries. You know of Shla. I was allowed her company when Fadar thought it right, but she never could take the place of Sirchii. As they say in all the great books of knowledge, there is but one love but there can be many lovers . . . Shla was never mine to keep.'

Both men sat for a long time thinking about their respective lost loves. The general was about to take him up on the comment he made about Shla but let it go, but thought to himself what an aggravating bastard he was; he always seemed to finish a sentence with a suggestive remark, leaving you hanging in the air. You never seemed to get caught up with him, he was sure he did it on purpose.

'What did Sirchii mean Hydra?'

Hydra looked away from him and up to the mountain.

'You know that mountain is seventeen thousand and forty feet high . . . Child of sweet water . . . and that she was.'

'Is she up?' The general pointed his finger skywards.

'You know, Aaron, I don't know, I've never been allowed to contact any of my people . . . still it won't be long now!'

'There you go again, Hydra, with your innuendoes, blast your hide.'

Hydra laughed and gently pushed the general forward. 'Come on, Aaron, let's make a move, the time is now.'

As they climbed from the foothills to the higher ground, the air became cooler and less pungent. The sight below them expelled all knowledge he had ever gleaned from the history computers. It was not the savanna of their projection, it was a great sea of green, lush and fertile as far as the eye could see, only marred by deep lines which appeared here and there showing the wanderings of the larger animals. The updraft took him unawares as he turned the corner of a huge rocky outcrop. Hydra stood looking downward, a knowing smile playing on his lips, as if he had found what he was looking for, although the general knew damn well he wasn't lost. He had said he had been here many times before but he seemed to need his sense of the dramatic. The valley lay in a large rocky indent; it must have been at least fifty miles across. Its centrepiece was a beautiful blue lake, its surface mirrored the white clouds that lazily played in the sky above. Hydra looked over his shoulder and waved him forward. 'Come, Aaron.'

They made their way downward again and, to his surprise, it got much cooler. Hydra explained besides being in the shade, what wind there was blew across the glacier above them, forcing cooler air into the valley. They carried on downward for another hour till they reached the long flat plain. The grass was surprisingly short, not like the savanna, it looked for lack of a better word, cultivated. It was well wooded but no trees grew near the lake only large bulrushes, or something like them. They stood over twenty feet high, their stalks looking more like bamboo, although it was probably their height and thickness that gave the impression. They swayed gentle in the sudden breeze; their rustling was the only noise he could hear.

As the wind died away another noise caught his ear: it sounded as though someone was throwing small pebbles down into the mirrorlike water. His eyes scanned the scene and caught nothing. Hydra put his hand on his shoulder and pointed with the other. 'Look Aaron at the bottom of the rushes . . . no, over there.'

The general shaded his eyes and concentrated; the sun still danced on top of the water, causing a blinding golden flash. He moved farther round, allowing the shadow of the reeds to fall on the water, then he saw them. They were obviously fish, what kind he had no idea, they were huge, with great gleaming scales; as the sun caught them, an instant flash of colour shot from the water. They reminded him of the great mirror carp he had seen in the aquarium of the domed city, but these were ten times bigger with much more colour.

'What are they doing, Hydra?'

'You are not as observant as you claim, Aaron.' He pulled the general slightly towards him.' Follow the stem of the rushes and watch carefully.' Some of the rushes quivered as he followed the outline of their thick stalks. He saw some form of crustaceans, probably some form of snail; the reason he hadn't seen them before was that they were on the shadow side of the stalks most likely to keep out of the sun. The large fish were ramming the rushes causing them to vibrate, thus causing the snails or whatever they were to lose their grip. As soon as they touched the water they were gone. The general smiled at Hydra. 'Very clever.'

'Not really, Aaron, the animals have been here a long time . . . come.' They wandered through the woods always climbing. Signs of wildlife were everywhere – animals of all shapes and sizes grazed on the plush grass. They had no fear of man at all. The general stroked the rump of a large, long-haired stag. It turned its head, looked at him for a second and went back to its meal. No fear, only acceptance of another animal, strange as it may have looked to him.

'The whole place is fantastic, Hydra, nature in the raw, the animals are so tame. Unbelievable, why couldn't it have stayed like this?' Hydra laughed out loud.

'Have you forgotten your own kind so soon, Aaron? Man and man alone destroyed all this. The trouble was this time you had . . . had . . . oh, come on Aaron.'

The grass began thinning out. They were half way up the slope at the far end of the valley; they had been travelling at a steady walking pace all day.

The general noticed that there were now very few animals about. 'What's happened to the animals, Hydra, they seemed to have just disappeared?'

Hydra pointed to a small pond; the banks had been well trodden and it was obviously a watering hole for the animals that lived at this end of the valley. They walked over and circled it twice. There was traces of animals all along the banks, mostly of the smaller variety. The general held on as long as he could. 'Well . . . so it's a watering hole . . . big deal, so what?'

Hydra once more encircled the general's shoulders with a friendly arm. 'How you ever became a general Aaron, I will never know.'

He laughed and pushed him away.

The general quickly retaliated. 'For god's sake, I didn't live in a world like this, mine was plastic and recycled air. The only animals we had were in captivity or just recalled on video, give me a break Hydra.'

'Ok . . . ok, I'll give you a clue, when did you or I start walking about with no shoes on.' The General relooked at the ground around him. It was obvious he felt the heat rise in his neck, bare footprints were leading away from the watering hole and up the hillside. He followed them up as far as he could; the light was beginning to fail and if last night was anything to go by it would be dark in no time flat. '*Homo sapiens?*' Hydra shook his head. '*Homo erectus* they came before.'

84

A Friendship Made By Time

The General shook his head. 'I don't really follow this. You told me that *homo sapiens* was evolved by the mating of *homo erectus* with *homo sapiens*. How can this be if *homo sapiens* was not evolved yet how can they mate with them. There's got to be something wrong here somehow . . . I don't get it.'

'You will . . . look, up there.' His finger pointed to what looked like a large black hole in the hillside. The general stood stock still. He felt his adrenaline begin to pump its way through his body. He tried to analyse his feelings, it wasn't fear as such, it was excitement, but taken to an extreme: he was about to see history in the making. Hydra touched his arm. 'Sit down here for a moment Aaron!'

They sat for a moment in silence. 'I just want to remind you, Aaron, that nothing can be altered by you, all that you will see and hear has been. The suffering and pain, the complete lack of compassion, is as it was, remember this was the beginning of their time. Another thing, you will not be seen.'

'Will you?'

'No, but I will do as I have done before, you'll see. I have told you I have been here before, it cannot change.'

'Is this one of those helping evolution projects of yours, Hydra?'

'Yes, Aaron . . . just have patience.'

The evening now was very dark indeed. The general looked up the steep incline and saw a pinkish glow against the blackness. He turned to Hydra.

'Fire?'

'Yes, Aaron, but not manmade, gathered in a storm, then tended with fanatical care. At this time it is revered more than life itself. To them it is a godlike thing that comes from the sky.'

A cold wind suddenly rose from the valley floor, making the general shiver. From where they sat, the great mountain seemed to black out half the stars but it was still beautiful in its starkness. They stood at the cave entrance and listened. The flickering of the fire danced on the walls and caught a pile of bones thrown to one side of the opening. They looked as if they had been split open and the marrow removed. The smell coming from within was unbelievable – it seemed to be a mixture of human excreta, urine, sweat and, well, rotted meat. The word revolt-

85

ing seemed totally inadequate to even consider. The general's stomach
heaved. He tried to be sick but couldn't. It suddenly dawned on him
the last time he had touched food was in the domed city and that
was . . . was, god knows, strange he had never felt hungry. He didn't
know what he was thinking about. He wasn't even in his own bloody
body, but how could he feel and smell and see? The flat of Hydra's hand
in his back pushed him from the gloom into the flickering brightness.

The cave was huge. It seemed to be in two tiers: the ground level
held mostly males, with a few females of the species scattered amongst
them. They were kneeling with their heads bowed, as if trying not to
be seen. They were all completely naked, small in stature with heavy
brows. Both male and female were covered with coarse body hair. Their
eyes were set deep in their heads but they had no sparkle. It was only
when they moved that there was any sign of intelligence. Moving farther
in, he noticed there was more than one fire: there were, in fact,
three in all. Each fire was surrounded by a ring of stones, joined by a
smaller ring which contained wood of various thicknesses, but all more
or less the same length. Small pebble-cutting tools lay within the circle.

What was even more amazing was each fire had a feeder. He looked
at the nearest to him, a female. Her large sagging breasts lay heavy on
her knees as she sat cross-legged in front of the fire. Her hair was matted
with grease, her whole body was filthy, covered with matted sores.
Hundreds of small burns also pitted her body, obviously from tending
the fire. Much to his disgust, he noticed even her pubic hair was singed
to the skin. She turned and looked in his direction. She was blind. Great
cataracts covered her sightless eyes, like leather patches. This was probably the fate of them all, as they constantly looked into the fire, hour
after hour. The smoke hung from the ceiling like a black cloud running
down the damp walls and escaping through the entrance. It seemed to
accelerate as it met the fresh air, happy to be free of the awful stench.
There must have been about fifty bodies scattered about the floor of the
cave. The only noises were grunts and the slapping of flesh on flesh. He
watched a male pin a female to the wall, using his huge erection to
demean her in every possible way. When he had finished with her he
threw her to the floor. Immediately she was pounced on by another,
then another male, six in all took her body. A group of males stood

masturbating as if to give encouragement. She tried to rise. She got half way, her back arched and her legs trembled with the exertion, blood and sperm ran from her like a river. Her eyes rolled and she fell forward, scattering the small stones that surrounded the wood pile, what happened next was the strangest case of opposites the general was ever to see. Two of the males picked her up. One grabbed her breast, the other her arm and they literally threw her full force at the cave wall. There was a sickening crack as her forehead smashed into spiked outcrop, the point pierced her frontal lobe then reappeared through the back of her head. Her body was impaled, she hung like a rag doll, only an involuntary twitch passed through her remains. Aaron looked at Hydra for an explanation, he shrugged his shoulders.

'She'll be eaten . . . eventually . . . now watch!'

The two men who had killed the female sank to their knees and crept towards the fire. Six stones had been disturbed from the ring. Each took three and in turn reformed the circle wiping them clean and inspecting them for any damage. They looked as if they were in prayer as they replaced them, one by one, turning occasionally to look at the body impaled on the wall, a deep growl forcing its way through their yellow teeth. Their gentleness was amazing after the act they had just performed. As quickly as it had happened it seemed to be forgotten, only the body was left as a reminder.

Aaron walked around the floor of the cave watching their movements and looking for some sign of motivation. Their dead eyes gave nothing away. It was hard to put an age to any of them, their grotesque looks did nothing to help or the matted body hair. One thing he did notice that the ones nearer the fire seemed to command more respect. None of the others sat within six feet of them. The farther back from the fire the closer they huddled together. He also noticed that the ones enjoying the pleasures of the fire were sporting scars of different lengths and depth, they had to be from hunting or battle. So what's really changed, he thought, to the victor the spoils.

Hydra motioned him to follow. They made their way to the upper shelf of the cave. It was obvious this was the females quarters and yet another two fires with their attendants. But these were not blind, although they followed the same ritual. He looked to Hydra once again for an explanation.

'The ones below are blinded by hot coals so that they may not look upon the bodies of the warriors. They think it is bad luck to have a woman gaze upon them before doing a brave deed. Women are here under sufferance, purely to be used and to breed and that is *all.*'

In the upper section there was dry grass strewn over the floor. With the heat rising form the fires below, plus the two on the upper level, it was very warm indeed. The general had expected the upper level to be choking with smoke but it wasn't. He looked around the ceiling and spied a funnellike hole. It was obviously a quirk of nature, acting like an extractor fan, sucking the stink and the smoke into the night air; a sort of venturi action, what it would have been like without it he dreaded to think. There were several smaller compartments leading off the main cave. Hydra stood looking into one of them and the general joined him.

'Look Aaron . . . in the corner . . . there!' His voice was soft as if tinted by a sad memory. The general was sure he saw tears well up in his eyes. He sank to his knees, allowing more light to enter the small opening and pulled his friend down with him. The opening was guarded by branches from which protruded large barbed thorns. The light from the nearest fire bathed the inside of the chamber with a pale yellowish glow. Two doglike creatures lay to one side gnawing what remained of any goodness from two large bones. What they had come from they had no way of knowing.

The general put his head closer to the thorns to get a better look at the other side. He wasn't sure at first as the flickering light did little to help . . . he shut his eyes for a moment and looked again. It was a baby and by the look of it not long born; it was hideous to look at, terribly deformed. Its spine was twisted like a corkscrew, its small chest badly misshapen, its legs out of proportion to its body, its bulbous skull forced its head to one side. Its face . . . its face was beautiful, almost angelic; it was a manchild.

The general looked over his shoulder at the fire. One small female was looking at the opening: he had never seen such resolution and despair on any face. Her shoulders were rounded, great tears ran quietly down her solemn, expressionless face; her legs were crossed with her hands laid open as if to say why me. Her crotch and legs covered with blood and afterbirth. There was no doubt in his mind this has to be the mother. She was destined to sit and watch her child eaten alive. The general's head snapped round as he heard a growl from the chamber; the dogs moved towards the child, saliva dripping from their jowls.

There was no hesitation. Hydra glowed for a second and passed through the thorns. He knelt and picked up the dying child from the filthy floor. The dogs retreated, cowering in the corner, whimpering their protest at the strange apparition that had stolen their meal. Hydra stretched to his full height, his arms encircled the tiny twisted body like a shield, his aurora flickered in unison with the firelight. He seemed to take a deep breath, held it for a second, then there was a sudden flash.

The general was momentarily blinded. He shook his head and blinked his eyes to clear his vision. Hydra's aurora dissipated slowly till he stood as he had been in the glow of the fire. There was no realisation from the other females, only the child's mother watched the strange ritual.

The general watched Hydra in silence, he was holding the child to him pressing his lips to its forehead. He spoke to the child in a quiet voice.

'For you Sirchii, my love, for you . . . for the love we had and I destroyed . . . one day, my love, one day!'

He glowed again, not so vividly and was knelt next to the general, still holding and kissing the child. He held out his arms full stretch.

'For you, Aaron . . . lay it in her arms . . . for this I give you as a friend, for there are two seeds. This one will die but he will lay his seed before going on. Hold it for a moment and let it feel as you feel, give it your heart and it will remember you for ever. This I promise you . . . you will meet again.'

The General took the child awkwardly as any bachelor would, his hand finally supporting its back. His fingers moved down feeling for the twisted bones, his fingers marvelled at the straightness of its spine, its strong legs pushed against his arms, as its little chest filled with air. It was perfect, it could have been his child, its eyes were full of curiosity, there was nothing dormant in this new life. A small hand stroked his face the lips puckered and the human suckling sound was loud in

89

his ears. He saw water fall on the child's chest and he looked upwards at the cave roof before realising, it was his own tears. He had never ever felt emotion like this, His throat was so constricted he could hardly breathe. He heard Hydra's voice repeat in his head, there are two seeds, one will die, why did it have to be this one . . . his?'

He turned and looked at the female, she seemed to see nothing but the child. There were no questions only that this was her offspring, the strange face was awash with tears her great breasts heaved with anticipation. The open hands raised towards him, she showed no sign of knowing that he was there, her eyes were only for the child. She took it to her breast and watched it suckle for a moment, her quiet grunting seemed to pacify the boy. Then she raised her head upwards to look long at the ceiling. She nodded once or twice and looked down. He had seen that gesture so many times in his own time . . . was it possible?

A scream of pain penetrated the upper level but not a pain of fear. Hydra knew the general had no idea.

'The time is now, Aaron, the seed is about to live . . . there, look!'

The upper cave narrowed, almost touching the floor, all the general could see were two filthy legs protruding from what looked like a pile of leaves. Looking closer he could see that the large leaves had been placed on the body from the waist up, completely covering the woman's face. She must have been very young, her frame was much slighter than the three females that sat patiently at her feet. Her legs were bent, her knees wide apart, her breath came in short pants, she was fully dilated. Her distress was obvious. The child's head was in place. She rested for a moment to regain her strength. She gave a strong push and a sharp scream of relief and the child was gone from her. It laid for a moment on a blanket of leaves, coughed and spluttered the mucus from its lungs and cried to the world. She lay still for a moment, he watched her heels dig into the cave floor, her hands appeared from beneath the leaves and pushed hard downwards into her groin. The afterbirth shot free and lay next to the child. The nearest female picked the afterbirth and the child up, biting through the cord and licking the child clean. She turned and handed it to the woman, who still had the first child in her arms. She took it without hesitation. It too was a perfect *homo sapiens*, but a girl child.

The general silently mouthed 'Second' to Hydra; he nodded in reply. The three females sat sharing the afterbirth between them, leaving the fourth covered with leaves, they moved away settling around the fire.

Hydra had moved forward and was removing the leaves from the female's body, she like the others was covered with gore from the ancient childbirth ritual. She lay completely naked but was in the dark from the waist up. Hydra suddenly bent forward and kissed her hand; leaning further forward, he pulled her from the floor. The general could see nothing for Hydra's back but he could tell he was talking to her, he was using the same soothing tone he had used with the child. His curiosity became too much for him to bear, he sidled up next to Hydra and looked over his shoulder. He was wiping the filth and the sweat from her face; she had very fine features. The fire flared as another piece of wood was added; the yellow tongue bounced from the ceiling, illuminating the rear of the cave. The exhausted girl raised her head and looked the general straight in the eye, a slight smile played on her dry cracked lips. The general in turn looked at Hydra . . . Good God it's Amy!

'Shla . . . Aaron, will you never learn.'

His stomach heaved once more and he felt as if he was falling down a well spinning around and around . . . all he could hear was her name repeated over and over again.

'Aaron . . . Aaron, come on now . . . open your eyes, we're back.' He felt his body being shaken, he opened his eyes and there was the blue sea just as it had been. He sat for a while cradling his head in his hands, he knew it had been no dream, there had been too many details. It was the most amazing thing that had ever happened to him, his body still ached with emotion. Hydra sat watching him for a while, realising what a toll it had been on him. Eventually he turned to his friend.

'What of the children, Hydra, that female could never rear two, she was completely subnormal.' Hydra smiled at him in his aggravating way.

'That's why she was given the two . . . twins then were completely unheard of and besides they also looked so different. It was better that it was thought that they came from the same mother.' The general shook his head.

'I still don't understand.'

'Aaron, then and for many many thousands of years later, even in

91

your time, what could not be explained was worshipped, was that not true?'

The general nodded his head. 'You're right.'

Hydra carried on. 'So you see if we take that as the only conclusion, only they would be cosseted till they were old enough to reproduce. By that time their superior intellect would have made its mark. They would be well able to take care of themselves, in fact they would revolutionise the whole family structure even the point that the female did exist as another person.' The general nodded his head in appreciation. He could see the point and the difference that the new laid seed would make, but he had another matter on his mind.

'You know, Hydra, it struck me while we were there, I haven't had anything to eat since god knows when. It's not so much that I am hungry, it's more a habit.' His next remark made him laugh before it came out.

'Hydra!'

'Yes, Aaron?'

'I know this is going to sound stupid considering what we have gone through . . . but.'

'Yes, Aaron.' Hydra sat waiting for some irritating comment that questioned the facts.

'Can I have my bloody body back, it's got to be starving, if I'm not!'

Raucous laughter ran down to the shore below, birds by the thousand took to the wing animals darted in every direction; noise, especially at this volume, was not the norm here.

6

A Faith Reborn

The first realisation of consciousness was the coldness of the pillow beneath his head. Malise sat himself up slowly, trying to peer through the darkness; sand stuck to the left side of his face like a crust. He sat for a moment, taking stock of his surroundings. Then a sudden realisation, where the hell was Campbell and Shla? They had started out together, had he been the only one to make the journey? He felt for the crystal – it lay stuck to his chest; it too was covered in sand. It was so dark he couldn't even seen what he was wearing, whatever it was, it was rough to his skin and had the odour of wool. He decided there was no point in moving, for a start he had no idea where he was literally, he had no idea what time it was only that it was jet black, not even a star to be seen. He decided the best thing he could do was to keep still and try to keep warm, he curled himself into a ball and waited for the morning.

The inn was small, the shuttered windows letting sharp spears of light escape into the cold evening air. Campbell hadn't hesitated in asking the way to the nearest inn. He had been told by a pointing finger whose owner had scuttled quickly away into the darkness, but not before reminding him to avoid the night guard at his peril, also he rebuked him for having his wife out well after the curfew. After several attempts the inn door slowly opened but not before the lights were dimmed. Campbell bartered with the voice in the darkness before they were allowed entry. They passed through into the semi-darkness. The door shut quietly behind them. There was a moment's silence, disturbed only by the wooden bar sliding into place. They heard the innkeeper's voice say something to a third party and the lights came to life again.

The inside of the inn was small but warm; the hard clay floor was scattered with straw; it held only half a dozen tables served by small stools. Campbell went forward and spoke to the innkeeper and pointing to Shla. She stood close to the door, her head bowed, her face partially covered by her rough shawl. The innkeeper was not amused at being disturbed at this time of night. She heard Campbell say something about a child. His attitude changed completely, he smiled over Campbell's shoulder and signalled for her to be seated, why hadn't he said this before?

His wife brought bread, wine and water, also two small pieces of cheese, she patted Shla on the shoulder in a knowing way that one woman keeps for another at these times, as if sharing a sisterly secret of things to come that was beyond the knowledge of man. Campbell returned and told her he had arranged a room for the night and he had told them that they were married and on their way to see her sister in Jerusalem, which was only a mile and a half away. The place they had arrived at was Bethany, a small village outside the walls.

She smiled at him and thanked him for making her pregnant; he tried to explain the reason but she wasn't really interested. She poured some water into her wine and dunked her bread. The cheese was strong, obviously of goat extraction.

'Where the hell's Malise, Shla?' His tone was that of the rejected. She looked up and smiled.

'Not far away . . . we'll see him soon . . . be patient!' Campbell looked almost disappointed.

'How do you know?'

She touched the crystal that lay between her ample breasts.' I know . . . I know . . . let's get to bed.' She watched his face for a reaction – there was only the slightest flicker of concern. One thing he knew he wouldn't enjoy sleeping on the floor . . . he didn't.

It didn't take Malise long to realise why he hadn't seen the stars. The morning had crept slowly into his new world. Eventually the filtered light danced on his well-rested eyes. The ceiling above him seemed to be alive; looking again he realised it was, hundreds of bats hung from the sandstone roof. He was in a large cave. How the hell did he manage to get there? He rose and looked towards the light. The opening seemed high up in the cave's side. It took him quite a time and considerable strength to reach the irregular gap in the cave wall. He looked out. It was at least a hundred and fifty feet to the floor of the valley below and it was a sheer drop. As he sat wondering how he was going to get down, he noticed deep ridges cut into the mouth of the opening; of course, they had to be made by ropes. He had been too busy trying to get out to notice anything unusual. They were there, great coils of rope neatly piled in rows, containers of various shapes and sizes with rings for the ropes to be attached and lowered to the floor below for hauling people or food up into the cave. How safe could you be? It had to be a hideout for bandits or the like. He dropped the nearest rope over the side. It was more than long enough. He rechecked the large ring in the wall before letting himself down into the bright sunlight. He was glad to be back in the open again, the cave had a strange smell, a sweet sickly smell, probably the bats. He walked a few hundred yards before looking back. The hair stood up on the back of his neck, the rope was no longer hanging from the cave mouth and there was more than bats in that cave. The tunic he found himself wearing was of some coarse cloth, a rough woollen fabric. It came to just above his knees, his underwear felt like cotton, his feet were clad in soft leather sandals, all a little rough but ideal for the heat. Various paths criss-crossed his own. Soon he was surrounded by a crowd of people, their eyes fixed on the walled city ahead.

'Water, friend?' Malise turned at the voice. A small man, leading a donkey, was by his side.

'My wife and I would be pleased to share our water with you.'

Malise looked at the wife, she too was small. She walked in the shade of the animal, holding on to the leather ring. Her striped shawl hung to the ground; it also covered her face completely. He thought to himself that she must be sweltering.

'Thank you.' He took the leather waterbottle from him and drank deeply. It cascaded down his parched throat like a cool river. The man looked at him in amusement.

'You were thirsty, my friend, when was the last time you drank?' Malise had to think for a moment. 'Yesterday, I suppose.' He tried to think it into place but again time was a confusing matter.

'Are you going to Jerusalem for the celebrations . . . you travel light my friend have you come far?' The questions weren't doing Malise any good at all, all he wanted was to be inconspicuous and to find the others as soon as possible.

'I spent last night up there . . . it was cool and dry.' He pointed to the mouth of the cave that was still visible. He handed the water container to his generous companion, who dropped it to the sand in disgust.

'Leave us . . . leave us now, and take the water.'

'Why . . . what have I done?' Malise was completely confused, one moment generosity the next total rejection. The small woman moved to the other side of the donkey and looked away into the sun, pulling her shawl tighter round her face.

'Come, woman, don't linger, we still have a way to go.' He struck the half-asleep donkey with a hefty stick and turned to look over his shoulder. 'Please leave us alone . . . you must know why.'

More and more people were shying away from him as the conversation was passed from mouth to mouth, back down the line of travellers. Malise's temper was beginning to rise and the heat didn't help. 'Please, just tell me why . . . I really don't understand.'

The man continued to strike the poor animal harder, trying to make it break into a trot, his wife was hanging on for grim death. 'You cannot come from this area?'

'I don't!' Malise had almost to break into a run to keep up with him; the man's eyes still held fear. He pointed back over his shoulder at the slowly disappearing cave entrance. 'It's a leper colony . . . there must be at least two hundred rotting souls up there . . . how could you not know?'

Then it dawned on Malise . . . of course, the smell, it wasn't the bats, thank god he hadn't known, they must have been watching him all the time.

The city of Jerusalem was a massive complex surrounded by a huge wall with numerous gates: four in the west wall alone which provided

96

access to the upper city; two leading on to arching viaducts over the western valley; it was the jewel in the Jewish crown. It was said he who had not set their eyes upon the structure of Herod has not seen a structure of beauty in all his life. Campbell felt that this had to be true. There had been no problem of entry. There were so many people coming for the passover celebration, all they did was mingle, the Roman guards just stood aside and let the throng pass unmolested, for they knew there was no way of stopping them.

The temple was alive with people, the great Antonia Fortress lay alongside. The majestic Palace of Herod and the Hasmonean Palace also lay within the walls. The city was abuzz with rumours of all kinds, that Jesus was within the walls, that he had been condemned to die by the Sanhedrin Council of Jewish Elders. That being the case, he would surely be stoned to death as was their way, and yet he hadn't been . . . they would have to wait and see.

It was almost noon when they first sighted Malise. He couldn't be missed as he stood out well above the people in the crowd. The average height of people in that day and age was about five foot seven, depending on the tribe or creed, so he looked like a giant amongst them. Campbell left Shla in the shadows of the great wall and brought Malise to her.

'For god's sake you two, remember where we are . . . sit down, you've brought enough attention to us already, Malise.'

Malise spoke through clenched teeth. 'If you had any idea what I have been through to get here I . . .' Campbell butted in, 'Who the hell brought us here in the first place . . . and why here, why now, are you a sadist . . . or what?'

Malise's temper subsided as it always did, maybe Campbell was right, maybe he was a sadist, maybe he would take pleasure in seeing him crucified. But he knew one thing for sure, he was going to see him . . . and talk to him.

Campbell put his arm on Malise's shoulder. 'All I'm saying, Malise, we will have to be careful, it's just that you stand out like a sore thumb. Just stay here till I come back . . . I won't be long.' Before Malise could stop him he had vanished into the milling crowd.

'Why did you come here, was it for Ula and your parents?' Shla's voice was soft and caring. She pulled his hand under her robe. 'Well?'

Malise looked down at her and wished he was somewhere else so he could take her in his arms; he knew she felt the same.

'You know, Shla, I'm not really sure, I was, but now I'm not, I think it's more for myself, I want to see who started this chaos, try to understand his answers, do you understand mine?' She nodded her head and squeezed his hand even harder.

Campbell returned with a supercilious grin on his face. He handed Malise a large striped robe. 'Put this on and slightly bend over when you walk, it will take some of the height off you.' It was very coarse just like his tunic but it did make him less conspicuous.

'Where did you get it, Campbell?'

'Gambled for it!'

Malise laughed and looked around. 'Where?'

'Malise, everywhere in every back street there's a game of chance.'

'But how did you know what to do.'

Campbell squatted in front of them. 'Don't you remember, Malise, I was the cardinal's personal guard, I also hold a doctorate in theology, aren't you lucky! The language we are speaking is Aramaic; it is the most common language used in this area. It died out eventually mostly due to the population being scattered after the revolt in AD 66. The Romans sacked Jerusalem in AD 70 and demolished the temple.'

Malise raised his hand to stop Campbell. 'Campbell, I'm sure you can run rings around us with your obvious knowledge but do you mind keeping to this moment in time; for instance, who are they?' Malise pointed to a group of sombre-looking men squatting on the temple steps.

'You mean those in white . . . the ones sitting on the steps?'

'Yes . . . who are they?'

'The group in white are Essenes. They are a sect that keep very much to themselves; they are bachelors elected to a life of poverty, you can always pick them out by their white robes. if you look around, white wasn't used very much at this time, mostly by teachers and priests. Now the other, the ones standing at the other end of the steps, the ones wearing swords, they're zealots, political activists, Jewish Nationalists, if you like. They cause the Romans a lot of problems all over Palestine, or Canaan as they call it now. They have heard rumours that the High

Priests were trying to get the procurator, Pontius Pilate, to stop Jesus preaching and to keep him away from the temple. They would fight if there were enough of them, they are tolerated as long as they don't gather in force . . . look there!'

A small company of soldiers mounted the steps, using their large shields, they forced the gathering zealots from the temple front to the courtyard below. The soldiers formed a V formation and taunted the zealots below them. Each man raised one of the two javelins he carried hoping at least one of them would draw his sword, but they would not be baited into action. The Roman red tunics, covered with heavy armour, clashed against their dull surroundings, their small swords hung ready by their sides. They were then the greatest fighting force in the known world. Two Syrian archers stood on the top step of the temple, their right arms bent, touching the arrows in their quivers; the mercenaries of the Roman Empire were waiting their chance to show their superiority, any excuse would do.

They roamed about the city taking in everything of interest, the many strange sights and smells. Some of the streets were broad and spacious, others narrow and dark, even in the daylight, but all were amazingly clean, considering the amount of animals that were about. There were many small taverns and inns, this probably due to the amount of visitors the city got throughout the year. Wine and water seemed to be served everywhere even in the street.

Campbell kept leaving Malise and Shla to explore on his own. When this happened, they stayed in one place to await his return. He kept repeating what a tale he would have to tell the cardinal on his return. Malise had thought of that himself, would they ever return to the domed city? He doubted it, if Hydra had his way. The great Roman villas were in contrast to the ordinary citizens' homes. They were beautifully built and ornate, some with colourful mosaics paths leading up to a high frontage, supported by pillars finished off with a tiled roof. The grand council chamber sat firmly on Solomon's Porch, the forum nudged cheek to jowl with the great theatre.

The huge wall that surrounded the city cast its shadow in exact precision as the baking sun moved across the brilliant blue sky. the Pool of Siloam blew a breeze in their direction. It surprised Malise how very few people were taking advantage of its coolness. More and more people were gathering around the temple as if waiting for some appearance or a sign.

Shla sat in the shade of a large fig tree. He was worried about her – she had been unnaturally quiet since meeting up again. Malise moved closer to her and slipped his hand into hers, trying not to be too obvious. She moved her leg against his searching hand and smiled encouragement.

'What's the matter Shla, have you lost interest already, has young Campbell stolen that fickle heart of yours?'

'Nothing!' She squeezed his warm hand. 'I have only one man now. Malise as is my destiny. The final choice will be yours, as you will see!' Malise shook his head in confusion.

'I don't understand Shla, what does that mean?'

She rubbed the back of his broad hand, looking intently at his fingers, as if trying to see something that wasn't there.

'Only you and Hydra can bring this to a conclusion, for you, my darling, are the only one with the choice!'

She smiled and placed his hand on his lap patting it gently, he pulled it away to show his irritation.

'What the hell are you talking about . . . you, like Hydra, talk in riddles. You never have a conclusion.'

'I'm sorry Malise . . . it's just this time, it's confusing, it has so much beauty, so much ignorance and so much brutality it's just not real.'

'What do you mean not real? You're not telling me this is a hallucination . . . that I'm dreaming all this. Come on now, Shla, I won't wear that, I know I should have gone crazy long before now but this is not a dream!'

Shla looked away into the city as if looking for some form of comfort. 'No, it's not exactly a dream; I didn't mean it in that sense. Why did you come to this time, Malise?'

'You know why Shla . . . I want answers and I don't want to go back without them . . . ok?'

'You won't get the ones you expect here!' Her voice had a hard tone he had never heard before; it took him by surprise.

'Why, I don't understand, if there was a time for answers, it has to be now.'

'Oh, Malise, you couldn't be more wrong. You were told that time

and the written word don't always go hand in hand. You asked Campbell
to find you the Nazarene, and he will, all you have to do is ask him.
You won't believe anyone else, in a way I don't blame you. If you don't
meet him you will always have that doubt.' She threw small pebbles into
the dark water and watched the expanding circles try to reach the shore.
She spoke no more.

Campbell eventually returned, wine was heavy on his breath but he
had made the arrangements. He was to meet the Nazarene later that
evening. Campbell told Malise that Jesus had said he had expected him,
whatever that meant.

They made their way from the pool to one of the larger inns. This
time Malise was Shla's husband and for three passionate hours they acted
that way, forgetting where or when or even how they had got there. It
left Malise in no doubt about Shla's feelings, or his own, for that matter.
Campbell came and aroused them from their pleasures. The time had
come, a time that every man in his time would give his life for.

The spring night was cold against the day's sun, the streets were
deserted. Great black shadows were cast everywhere, the tangled smell
of herb-coated food danced on the gentle evening breeze, as suppers
were made and eaten. Malise followed Campbell's shadowy figure as
best he could. Shla had been left behind at her own request. Malise
wasn't surprised – his own body was far from awake but well satisfied.
They found themselves on the wide road that led to Herod's Palace, a
place that had cost hundreds of slaves, lives to build to his satisfaction.
The lights from the high city windows danced like fireflies in the still
of the night. Campbell stopped him with a strong arm across his chest,
his long fingers pushing into his ribcage to make his point. Malise could
feel his hot breath on his chest and the lingering smell of stale wine as
he whispered in his ear.

'We turn left here and go about four houses down . . . someone
should be there to meet us.' His voice didn't sound very convincing and
Malise felt uneasy in the dark. He had no idea where he was and if he
lost Campbell he doubted if he could find his way back.

'How do you know where we are . . . I don't recognise a thing?'
Campbell pointed to a well-lit house in front of them. It had to belong

to a Roman or a city dignitary it was well sighted on its own grounds. Campbell's voice came out of the night.

'It's the house of Calaphas and Annas, very important, watch for the guard . . . ok?' Malise squeezed his hand in reply. As they rounded the corner and blended into the shadows they caught sight of them, there were two one each side of the ornate arch. They stood like statues . . . they were Romans. Their rounded helmets caught the house lights, their armour glinting from the light of a brazier that was hidden just inside the gateway. The red and yellow reflections danced on their breastplates, giving the impression they were on fire. Campbell knew they were just thankful for its warmth, as any soldier knows who has ever been on night guard even in his time, cold makes you vulnerable.

'This way . . . here.' The deep voice was just loud enough for them to hear.

'Come . . . quickly . . . and quietly . . . hurry!'

The walls were rough to the touch and the ground uneven as they groped their way down the darkened sidestreet. Malise had a feeling that they were not the only ones on the move. He sensed other bodies pass them, he saw nothing, but his third eye seemed to pick them out of the darkness. The small hairs on the back of his neck stood out like porcupine quills. Campbell was enjoying creeping about in the dark but it held no joy for Malise. Suddenly they were inside a dimly lit house, a door opened slightly as they entered. The light shone for a second on a flight of narrow steps leading to a top room. Their silent companion waved them up after him. Malise caught sight of Campbell out the corner of his eye. He had entered the lower room and shut the door behind him. This had obviously been prearranged. As the top landing flooded with light, he caught sight of his guide: he was short but broad, his longish beard was tinged with grey, his face was sunworn but kindly, his eyes looked only ahead and were full of love.

'Master, the man they call, Malise.' He bowed slightly and waved Malise into the well-lit room. Many lamps hung from the walls, well trimmed as little smoke was visible; there was a large table well covered with food and wine, twelve places set in all and the air was filled with perfume of incense. Beyond the table looking out of a half-open window was a slim willowy figure; his back was to Malise, he spoke in a soft voice.

'Go, Lazarus my beloved friend, but tell the others the time will be soon . . . this very night.' Without a sound, the doorwas closed and the two men were left alone.

'You have come a long way, Malise and, as you see it, from one tragedy to another . . . don't be afraid, I am here for you, at least for a while.' His long white robe glided with him, as he turned to face Malise. His face was like his body, lean; his cheekbones high; his nose long and straight; his skin was so pale and tight, it shone. His mouth was small but full, his eyes were large and brown and held great warmth. He looked at first glance effeminate, his facial hair was sparse and fair. He motioned Malise to a chair then sat himself. Malise watched him for a few moments, he was like a statue, only a smile played on his lips, his eyes like dark pools. Malise's dual reflection looked back at him.

'You seem to know me?' Malise's voice was hoarse, his host poured a fair measure of wine and water from an alabaster container and handed the almost-full goblet to Malise.

'Drink my friend . . . have no fear of me. I know as much of you, Malise, as you know of me, but neither know each other for what we are. But we will meet again when all men shall be equal . . . save you!'

'For god's sake, no parables . . . I've had more than I can cope with. I won't even try to unravel that last lot . . . you've never set eyes on me before in your life . . . I'm from another time!' His expression didn't change at Malise's statement, then the angelic face lowered his eyes in mock submission.

'As you will, you are here for your own reason. Ask your questions then there will be peace between us.'

'Are you the one called Jesus?'

'Yes, that is I.'

'You know your future?'

'Yes.' He lifted his head and looked steadily at Malise.

'Do you know the future?'

'No, I don't, but you have the power *now*. How could you let the world die? Also people who have hardly lived. Disease of every kind become rife, wars, pestilence, suffering beyond all limits of endurance. Great blood baths throughout history in your name. You contend that this great father of yours loves the world and all living things, that he

103

bleeds when we bleed. In the years to come, teacher, there will be oceans of blood in both your names as you set brother against brother and you teach this as love?' Malise felt his neck throb as his veins stood proud. He could not remember when anger had crept so deep into his soul. The silent figure made no move nor did he change his expression throughout his outburst.

'The hurt of the world is not for you to bear, Malise, but the direction that it took was in as much your hands as mine. Malise, what happens tomorrow will change the future in so many ways. You see the ironic part is if I had been accepted as their king, I would have brought union and peace in my time. The Romans the Jews and every other sect would have lived in peace. I would have blazed bright like a shooting star for a while before disappearing into the dust of history and time. But rejection will make my name burn in people's hearts with love till the gathering.

'The Jewish people await a Messiah to return and release them . . . they will not receive me. In a way they are right, for I have never really been away. Their wanting will cost them dearly in generations to come for they will be remembered as those who crucified me. This will be cemented for all time when the Romans pick up my crown and sing the praises of the King of the Jews, who died for them. They will spread my word throughout the entire world and Rome will be my haven. The great father will be remembered through me. The name they call him is of no consequence as each prayer has his own world and his own conscience, for he is my master too. There is no kingdom he does not rule, no land in al the heavens he has not touched in his passing, there is no soul in all the universe he will not gather, for look!' He caught Malise's arm, led him to the window, his grip like steel. He threw open the shades and pointed to a star-studded night sky.

'His garden, Malise, open your mind. There is but a small scattering of seed, it is infinite, there is no end.' Malise stood looking at the night sky for a long time. The bitterness that had haunted him for so long had subsided into a quiet pool of curiosity. Malise walked back from the window and sat down. His wine tasted better for the second sipping. He looked at the gentle face and saw the wisdom in his eyes. There was also something else lurking there that he couldn't quite catch.

'Have you no way of stopping your crucifixion in order to be the Messiah and to bring the peace you want for your people?'

'Malise, you know you cannot change the past.'

'It's not the past, it's now!' Jesus placed his small hand on Malise's.

'It's your past . . . and mine too I suppose, but most of all I cannot change the choosing. This is the only planet in your whole galaxy that has this privilege.' Malise shook his head.

'I don't understand, *the choosing?*'

'This is what has caused all your catastrophes, all your wars, your brother against brother, your eventual overpopulation and your deliberate genocide. You abused the choosing. All the other planets in your galaxy, when they had life, had no choice. They were told how to live and when to die. They had no wars, no disease, no conflict of any kind. Their lives were totally programmed for them, understand?'

'You see, Malise, I opened the floodgates for the human race to do atrocities in my name through their choosing. They used me as a seed to grow a multitude of religions, that was also their choice. They used my name to perpetuate and alleviate their crimes and sufferings. Without the burden of my cross this would have not been possible . . . I will for generations to come be their crutch to lean on. I will be their ear to whisper in their despair; their song to sing to in their joy, their shield to raise against the darkness that has been called Satan. Satan is the other side of choice . . . the darkness within you that you have a choice to use or reject . . . it has and always will be your choice. Now it is your choice to take my life I have no other option but to obey as the father of all men gave you that right.'

Jesus broke some unleavened bread, blessed it and handed half to Malise. He thanked him and searched his mind for more questions.

'You said something strange, that you had never been away, what did you mean by that?'

'You asked if I was of royal blood and if I had a right to the throne. There is only me, Malise. I am what the people call a patriarch of the race. For I was Terah from the city of Ur; Solomon the great and wise leader; and now Jesus the Nazarene, who will be called the fisher of men . . . who better for the king of the Jews than he who has lived so long among them and loved them so dearly.' His great brown eyes glazed and the dams of his emotion overflowed. Malise had never felt such sadness or seen it displayed on a living being. His tears flowed freely without shame and Malise knew the pain was not for himself. He had never felt so humble, he was glad he had come, for his own soul.

Jesus rose and put his left hand on Malise's sitting figure. Malise could feel the heat from his body radiate through to his skin. Jesus pulled his right arm from his flowing robe and unclenched his small white hand.

'Malise, my companion in time, we have the same patron!'

The crystal caught the light from the many lamps and blazed its warmth at Malise's eyes, the thin golden chain shone against his pale skin. Malise looked at him and smiled. Jesus bent and kissed him on both cheeks, Malise returned the gesture, the salt from his tears was strong to his lips.

Malise smiled and pulled Jesus closer to him.

'I should have known . . . I should have known by the things you said . . . everything's falling into place . . . thank you, Hydra!'

'Malise, Malise, listen to me.' He held Malise's hands within his own and looked up into his eyes. The genuine concern fitted their friendship even on such brief acquaintance.

'I am to be sacrificed tomorrow but not as was written, whatever is. My wife, the Magdalene, my Son and my beloved friend and brother-in-law, Lazarus, will sail for Gaul and safety, this I have promised. I will return from where I came till next I walk and am needed.'

The room door opened and his twelve followers entered and took up their places at the large table. They made no sound. They sat with their heads momentarily bowed. They seemed to sense what was to come. Jesus made no move to explain Malise's presence. He conducted Malise to the door and once again took his hands in his.

'I will say farewell to you here, Malise. Will you do something for me . . . no, two things?'

'If I can!'

'Firstly, remember, the Gospels were written a long time after the crucifixion; assumption, exaggeration, frustration through lack of first-hand information, and time warps any tale. Remember me as I am, not what they thought I was.' A smile crossed his face. 'Now you have the choice. Secondly, please don't stay for the crucifixion, it is not what it

106

seems, it is for them, there is no hurt for me, I am Fadar's son. I have your word . . . Malise?'

Malise took a last look around the room: the disciples were all focused on Jesus. He had never seen such love in men's eyes.

'I promise . . . for you my friend . . . safe journey.'

As he turned towards the stairs, Jesus whispered to him.

'Tell the general, remember the dogs!' Malise hadn't the faintest idea what he meant. The journey back was fraught with the same dangers as before but Malise hardly noticed them. Shla laid by his side listening to the rising outside noises; they both knew what it was, the voices crying in the night. She gripped his hand and squeezed it tight.

Malise lay quietly being tormented by the noise. If the book had been anywhere near right it was to be a long night for his newfound friend. The gentle face of the Nazerene would not leave his mind; everywhere he looked in the darkness he was there. The gentleness that only comes from knowledge shone from his eyes. If only he had known before, his life could have been less bitter; his mother had understood, the same look had been in her eyes right to the last.

The Garden of Gethsemane was beautiful; the new shoots were sprouting from every crevice, bush and tree; the morning air was fresh and clean. The guards had looked at them strangely as they had passed through the tall gates. They had explained that they had urgent business in the near city of Jericho. They asked them why would they want to leave the city the very day they were going to crucify the Jewish pretender. Malise made the excuse that his wife was with child and she insisted on going home to have the baby. 'The typical of a woman to spoil a man's pleasure' ended the conversation. The three stood hand in hand with Campbell in the middle. The noise from the city was becoming louder as the crowds caught the chant and joined in, most of them not knowing why. Malise looked at the great walls and knew what was beyond.

'Are we ready?' His companions nodded, he turned and looked at Campbell.

'Thanks . . . I couldn't have done it without you!' As Campbell squeezed his hand in reply, the great city rose up from the desert and was gone.

7

Final Concessions

It took Malise only a second on opening his eyes to realise he was under water. He was actually sitting on the sandy floor, a school of fish had stopped to take in the unusual sight. He resisted the urge to take a deep breath and kicked hard against the sloping bottom, his strong legs propelled him quickly to the surface; on reaching it, he opened his mouth and vented like a whale. His ears popped and he was back in his own world, he lay on his back and felt the warmth of his body. Loud laughter skipped across the water's surface and bombarded his ears, he turned onto his belly and tried to catch the sight of the sound. The beach was only twenty feet away. Campbell and Shla were holding each other up trying to control their hysterical laughter . . . he had done it again. They ran into the water up to their waists and dragged him out onto the warm sandy beach.

'How do I manage to land in a different place to the other two, Hydra?' They were sitting round a large table eating, it was good to have their own bodies back again even though tiredness went with it and the aches and pains of the flesh. Hydra finished his mouthful of food before replying.

'You try too hard, Malise, instead of letting yourself be taken, you try to take yourself with an image in your mind. Am I right, think about it.' Malise sat for a moment and thought.

'You know you're right . . . I won't do that again!' They spent the next few hours relating their different experiences. Shla and Hydra sat listening in quiet amusement, they had made journeys such as theirs many many times over and in some cases had been the instigators of their outcomes. Malise turned to the general.

'Just before we left, Jesus gave me a message for you, I don't understand it, maybe you do.' The general looked puzzled.

'What is it?'

'He said to tell the general . . . how the hell he knew about you, god knows!'

'Get on with it, Malise, do you have to elaborate everything? Come on, spit it out.'

'It must be the scientist in me . . . what do you think?' He was deliberately baiting the general.

'Malise!' He had started to rub his metal hand, a sure sign of irritation; Malise gave in. 'He said to tell the general to remember the dogs . . . whatever that means.' The general sat for a moment, thinking. He eventually shook his head.

'I haven't even seen a dog in years, I can't think what.'

Hydra touched his hand. 'You have, Aaron . . . not that long ago.' The other three had noticed how close the two men had become, that's if you could call Hydra a man.

'The only dogs I've seen were in a cave in Kenya . . . you're not telling me.' Hydra patted him on the shoulder.

'Then how did he know . . . and you Aaron should know that anything is possible, think!' The general's eyes glazed over in remembering. He could see the blood-covered child that had been so badly deformed, lying straight and warm in his arms. Most of all he remembered the eyes of this perfect boy child and the intelligence they reflected in comparison to its subhuman mother. He remembered Hydra's words (give it your heart and it will remember you for ever). He looked at Hydra. 'The same person or at least life force?' Hydra smiled.

'Yes, my friend, and he did remember you.' Malise changed the subject as he could see the general was struggling with his emotions. He directed his question to Hydra.

'He also spoke about the choosing, he said we were the only planet in our galaxy which had free choice, is this so?'

109

'Yes, Malise, that is so.' Hydra's voice sounded slightly strange.

'Maybe I wouldn't have made the mistakes I did if we had had a choice on my planet. Obviously I carried the memories with me from my home planet and paid for it dearly.' Malise carried on pressing Hydra.

'What was it like, not to have a choice?' Three faces watched for an answer. Hydra took but a second.

'You know that really is a stupid question for an intelligent man, Malise. You have to be given the choice to know the difference. We didn't know so we were very happy in our organised world without fear, without famine, without war.' Malise wouldn't give up.

'Now you've watched a world with a choice as an observer, what do you think . . . which would you prefer to live in now?' Hydra had no hesitation in giving an answer he had obviously thought long and hard about.

'This planet, without a doubt, is barbaric with a long history of death and destruction. But it has produced despite that some amazing people and situations, some of which I have helped to inject into its evolution. It has produced some of the greatest fighters ever known in the fabric of time, this will be a credit in time to come . . . you will see. Most amazing of all, in little over a million years, you have destroyed a planet's surface that took hundreds of millions of years to create. You made a flowering garden into a barren plain.' Shla watched Malise's face for a reaction as she remembered saying the same thing to him not so long ago. He turned, grimaced and looked away. He had no answer this time either.

'Can I ask you a question, Hydra?' Young Campbell's voice brought the previous discussion to an end. Hydra turned to face the young man, he smiled at his eagerness. Campbell smiled back. He felt Hydra knew his question before his asking.

'Why are we here? I don't know how many times we have to ask this question to get an answer.' There was a stony silence. The real, relevant question had been brought to the surface yet again, all thought of food was forgotten. Shla stood and left the table. She walked into the darkness of the crystal, without a word to the sitting company. Malise had a feeling it was for a reason.

'Well, Hydra, we are waiting.' Campbell's question was not going to be ignored, not this time.

'Shall we move from the table gentlemen . . . come, this way . . . please.' They followed Hydra's footsteps into the darkness. Within seconds they were in a room that took their breath away. It was full of artifacts of every kind, each one lit to show it to its full effect. The result was unbelievably beautiful to the eye, no one in the world had ever had a collection such as this.

'Where did Shla go, Hydra?' His voice sounded only half interested as he was looking at a large drawing on the wall. He lent over and adjusted the light for a better look. Malise knew this was more his forte.

'She has gone to her quarters. She never enters this room. You might say it is my den, my retreat, to enjoy my collection. All you see here is what I have collected, or was collected for me, over the centuries, they are very dear to me and have given me many moments of pleasure. I come here when I want to think so you see I am not so unlike you, even in a place such as this, I like my own moments of solitude.'

'Just look at this, it can't be real.' Campbell looked over his shoulder. Malise was looking at a drawing of a naked woman, drawn in such a way that all her internal organs were visible. The notes either side of the drawing were in Italian.

'So . . . apart from it being very old, and what are those wax things underneath the drawing?'

'Campbell, you are unbelievable. Read the name, you can read I take it?' The colour rose in Campbell's neck.

'I think I can . . . just, my god, Leonardo da Vinci 1492. Do you think it's authentic, Malise?'

'Without a doubt, Campbell. Hydra wouldn't have reproductions when he could have the real thing. The yellow objects are wax moulds of her internal organs . . . you know he dissected thirty corpses to find the makeup of the human body. What I would give to have this back in the lab . . . that would make some eyes pop. You know he designed a parachute, he also designed a flying machine. He was a great artist and engineer. He was a most extraordinary man of his time he was miles ahead of anyone else.' Malise stopped mid-sentence and looked at Hydra, he was smiling.

'You know, Hydra, you would have let me go on and on.' He pointed to a portrait of Leonardo. 'One of your boys?'

Hydra laughed and nodded. 'Sorry Malise.'

'Come and look at these, Malise.' Campbell and the general were at the far end of the room. Malise walked across and looked at what they held in their hands. He had never consciously compared the two men. For the first time it struck him how alike they were – their features could have been struck from the same mould. He thought it better to keep his observation to himself.

'What have you got there, General . . . a pistol?'

'Not just a pistol, Malise, this is a German wheel lock Petronel 1600, and this an English flintlock 1650; look at the condition. And look at these two, a Colt 45, six chamber 1873, and a Browning automatic pistol.'

'Look at these rifles, General, have you ever seen anything so beautiful? Look at the workmanship! Look at this.' Campbell lifted a long, muzzled weapon from the wall. 'It's a muzzle-loading Baker rifle about 1800 and a breech-loading Enfield. These are the ones they used in the Great War, and a SLR. I have never seen anything like this and look at the collection of swords.' Their sharp blades glinted in the defused light: the general picked up an ornately carved sword and looked at it as if it was a sacred symbol. He ran his hand over its length feeling its cold steel, turning to Campbell to whisper a name, the look of respect in his eyes shone.

'Samurai, Campbell, the greatest warriors the world has ever known. He gave his loyalty to only one man and that meant his life. He would give his life fearlessly in battle and sometimes take his own life rather than suffer the disgrace of defeat, the best of these swords were folded two hundred times to give them strength. Can you imagine having a regiment of these fellows behind you, Campbell, when you needed them?' The two soldiers laughed and carried on inspecting the ancient weapons. They had found their common denominator. Hydra watched and waited for his companions to have their fill of his collection. He was pleased that not only he could enjoy it.

'Quite a collection, Hydra my friend, thank you for letting us browse

112

through it. I think there was something for all of us there.' His companions agreed, each throwing his eye to his favourite piece.

'Please be seated gentlemen, now is the time to get down to the business brought up by Campbell. In fact, all of you have asked the same question since you have been here. I think I can say that you realise that this is no ordinary place and I am not quite as you. Although Shla is more your genetic makeup than I but one thing is a fact, we are all members of a race that inhabits this planet.'

'Not for long!' Malise's voice held a bitter tone.

'No, as you say, Malise, not for long but the final end can be changed if you help me help you. Please let me finish Malise, then you can ask me all the questions you like, all right.' Malise nodded his head in submission. At least now they were going to find out what it was all about.

'This planet has been dying in earnest for over a thousand years. It was bad enough what you were doing to each other but when you started on your own planet, it was the beginning of the end. You started with your bombs, your atom bomb your hydrogen, your nutron bomb all polluting the atmosphere, the very air you breathe. Then your sprays and chemicals by the millions let loose into the atmosphere. Then as a final gesture of defiance against nature, you cut down the rain forests that gave you the very oxygen you needed to survive. You damaged the ozone layer beyond repair: that was the beginning of the end, instead of reducing your population you increased it by billions. One last but masterstroke, you panicked and built domed cities for the intellectuals and let the common man literally perish in his own filth, another gallant choice by the hypocritical demagogues.' Hydra stopped for a moment and shut his eyes in reflection.

'You see, gentlemen, your choice wasn't that different to mine. Anyway I kept sending scouts out as the world became more and more contaminated. They did what they could but by then it was a pointless exercise. The atmosphere was dying and there were billions of mutants roaming the world, killing and eating anything they came across, including each other. Sometimes it was an instant return sometimes the body they travelled in was torn to shreds; if they had been normal humans they would have died. I stopped sending scouts out onto the earth's surface

113

until I heard from Shla. I had sent her to your moonbase. It was easier to scan the globe from there; with her power of telepathy, we kept in constant touch. On her observations, I sent two of my scouts to Kypros, or Cyprus, as you came to call it. Shla told me there was a small pocket of survivors there. They had made their own form of protection from the surface: they had gone underground and had made their own air-purification system. But they had been detected by the mutants who had started to dig down to them for only one reason . . . food. Their lungs had long gone past the need of fresh air, it was only a matter of time. The one remaining transmitter wasn't strong enough to reach the two remaining domed cities, one being yours. Their message was simply: is there anyone out there, please help us. By the way there is only one domed city left functioning, the one in Rome no longer exists . . . I'm sorry.

'To cut a long story short only one of my people returned and he was in a very bad way. He had to be revitalised before entering the crystal. Then, as you know, I sent Shla to your city for help, a help I have never till now needed, or wanted.'

'I knew it had to be something like that.' Hydra turned and patted Campbell's shoulder.

'Thank you, Campbell, your military mind strikes again.'

Malise turned, uneasy in his seat. It didn't make sense to him, all this for one crystal. He could see the general was puzzled too and he had no hesitation in jumping in with both feet.

'I don't understand this, Hydra, with all the power you have at your disposal, getting hold of one crystal should be child's play. Just send some of the others, or in fact all, surely twelve have got more chance than three of us?' The other two men agreed with Malise's assumption.

Hydra ran his finger down the curved blade of a Hungarian sabre and tilted it by its broad point to catch the light.

'I can't do that, at least not now, it's too late.' For the first time he looked vulnerable. 'I'm sorry.' His voice was short and curt.

'It has to be you . . . I can't lose any more of my people, and you'll have to go by your ship not by crystal. I know it's more dangerous but that's the way it has to be.'

'Well, that's bloody charming . . . it's all right if we get slaughtered and don't return.' The general shook his head in disbelief.

'You know that's not true Aaron, you of all people should know how I feel . . . but it has to be this way. I have no option.'

'Are we allowed to know why we should take this risk?' Malise knew he had the support of his companions. This wasn't an easy choice to make. He turned once more on Hydra.

'You have told us that ours was the only domed city left operating, well that won't be for long. Why should we risk our lives by leaving this place? If it has survived millions of years, it could survive millions more. For what we have seen of it it is virtually a Garden of Eden, we would be mad to leave, and there's still moonbase!'

Hydra's expression changed. 'No, Malise I'm afraid there won't be, not by now.'

'Why the hell not? It's independent from earth, it was fine when we left. I spoke to a shuttle commander – they had just come from there, all right he said it would probably be his last trip till things sorted themselves out and they couldn't take any further personnel back with them.' Hydra cut him short.

'Malise, they are gone . . . all are dead, their physical bodies no longer function.' The tone of Hydra's voice made his statement a fact.

'How and why Hydra . . . you had a hand in this it's slaughter; there were four thousand healthy people on that station. Why kill them off . . . there was no earthly reason, they could have survived indefinitely.' The general's voice was high with anger.

'Earthly reason . . . earthly reason..yes, Aaron, that was the reason, they belonged . . . here. I need you all and the number was five thousand and thirty, two hundred of those were children.'

'You didn't kill them did you, Hydra?' Campbell was standing, spinning a silver globe of the moon, the certainty in his voice made the two men search Hydra's expression for any sign of denial.

'It was Shla, wasn't it Hydra? Your beautiful Shla. Malise, how do you feel about her now . . . a mass murderess . . . the evil bitch!'

Before Malise realised what he was doing, he threw himself at Campbell, knocking the beautiful globe from his grasp. It shattered into a thousand pieces, a two-thousand-year-old relic gone in a second. At

115

close quarters Campbell was easily overcome by Malise's greater weight and strength. His face turned redder and redder as Malise's thumbs dug deeper into his windpipe, his eyes bulged till only the whites showed, then at last he was still. Malise's first realisation of sanity was twofold, his face was awash with his own blood. A deep gash lay open on his forehead where the general had struck at him wildly with his metal hand time and time again to make him let go of young Campbell. The second was the bloated face of his young companion, his open eyes staring at the ceiling, as if wondering were his life had gone. The general unceremoniously kicked Malise to one side and cradled the young trooper in his arms, wiping Malise's dark blood from his face. His fingers searched in vain for a pulse in his badly bruised neck.

'You bastard, Malise . . . you evil sadistic bastard. He was only a boy, for Christ's sake.' He cradled the young trooper's head in his lap and to his surprise tears pumped themselves freely from the corner of his eyes. They dropped from his chin and seemed to try to wash the drying blood from the boy's face. Malise watched his face contort in grief.

'If I had my laser, Malise, I would blow the biggest hole you had ever seen through your miserable gut. And you, Hydra, I thought you and I were . . .' He stopped mid-sentence. Hydra's face was intermittently lit by the swinging lamp. He smiled down at the scene in front of him.

'Not you too, Hydra.' He pulled the youngster's body closer to him. 'Not you too!' Hydra steadied the swinging light and carried on smiling at the confused general, his voice was soft but accusing.

'So you are also a potential murderer, Aaron Zerta, interesting you choose to believe your ears and your eyes instead of your logic. You should never arrive at a conclusion without knowing *all* the facts things are not always what they seem, are they Campbell?'

'No sir!' The respect in Campbell's voice was evident, Malise pushed the general to one side and helped Campbell to his feet, pulling the youngster to him in a grateful bear hug.

'You're alive . . . my god, you're alive . . . I thought I'd killed you,' Campbell pushed against him to relieve the pressure on his ribs. 'If you don't let go, you'll do a proper job this time.' They both laughed and the tension was gone.

'Malise, look at your face.' The general's voice held complete disbelief.

No gash no blood . . . nothing. All three looked at Hydra, he in turn was still smiling.

'In danger of repeating myself, never come to a conclusion without knowing *all* the facts, come Aaron.' Hydra sat the still shocked general on a wide leather seat, there was more embarrassment than anger on his face.

'I am sorry, Aaron, but I had to make a point.' Malise couldn't take his eyes off his reflection. He searched for any sign of the large gaping gash that had covered young Campbell in his blood. Hydra had certainly made his point.

'The point I have made and that I would have thought you would have concluded by now is that everything is done here for a very deliberate purpose. You were brought here for a purpose; I am here for a purpose; the world is dying for a purpose or at least every living body will die for that purpose, including moonbase. As I have explained before, all the souls are held in the Umbra and the Perumbra but this time there is no going back, no reincarnation, not on this planet. This time there is no choice, you have done your choosing, it is the time of the gathering or will be when you have done your task. I need that crystal, I need all the crystals or there will be no gathering, only eternity in limbo for us all.' The three men exchanged glances not knowing how much to believe. Malise was first to speak.

'So if we don't retrieve that crystal for whatever reason you want it for, all those millions will have died for nothing . . . yes?'

'Yes, Malise, as simple as that, the crystal bank is also a transmitter which is programmed to give out a special signal when this planet has got to a certain stage. That stage is now but without the missing crystal the circuit is not complete, you do understand why I can't afford to lose any more crystals.' Three heads nodded almost in unison they now knew they had no option.

'So our choosing has been taken from us after all, so much for our great gift.' The general's voice was almost inaudible as if he was thinking out loud. Hydra lent forward and touched his friend's shoulder.

'No one ever has a choice at death only how they die, at peace with themselves and everyone around them or go screaming into the next

117

world with hatred in their hearts. All this is irrelevant unless we get the one remaining crystal. All this has been for nothing . . . well?'

'We'll go,' the general's voice spoke for them all. 'I have only one request.'

'Which is?' Hydra's voice held a sharp edge; he wasn't used to making bargains.

'We can go back to the city and tell them what to expect, that there is hope after death. The signal has to reach that ship you told me of doesn't it Hydra, the one that returned your people to the sea?'

'Yes, Aaron the same ship, only this time for a different reason. I cannot let it go wrong. This is the penultimate challenge for your small world.' Hydra felt the unfamiliar surge of adrenalin flow through his body, his senses hadn't reacted this way for thousands of years . . . he liked the feeling. It was ironic that he was coming alive just before he would die, at least in the physical sense. He turned to his companions, taking full stock of the situation.

'Malise, go to Shla. She is at the pond she took you to. She needs you now, she will tell you why. Campbell, go check your ship and get it ready for flight. What we have to do won't take long. Aaron, if you wish to tell your people then so be it, you can go to Cyprus from there. Stay here with me and we will go over the details and will meet at the ship in one hour of your time!'

Malise walked to meet Shla, his mind in confusion. There had been more excitement in what seemed the last few days than he had encountered in most of his life. But now he was to die still young and be taken to god knows where. What would happen to them when the ship came, did he have to die? He had always had a habit of arguing with himself. Some people would say it was the first sign of madness.

'You don't have to die.' The voice in his head still laid its doubt. He answered himself instantly. 'I've got no bloody choice, the decision's been taken out of my hands, if my choice.' He waited for his reply, 'You have a choice.' He was about to answer himself when the sound of female laughter in his brain brought the realisation that the conversation hadn't been one-sided – Shla had invaded his privacy once again. He shut his eyes and sent back his own message to her – it brought her running to him. She wrapped her lightly clad body around him and

118

pulled him to the ground. An array of beautiful fragrances filled the air as their bodies crushed the flowers beneath them. Her warm supple body touched every corner of his as she twisted for his delight, probing his body with her darting tongue, her sweet breath almost burning his skin. Then she stopped, suddenly. She gently pushed Malise away. As his body failed to respond to her attentions, she kissed him softly and laid herself by his side, his closeness was enough for now. Malise's mind kept returning to the same thing.

'You know Shla, it seems such a waste all this being left to grow wild, and us, we've only just found each other . . . what do you know about the gathering?' She turned and lent on one elbow and looked down at him. His face was tired, there was a darkness under his eyes, so much had happened in such a short time.

'I wish we had met earlier, Shla to do things ordinary couples do . . . what about the gathering?' She looked beautiful, her long black hair cascading onto his chest, her red eyes shone bright against her white skin, the warmth of her body radiated through his thin flight suit. A sensuous urge radiated from his manhood as it started to rise. She pressed herself to him, but it suddenly died. He kissed her gently and pushed her away.

'I'm sorry, Shla . . . but.' She pressed her small hand over his moist mouth.

'There's no need, you have given me so much already, and you could again after.'

'What do you mean . . . after the gathering?'

'Yes, if you wanted to, it's up to you.'

'Are you allowed to pick your own partners . . . after?' Malise watched the look in her eyes change.

'Yes, you are . . . but I won't be there for you to pick!'

'I don't understand.' Malise sat upright and grasped her slender arm as if she was about to run away. He realised he was hurting her and let go.

'Shla, tell me, please.' She stroked his hair and gently kissed him. She had dreaded the coming of this time, but like it or not it was here.

'It's simple, Malise, my darling . . . I am not part of the gathering.'

119

Malise sat for a moment trying to digest her words. 'And Hydra?' Her eyes were wide and moist.

'He is part of the gathering, without him there would be no gathering. He above all deserves the gathering. He has been the keeper for so long and has suffered so much for all mankind.'

'I don't understand any of this.' Shla stood took his hand and pulled him to his feet.

'Malise, come with me, then you will understand.' They walked in silence through the long golden corridors till they came to the forecourt of the temple.

Shla sat Malise on the small wall and pointed to the orbs.

'These are the reason or rather that is.' Her eyes were fixed on the shimmering orb with its cross standing straight and proud, it looked alive, as if knowing it was its turn next. Malise felt his body surrounded by a sudden surge of heat, it held him for a moment and then was gone. Malise turned to Shla for an explanation, she stood smiling at him.

'Yes, Malise, it's alive, it is only waiting, it was probing you for data, knowledge of you as a being.'

'And?' She took his hand and pressed it warmly.

'I am sorry, my darling, only it knows the answer. You see Malise, I have to stay. It was decreed a long time ago. But you . . . you have been given a choice, an option only you in the hundreds of millions of souls have been given this last choice.' Malise's brain refused to take in the obvious it was too bizarre.

'Shla, for god's sake, what are you talking about.' She moved away from him and pointed to the shimmering metal.

'A keeper, Malise, *we* need a keeper. You were chosen when the first seeds were laid thousands of years ago. Hydra's time is up, this world will live again but with no direction without a keeper. There would be just you and I till the next awakening – if you stay.' Malise looked at the dull and dented orb with its twisted cross all life from it had long gone. It was strange to think that his original seed had been laid by this, for want of a better word, machine. There was an awkward silence. Malise looked around him slowly as if seeing things for the first time. The great temple lay majestic in its setting, the calm sea threw its colour upwards in a beautiful blue hue. The patchwork of plant colour was as

120

far as the eye could see, the white horseshoe bay was a gorgeous sight. But to live here for . . . no number would enter his head and his brain felt numb at the thought.

'The keeper, Shla . . . me the keeper. Is this why you have . . .'

She grabbed his arm and put her hand across his mouth.

'No Malise, no, I love you and whatever your choice I will always love you.'

'And very nice too, you're a lucky fellow.' Malise spun round at the sound of the general's voice.

'If I was only a few years younger, Malise, you should have seen me in my heyday, you wouldn't have stood a chance.'

The general's whole attitude seemed to have changed: he looked years younger. Whatever Hydra had told him had had an amazing effect on him. Malise noticed the look that passed from Hydra to Shla, she lowered her head in reply. He knew he was the topic of their telepathic conversation. Hydra touched Malise's arm and smiled.

'Take your time Malise, you know what's here, even I don't know all that happens beyond the Perumbra.' Malise nodded in reply.

'Well, Malise what do you think?' The general stood hands on hips, his laser strapped to his right leg but with an addition, the exquisite Samurai sword held firmly in his belt. 'A present from a friend . . . thank you, Hydra. Come on, Malise, let's get to the ship, we'll go along the beach.'

Campbell had everything on standby. The farewells were long and awkward. Shla gave Malise a soft and lingering kiss, then walked away along the water's edge, not looking back. The dolphins followed her, watching her every move, their plaintive cries setting the scene of sorrow. The expression on Hydra's face was beautiful to see. The two men stood holding hands for a long time, Hydra looking deep into the general's eyes, then he said the strangest thing:

'Your wait will be short, Aaron, then we will be friends for eternity.' Tears gently ran down his cheeks to gather in the cleft of his chin, could this be the entity they had met such a short time ago? 'You will find great joy before we meet again, my dear friend.' The general shook his head and embraced him, his fingers pressed white on his back; no more could be said by either man.

The journey back was simple: all Malise had to do was reverse the computer's flight plan and include the massive drift that had taken them to Hydra's domain. The craft dipped suddenly on its final descent, the thick yellow smog made outside viewing impossible. The craft hovered for a moment as the double airlock allowed them to enter the domed city's landing area. The craft came to rest and its engines died; the silence was loud to their ears. The landing areas lights sprang to life illuminating every corner of the bay. Campbell looked out of the nearest inspection port for any sign of ground crew; they should have been picked on the radar on their final approach.

8

Unlikely Allies

'General, look at this, up here, sir!' Campbell's voice had an unbelieving tone to it. The general made his way to Campbell's side and looked through the small inspection hatch. He turned and beckoned Malise, all three men looked in disbelief. The cardinal was on her knees obviously praying, she rose to her feet and tucked her small hands into her wide sleeves. She stood like a statue awaiting their descent from the ship. The general spoke quietly as if to himself.

'How the hell did she know we were arriving?'

'God knows.' Malise's reply echoed the disbelief in his voice. The cardinal's entourage filed into the bay, forming a half-circle around her, coughing and shuffling their feet in pure self-indulgence. The crew offloaded themselves and made their way to the waiting reception. The general held out his hand in greeting to the cardinal; she remained immobile making no move to return the gesture of good manners. It stopped the general in his tracks. Malise could see the red rise in the general's neck. The cardinal had chosen the wrong moment to antagonise the general. They had nothing left to lose but their lives . . . not that she knew that . . . yet.

'What the hell's the matter with you, woman, don't look down your bloody nose at me, you have neither the time nor the power any more.' She ignored his outburst.

'I know you could be a fool sometimes, General, taking risks that no

123

other man would take. That is why you are what you are. But I never took you for a coward . . . no Aaron Zerta, that I didn't!' Campbell lunged forward. Malise caught him by the wrist.

'Campbell?' The cardinal looked surprised at the young trooper's reaction. 'And to think you offered your life for me, you were ready to kill this man in my name.' Campbell spoke through gritted teeth.

'That was before.' He pulled his wrist from Malise's grasp.

'Before what, Campbell, before you met this, this person.'

She pointed disgustedly at the general. Campbell turned his back on her and spoke over his shoulder.

'Before the mission we have just returned from, and one we risked our lives on. What the hell do you think, where the hell do you think we've been?' The general looked closely at the cardinal's face. He had known her for many years, she had always been pious but always fair in her judgement.

Malise stood watching the confusion of his companions. He put his hand on the general's shoulder for moral support and tackled the cardinal himself.

'Cardinal, where do *you* think we've been all this time?'

Frustration was beginning to infiltrate itself into the cardinal's stony composure. He watched her knuckles whiten to his question.

'You have been nowhere . . . your ship left this bay ten minutes ago, I am not a fool. I hadn't even left the area when you returned. I felt under the circumstances I would like to give my own private prayer for your safety, that is why you found me alone. But I was wrong you had no need of it, the only danger was yourselves, may God forgive you.'

The three men looked at each other and came to the same conclusion. The general was the first to speak.

'Hydra . . . that man gets everywhere.'

He took the cardinal's arm and pressed his laser into her ribs. She gasped at the sudden pain, the action was completely unexpected.

'We have to talk, Cardinal . . . *now*!' He unceremoniously pushed her into an empty travel tube.

'Malise, Campbell, collect up the others, they're no threat'.

Campbell's eyes lit up as he bundled the cardinal's followers into the remaining cars. Malise smiled as he watched the eagerness of his efforts.

His laser was in its favourite position, entrenched firmly in his eager hand. He had waited for this for a long time. At least it was action of a sort, how long they could hold the cardinal was another matter. He could see the general in the front car. He was just glad he wasn't in the same car as the cardinal but he knew the general was an equal match. As they entered the outskirts of the city, the general once more tried to get through to the silent cardinal.

'As I said we will have to talk. Whatever is going through your brain is wrong, we have been away and we have found out a great deal. The world as we know it *is* coming to an end and quicker, a lot quicker than we thought but there is nothing to fear. It has all been taken care of, that is if Malise, Campbell and I can do one more job. You, Cardinal and your merry men were more or less right, there is a greater being, a greater being than even you could imagine.'

She remained silent and unmoved. The years of teaching and being the teacher had made her inflexible. She had decided the rights and wrongs of her flock for too long to have the will of mortal man oppose her. He had to get through to her or else coming back would be a waste of time.

'Sophronia, we came back to help make it easier, to make you all less afraid and to ease our conscience I suppose, as we in this domed city are the last of the civilised people left alive.' She turned and looked him in the eyes, for the first time there was a sign of belief.

'How did you know my Christian name? My father was the last person to use it and that was at least sixty years ago.' The general felt for her in her confusion, she and all of them had to learn in a very short time what Hydra had allowed them to do in semi-leisure.

'I used your Christian name for a reason, it means in the Greek, "of sound mind". This you need now more than ever before. Sophronia, where do you think I got this from, have you ever seen anything like it before?' He removed the beautiful Samurai sword from his belt, handed it to her and laid the point against his chest to prove his sincerity. Her eyes played on the finely carved ivory with its gold inlays, each telling a story of so long ago. The razor sharp blade shone blue in the dim light. Indeed, she had never seen anything like it before. If one doubt

125

was placed in her mind it could harvest more. She owed it to her people to know the truth.

'I could have killed you, Aaron Zerta, one small push and your arrogance would have been halted mid-stream, but you weren't afraid?' The general smiled and returned the sword to its scabbard.

'I probably trust you more than you trust me and, with a name like Sophronia, I was in no danger. Don't forget when I was chief of security I was supposed to know all those little things. All I want to do is talk, is that so bad . . . well?'

He held out his hand to the cardinal, his palm wide and open. After a slight hesitation, she placed her hand in his, but she still had the last word.

'I suppose I haven't a great deal of choice!' He smiled to himself – a woman's prerogative. The travel tubes had come to a halt in the main body of the complex and it was, as usual, full of milling bodies. They disembarked and waited.

The cardinal's transport was soon at hand and all were easily accommodated. The general cast a black shadow over Campbell by making him holster his laser. The general council building was surrounded by curious crowds: the word that the expedition had failed to take place had spread like wild fire and the populace wanted to know why.

Malise's reunion with Chez was short, the main council hall filled to capacity; the public gallery was dangerously overcrowded for the first time in years. The easy life in the dome had made the inhabitants complacent but not today. The cardinal had decided that all should hear what was to be said and all video stations were to relay the meeting so that no one would be left in doubt.

Malise was chosen to relate their experience: his scientific approach made the re-enactment more feasible. He decided to keep to the basics. The facts were unbelievable even to one who had lived through them. The vast audience listened and tried to digest as much as they could. They sat in complete silence till the last word was spoken, then all hell broke loose.

The three men exchanged glances as the bedlam grew louder and threatened to get out of control; the result was only to be expected. The cardinal realised she had made a mistake by allowing so many

126

people into the chamber and she ordered it to be cleared except for council members. The security guards unceremoniously ejected them into the main square and several died in the process. No one seemed the slightest bit concerned: their bodies lay as they dropped – basic survival had set in.

The cardinal's voice cried out for order, she could be heard throughout the city: every video screen was filled, every public address system vibrated with her promise. The discussion would go on but she would give them time to get to their homes before proceeding further: they would know what she and the council would know. Chez took the opportunity to monopolise Malise he wanted the facts firsthand. At least Malise owed him that much.

'Amy, Malise, what happened to her, tell me. The truth is obvious: we are going to die but did you have to wrap it up like this. To say the least, it's bloody far-fetched.' Malise smiled at his friend; he could understand his doubts.

'Chez, it's all true, Amy as you knew her doesn't exist. As you've heard, she has been Hydra's companion.'

'I know, Malise, for thousands of years, give it a rest, it's me you're talking to, your froggy crap friend.'

Malise looked at him as if for the first time. His ginger hair still hung in its unkempt way, he had indeed been his friend for a very long time. He was also a fellow scientist, if he didn't believe him, why the hell should the others.

'Chez . . . look my friend it's all true. I'm not going to try to convince you. The best thing is to come with us and see for yourself, there's room.'

'What!' The look on his face made Malise smile.

'Why not . . . the ship's rigged for four as you know, you helped with the conversion . . . well?' Chez sat down heavily on the long wooden bench. Malise watched his mind tick through the facts as he always did when confronted with a problem. He finally looked up – he was not altogether convinced should he take the chance.

'It's all true Malise?'

'Yes, Chez . . . it's all true.'

'But what about the time factor, you came back almost before you

127

went . . . well, you know what I mean,' Malise did his best to keep aggravation from his voice.

'As I have already tried to explain, Hydra seems to be able to control time at will. Don't ask me how . . . I haven't the faintest idea.'

'Yes, but talking about living thousands of years and going backwards and forwards to where and when you want, it takes a lot of swallowing, Malise.'

Malise sat beside his friend and put his arm on his shoulder. 'Chez look at me, I have seen what I have seen, it was not a dream. We are all going to die in a very short time, that is a fact. Does it really matter where or when? But it could matter who you are with when the moment comes. We have been friends a long time, no one knows me better than you, we have laughed together and cried together, what better.' Malise got no further for the cardinal's voice boomed loud above the hum of conversation:

'Take your seats councillors and come to order, gentlemen.'

The cardinal waved the three men in the direction of the rostrum and they re-took their seats. The general in the centre, Malise and Campbell on either side. They sat quietly, each thinking his own thoughts, Malise most of all.

The cardinal rose and addressed the assembled, her magnetism could be felt by all, she was a formidable opponent, equal to the general in stealth and cunning.

'General, the council have taken a vote, the vote on your evidence so far is one of no confidence, and I must admit I concur their findings.' The general's jaw tightened, his eyes held only contempt for their stupidity.

'What exactly does that mean, your eminence?' He raised his hand and passed it in front of his body, as if blessing the council. His gesture had an instant reaction on the cardinal and her face contorted in anger.

'That is sacrilege within these chambers, you have no right, no authority not even a faith.' The general achieved his goal to unbalance the cardinal: her calm dignity had abandoned her, her eyes blazed.

'Very good cardinal, what does your outburst mean in down-to-earth facts, for all to hear. Never mind your robes of office and your priceless crucifix, take them away and you're a human life like the rest of us, no better and no worse, except for your giant-size vanity.' The general was in full stride. No one would stop him till he had had his say. He turned once again on the council.

'You are fools, being led by a fool, what do you think you are going to do?' He banged the rostrum top with his metal hand, the beautifully ingrained wood splintered under the impact but he didn't falter.

'What the hell do you think you are all going to do . . . stay alive when we have passed on?' He shook his head in frustration. 'We are not offering you survival, no not for any last one of you, and that includes you, cardinal. We came back as it now proves at great risk to ourselves to put your wildest thoughts to rest, the believers and the non-believers. That you are not alone . . . that some other entity does care. We brought you the answer that has plagued man since the beginning of time, the unequivocal truth that there *is* another life. Not just for you but for all, can you imagine all life that has lived and died will culminate and be gathered and be reborn; the knowing you are not alone at this time should be enough.' He looked around the council chamber for a face, any face that showed enlightenment . . . none.

'For what reason are all these lives being gathered, what's the point when the world is no longer habitable?' The voice came from the midst of the council; the general wasn't quick enough to catch the inquisitor and the answer wasn't his to give.

'I don't honestly know. Like you I have to take so much on faith I only know it is almost time. Can you add anything to that, Malise?' Malise shook his head in reply. The general could see he was getting restless; he lent forward and whispered to the general.

'This is a waste of time, we're doing no good here, they just don't want to listen. The council will do exactly what the cardinals wants . . . you know that as well as I do.'

'I second that, let's make a move we promised Hydra, as soon as possible.' Unfortunately, Campbell was louder than intended. The cardinal had regained her composure the knowledge that they were in her domain was grounds enough.

'Go where Campbell? I am the law here and I do not feel obliged to allow you to go anywhere. Least of all to your mystical island; if what

129

you say is right you have no more right to life than any other citizen.'
Malise stood up next to the general.

'Now hold on Cardinal, we have told you why we have to leave, we
didn't have to come back here.'

'No, but you did Malise, you did.' The general signalled for both men
to sit; his contempt for the cardinal was now quite open.

'Let me get this straight, Cardinal, are we, Malise, Campbell and
myself, your prisoners?'

'In a word, general, yes, we feel you have tried to make fools of this
council with your elaborate tales and above all ridiculed my office as
cardinal. With regard to moonbase and the Rome domed city, either
could be a technical fault, it has happened before. You haven't told us
one thing that can be corroborated, the time factor alone. Malise I am
surprised at you a man of science.' She raised her hand and dropped it.
The twelve doors in the round chamber sprang open. Within seconds,
the room was encircled with security guards, all with their lasers drawn.
The cardinal seemed to read the general's thoughts.

'Not this time, General, I am very sure of myself.' She smiled and
waved her hand at the troopers.

'These are my guards, General, you see I don't make the same mistake
twice. May we have your weapons please . . . please there is no point in
resisting.'

'Probably not!' The general turned to his two companions.

'We'll have to die one way or another, what do you think, Malise? I
know what you think, Campbell. Let's have a democratic vote before
you blast your way out . . . ok.'

Campbell nodded in agreement if not in spirit.

'Well, Malise, we don't seem to have much choice, do we? Have one
last gung-ho or just give in . . . well, Malise?' Malise's eyes were fixed
on the general's belt.

'What's the matter, Malise . . . for Christ's sake man!'

'Look, General.' Campbell's finger was pointing at his sword. As the
general was about to look down, the gleaming blade flashed before his
eyes. It spun high in the air, stopped and plunged into the highly
polished floor, quivered violently for a moment and was still. The
silence screamed in their ears. Every eye was on the general's mystified

expression. He looked at his companions in bewilderment and shook his head.

'Another one of your illusions, General, your performance is getting boring. You will need more than this. We are not amused by your futile gestures of defiance; they come too late.'

Malise was on his feet his eyes fixed on the sword. 'Your eminence, look at the sword . . . look.'

The slim blade that was reflecting the lights of the chamber began to pulse. Slowly at first but becoming brighter and faster. A high-pitched hum radiating from the vibrating blade increased steadily.

The cardinal raised and lowered her arm, obviously a prearranged signal. Twelve lasers blasted the area of the sword. The blinding flash lit the whole chamber and the smell of burned wood infiltrated into every corner of the room. It hung for a few moments a yellowish pall, reminding all of the outside contamination that was waiting to take their lives. The automatic ventilators opened and relieved the chamber of its acid-tasting smell.

All eyes returned to the sword. There should have been no sign of its existence but there it was, surrounded by a white light that became brighter by the second. It took on the pulsations of the blade, silently beating itself into a larger and brighter shape. Every eye watched in fascination as it grew.

'General, unless you stop this charade, I will have you and your companions shot . . . do I make myself clear?' Her anger was building by the minute. Confusion had settled on the council, their reactions were almost comical. At any other time, they would have been. Their eyes moved from the cardinal to the general to the sword in constant succession.

'Do I make myself clear, General . . . General!'

His eyes never moved from the sword; he knew this was Hydra's doing and he had faith in his friend. Maybe this was the time of separation he had talked about. If this was it so be it. The cardinal's voice seemed so far away and unimportant.

'General, I *will* have you shot . . . now!' The cardinal raised and lowered her arm once more. Campbell pushed the general to the floor and lay prostrate across his body, at the same time bringing the cardinal

131

into line with his sights. Without hesitation he pulled the trigger of his laser. He couldn't possibly miss her at this range. At the same moment, the twelve troopers brought their weapons into line with their target, that being Campbell. As Malise stood directly behind his companions he too would be in direct line of fire. As he watched, the fingers seemed to tighten in slow motion and he thought . . . so this is dying. The beautiful face of Shla filled his mind and he was ready, he heard himself shout, 'Sorry Hydra.' And closed his eyes ready for oblivion. Nothing happened, he stood quite still for a few seconds before opening his eyes, a familiar voice played on his ears.

'Don't worry, Malise, they can do you no harm . . . we keepers are invincible.' Hydra's laugh filled the quiet chamber, a faint image surrounded the sword. He looked around, wondering why he wasn't dead. Everything was still, the troopers with their fingers extended taking up the first pressure of their weapons. They, like the council, were stock still, their eyes glazed, their bodies frozen in time. Only the cardinal and his companions had movement. The cardinal was looking around, her eyes trying to grasp the scene before her. Her dark skin had a grey pallor to it. Campbell helped the general to his feet, he was mad as hell.

'I wish you would stop doing that boy, I've got more bruises since I met you . . . I am quite capable of defending myself I have lived this long without your help.'

'Sir . . . my apologies, sir!'

The general growled and whispered under his breath, 'Sarcastic young bastard.'

They moved forward and joined Malise by the sword, Malise turned and smiled at the general.

'You knew, you crafty old sod . . . didn't you, you knew nothing could happen to us before we completed Hydra's mission. You let us go through all this . . . you knew, didn't you?'

Campbell stood waiting for the general's reply, at the same time keeping his eye on the cardinal. The general lent forward and plucked the sword from the charred wooden floor. He held it lightly in his hand, as Hydra had directed him. They could hear Hydra's voice faint but quite clear.

'You didn't think I would leave you completely alone; you have done what your conscience required of you. Now think of yourselves. You know what is at stake, it would be a pity to let it all have been for nothing. There is only one piece of the jigsaw left to fit and yours are the only hands that can be used.' Malise turned and looked at the cardinal, she sat quite still there was no fight left in her.

'What of her Hydra . . . the cardinal, we can't leave her like this, she will have a whole city to contend with when we leave.'

There was silence for a moment and once more the sword gave off its silvery glow. 'I am losing contact with you, Malise, bring her to the sword and when that is done you will be on your own. Make your plans well, bring her now Malise!'

Malise turned to do Hydra's bidding but Campbell had preceded him. He helped the cardinal to the general's side. How odd, he thought, young Campbell had tried to kill her only a few moments before and now look. Hydra was right, they were strange beings.

'Put your sword in her hand, Aaron, and Aaron don't forget our promise.' The general placed the ivory hilt of the sword into the cardinal's small hand and wrapped her cold fingers around the beautiful carvings. Campbell stood back allowing her to stand on her own. She swayed slightly, her face was still ashen, almost the colour of her robe. Malise made a move to steady her but the general took his arm.

'Leave her, Malise, she is stronger than you think and you and Campbell move back from her . . . now Campbell!'

'Watch the sword . . . there is only a residue of energy left and that's for her alone.'

She stood for a moment, still like a statue her eyes half closed, the gentle glow moved from the sword hilt to her arms. It slowly made its way to her shoulders, then enveloped her head like a halo, her large brown eyes pulsed bright blue. An angelic smile took the place of the narrow straight lips that was her normal mouth, the full dark tone returned to her face making her skin shine. The general was visibly moved by the dramatic change in her. He mumbled something Malise couldn't quite hear.

'What did you say, General?' His voice was almost a whisper. He turned and looked, Campbell nodded in the general's direction and then looked away in embarrassment. The general's eyes were full of tears: he

133

Fadar

was obviously very moved, he kept repeating the same thing over and over.

'My god, she looks so beautiful I would never have believed it.' With the white aurora behind her throwing out the contrast of her skin and the blue of her eyes, she made a striking sight. She looked so very young she could have been in her twenties . . . or younger. The minutes ticked away. She occasionally nodded her head to her invisible mentor, then gently it died, the white to blue to yellow then was gone. She stood quite still for them to see, the age had returned to her face but her eyes were bright and clear their rich brown harboured a secret just learned. The enigmatic smile remained as if proof of her experience. She stepped forward and took the general's hands in hers, she seemed to search for words.

'I'm sorry, Aaron I didn't know . . . I thought I did, I have always believed what the book said without question. It has taken this to open my eyes. We clergy have been so ignorant to the truth. I wish I had known before . . . he is quite a person, our Hydra.' The general squeezed her hands warmly.

'Yes, Sophronia, he is our Hydra, there for you and me.' He pointed to the red lights that indicated the cameras were still alive and working.

'He's there for all of us . . . just trust in him.'

'You will help us?' Malise felt as if he was intruding.

'Of course, go into the anteroom while I explain to the council.' The three men hadn't noticed or heard the revival of the council and troopers. The security guards still had their lasers raised but did not know what to do.

The Cardinal unceremoniously ushered them out of the buzzing chamber; the embarrassment of their presence was quickly dealt with. The three men made their way through the maze of corridors and tried to find the door of the anteroom.

'Have you anything else up your sleeve general . . . we weren't ready for your last performance?'

'Cut it out, Malise, I wasn't ready for that either, it all happened so quickly. I had a feeling about it when Hydra told me about the sword, but I wasn't sure. Anyway what the hell are you moaning about? The

134

bloody thing nearly cut my nose off.' All three men laughed but to the general it was a near thing.

The antechamber was also a library, a real library, not the micro-dot horror chamber that the general public were used to. Again the shelves were of real wood not the synthetic of the modern age, real wood was worth its weight in gold in fact probably more, there just were no more trees, not that it mattered now. But the carvings were beautiful – they had lost their sharpness caused by loving hands doing their daily penance. Malise wondered how much was wood and how much was polish, they were very old. 'Look at these books, General, there's dozens of first editions, there must be thousands of volumes here, what a waste, in fact the whole city is a waste.'

'I don't understand. What do you mean by a waste, Malise?'

They hadn't heard the cardinal come into the room, a figure stood behind her; they couldn't quite see as she was so tall.

'I'm sorry, Malise, it's your friend Dr Kincade. The young man tells me you have asked him to go with you, is this true?'

Malise smiled at Chez and waited for a rebuke from the other two but nothing came. The general inclined his head in acceptance, Campbell just smiled. Chez was nearer his age all the better for him.

'Yes, your Eminence, we have been friends a long time. He is a scientist with a good working brain. Another pair of hands, the right hands, could make our task easier . . . have you an objection?' She raised her hands above her head as if in a gesture of surrender.

'No . . . no, Malise, I have made my mistake, I only want to help in any way I can. What did you mean when you said something about the loss of the city being a waste. I don't understand, if we are to pass over what good could it be?'

Malise walked the length of the room allowing his fingers to slide across the bindings of the books: they felt warm to the touch.

'It's difficult to explain, your Eminence, as you know so little of the over all plan.'

She waved her hand in irritation. 'My name is Sophronia to you and the general.' She turned and looked at Campbell and Chez. 'But not to you young pups . . . clear!' Campbell and Chez came to mock attention, Campbell answered for them both.

135

'Yes, your Eminence . . . of course, your Eminence.'

'The waste factor Malise . . . please . . . sit down shall we, I am getting too old for this kind of excitement.'

The General had never heard her mention age all the years he had known her. She had never given way to her one hundred and sixty years but now she looked old, like the great refectory table they found themselves sitting at. It was two thousand three hundred years old and the hardened glass that protected its surface magnified the fine grains. The dowel fixings were only just visible: if you knew where to look it was a masterpiece of craftsmanship but normally no one was allowed near it.

'Malise, when you're ready.'

Malise once more rose from the table and paced the room. 'I'm sorry but it helps me think and I have one hell of a decision to make and only I can make it . . . only me!'

'Malise, come on, don't be so bloody dramatic.' The general was getting impatient, as were the others.

'Sophronia, general, gentlemen, I crave your indulgence, I didn't mean to be dramatic. But it isn't every day you are asked and *decide* to be the next keeper of this rotting ball that you are all planning to leave.'

'For Christ's sake, Malise, you can't be serious, Hydra told me nothing of this. When did he ask you?' Malise could see the general was working himself into a frenzie. 'He has no right to deny you the . . .'

Malise stopped him in mid-stride. 'He didn't ask me, General, he dropped a few hints now and then, but he didn't ask me. He allowed me to exercise that special gift that he says only this planet was given, *choice*. As I said, he didn't ask me . . . Shla did.'

'Why? She had no right to ask you either, no right at all. Malise, you must be mad!'

'Oh, but she has General . . . she has every right. In fact, only she has the right, and I am doing it willingly.'

'For god's sake, no one has the right at this late stage. You'll never survive on your own.' Malise smiled at the general and shook his head. It was a one-sided conversation that really wasn't fair on his companions.

'That's the whole point, General, I won't be on my own, Shla is not allowed to pass over . . . not this time. I was chosen a long time ago by the first orb, don't ask me, how that is beyond even Hydra.'

'The first *orb* . . . what is this orb you speak of Malise?' The cardinal hung onto his every word.

'Yes, Sophronia, the first orb, or Noah's Ark if you like. There are two; the second is for the second coming in your terminology. When the world has regenerated itself and the atmosphere is breathable once more; when seas and rivers are clean and wanting the feeling and movement of life in their bellies once more – that's when the second orb (myself) and Shla will walk upon the surface . . . the second Adam and Eve . . . how could I resist?' Every one knew his humour was self-indulgent. There was nothing left to say for he had made his choice.

'I wish you had told me, Malise, I feel partly responsible.' Malise ignored the general's remark.

'What about the city Malise, I still don't understand.' The cardinal had no intention of letting the matter drop, Malise knew there was no way out of the inevitable.

'Sophronia it was a selfish thought, just forget it. I had no right, I didn't think of the consequences.' He tried to think of a way to change the subject but she wouldn't let it go. Campbell tried to catch the general's eye but he ignored him.

'Malise if ever there was a man who had the right to ask for anything and be given it, it's you . . . now tell me!' Malise felt uncomfortable: all eyes were on him.

'You no doubt will think it's a strange request, considering what I have decided to undertake and I don't really know how you would do it, or how you would get everyone to agree. I want this city intact without a single body in it.'

His request had struck his companions dumb, they sat for a few moments trying to digest the reality of the situation.

'Go on, Malise, you must have a reason, scientific or otherwise. Is it yours or is it Hydra's idea?' The general felt he really had no right to ask after Malise's decision.

'It was purely my idea. I've told you what I have decided to do, and despite what you think I have thought it through. There is nothing unusual in it really. This is my home and has been from being a child.

137

It's familiar, I know every inch of it, my father helped build it, both my parents died for it. I have as much right to it as anyone. In fact, more, for I could make it live again.'

'Come on, Malise, there are thousands of people living in this city. How will you convince them to walk into the desert, then to stand there and suffocate. You will never convince them because you, one man, wants it.'

Malise took the cardinal's hands in his and looked deep into her eyes. A smile played in the corner of her mouth. She knew what he was going to say. 'I don't have to convince anyone. This dear lady will do it for me. They will follow her . . . she is ready; am I right Sophronia?'

She withdrew her hands, bent his head and placed the sign of the cross on his brow. 'Yes, Malise, I am ready. There is nothing more for any of us here. I will do as you wish gladly but tell me why and how. I do not want my people to suffer unnecessarily.'

'Yes, Malise I'll be interested in that.' The general wasn't at all convinced. Malise could see it written on his face. Malise turned on him.

'Right, General, answer these questions: Will this city be any good to you when we leave here?'

'No.'

'Will the city be any good in any way to its inhabitants when they die?'

'No, I don't suppose so . . . there will be no one here, of course not, they'll all be dead.' Malise still wouldn't let go.

'Of course they will; if it was left to you there would be thousands of rotting corpses littering the streets and the whole city left to decay. In this room alone there are books that could never be replaced. Workmanship that could never be repeated; they are originals, they are part of my world now, a world I will need to call on in the future!'

'In other words I want to come back when the time is right to walk the streets that I know to touch familiar things. To let my eyes play on memories, to see you all again just as you are now, is that too much to ask . . . for what I have to give?'

The silence was loud as they shook their heads. Only the general broke the unity. 'But how, Malise, how do you get your clean city?'

'You mean my other. Don't forget moonbase, that's what gave me the second part of my idea. It lies in a vacuum. It will never decay, it will be there waiting, maybe for a long time but it will be there. This city is different; it is governed by its own laws and can be saved for me and mine by its own laws.'

'I don't understand Malise . . . I helped to make those laws none could be employed here.' The cardinal searched her memory to no avail. 'Well, Malise?'

Malise smiled wryly. 'I am sorry, Sophronia there is, but I wish there hadn't been all these years ago.'

The cardinal was getting agitated. 'Malise . . . I don't understand.'

'It's ironic. It's the same law that killed my parents, I am not sure I can quote it word for word but I'll try. *Any* worker or *inhabitant* who is not in absolute health when this city is in completion shall be exiled from the same there will be *no* exceptions whatever his rank or status. As you have always said, Cardinal quote.'

'And the *how* Malise?'

'Again, the same as my parents; they had the same choice to wander in the desert and die or.' He stopped for a moment and remembered – she was so small and so beautiful and so brave. He could see his father take her tiny hand and walk forward. 'The electro carpet; that's the solution, turn it off. Then surround the city with its populace. Have your last rites or whatever you want to do. Then by remote control, switch on the blanket, it takes only a second, I know, I saw them die.'

'Then the city, Malise.' The cardinal had accepted every word: she had no reason to doubt Malise, revenge had to be the furthest thing from his mind even though his parents' death had been a state affair. It was a law laid for all, regardless of rank or creed, a fair law, now a law executed by himself as the keeper of things to come.

'What of the city Malise, what will you do with its soul.'

'Sophronia, this is the same point I made about moonbase. The city has a vacuum system that was installed a long time ago, not long after the city itself was built. It was installed when the air outside was still breathable. As you know, the idea was if we were attacked by the then rebels who later, much later, became mutants, we had some form of defence even though it meant evacuating the city for a while.'

'I knew nothing of this . . . it's news to me!' Young Campbell looked

139

quite taken aback. As far as he was concerned, security should be all knowing.

'As I said, it was a long time ago, there would be no point now as the outer atmosphere would kill you in about half an hour but not then. The idea was to evacuate the city and virtually hand it over to the invaders. In theory we expected them to take the city and not bother with the fleeing citizens. The vacuum system was set to operate in five hours after evacuation. Every ounce of air would be literally sucked from the interior of the city, killing every living soul inside. It would have been a painful death but a sure one. The city could be re-entered by a computerised switch from outside the city, the combination known to only a few, am I right, Sophronia?' The cardinal nodded her head.

'Yes, you are right Malise but it took you to remind me. As you say, it was a long time ago. I do remember your family. I was a priest at the time, an unknown quantity in the church, not knowing my fate because of my colour. I also remember the thinning, as they chose to call it, all but your family walked into the desert in hope for a new beginning. I didn't understand at the time. It wasn't till much later that I found out that your mother was dying; I do understand Malise believe me I do.'

'Understanding is one thing, doing something about it is another . . . well Sophronia?'

She stood and turned her back on the four men she walked slowly across the room each step a deliberation. She stopped and looked up at the large wooden crucifix, trying to transfer her thoughts, trying to unload her burden onto the figure she loved so much. She traced the outline of her Christ and spoke in a far-off voice.

'I wonder if he really looked as angelic as this?'

Malise replied softly. 'Sophronia, he did, I have seen him, he did. You do understand what I am asking you to do, Sophronia? Let's not mince words. I am asking you to evacuate the city, to put the vacuum system into operation and you and the complete population of this city to commit suicide by use of the electro carpet.'

She didn't move, the only indication that she had heard him was a slight nod of her head.

'The vacuum condition will last for an eternity, as long as there are no leaks. With a double failsafe system there shouldn't be but I will check. I hope you all understand how I feel. Hydra had two previous lives to remember. This one will be mine. It may help me keep my sanity in time to come, just knowing someday I will return.' She still hadn't moved. 'Sophronia . . . Sophronia . . . did you hear me?' She turned and smiled at him.

'Yes, Malise, I heard you . . . and I agree with everything you have said. Stop feeling so guilty. We are the ones who have the release, you are the one with the worry. I will see my subordinates. You do what you have to before you leave. Please, Malise, go now, no more talk!' Without another word, she turned and left the room.

'Quite a lady . . . I wouldn't want her job.' Admiration was loud in the general's comment.

Malise nodded. 'Nor I. Come on, let's make a move.'

The lab was not quite as Malise had left it.

'Chez, you are an untidy little sod. It's got to be the froggy in you, I think we can all find somewhere to sit.' They just pushed Chez's equipment to one side; there was no point in standing on ceremony now; Malise winced as his normally spotless laboratory became a shambles.

The general took charge of the blackboard and pinned a detailed map onto its surface. 'I know more about this next step in our operations than anyone, so if you don't mind.' He was back doing what he was good at, organising . . . No one objected, Malise was glad to get out of the limelight.

'Chez, it's too long and too complicated to go through all that we have seen and done, so if you still want to come you, you will have to play it by ear, no questions just listen, all right?' Chez nodded.

'Ok then, our target is, as you know, Cyprus; our objective the return of the missing crystal, one way or another . . . ok? The first reference point we make for is Salamis. It's about seven kilometres north of Famagusta; then we turn inland approximately one and a half to two kilometers. The place we are looking for is called The Vouta, a great water cistern built in the seventh century. It used to be fed by aqueducts, obviously a long time ago. I know it won't be easy but I have a detector that should pick the crystal's vibrations up although the range is very limited.' Malise looked up from the notes he was writing. 'How limited . . . it's widest range?'

141

The general seemed to ignore him but Malise wouldn't give up. 'How limited, General?'

'Five kilometers . . . now, let's get on.'

'General, you have to be kidding, five kilometers . . . that place is crawling with mutants. Is that the best you can do?'

'I'm afraid so, Malise, so we have to be pretty well spot on before we land and know where to go when we get there. So please try to digest what information Hydra gave me. As I said, we have to find this place called The Vouta, which was a vast water cistern. Seemingly, the small community that had survived on the island enlarged it to such an extent that the whole normal population were able to live in it. Seemingly, too, the set-up was similar to ours except, of course, theirs was under-ground instead of a dome. Their electro carpet failed and they didn't have a back-up system; well, you can guess the rest. With no defence they were quickly overrun and presumably eaten and, as Hydra told us, only one of his, for the lack of a better word, scouts returned. The other was obviously taken by surprise and killed. The object of our incursion is to find the crystal and get out as fast as possible . . . agreed?' All heads nodded in unison.

'Any questions so far?' The general surveyed his captive audience; each sat thinking his own private thoughts and his own private fears, there was dying, and there was dying.

'What's it like out there, General? You're the only one of us who's ever had experience of life outside the dome?' Campbell's voice sounded almost apologetic and the general was quick to see his predicament.

'No, you're right to ask Campbell; it's bad, it's quite a while since I was outside, so god knows what it's like now, it can only be worse. You even walk on human filth, the smell is unbelievable – it sticks to everything. You will have to wear protective clothing and abandon it as quickly as possible when you return to the ship.' He subconsciously rubbed his metal hand, the unaskable question was on everyone's lips. The general knew he had to get it out of the way.

'I was bitten by a mutant. He or it bit through the protective clothing and took a great chunk out of my wrist, so I blasted off what was left to stop the poison spreading; it also cauterised the wound. For god's sake don't let them get close, their bite is pure poison.' He could almost

hear their silent response, how could a man blast off his own hand? The
general smiled as he watched Chez rub the back of his hand.

'It was either that or die, young man; I wasn't ready for death, I was
too young then; you would have done the same.'

Chez knew damn well he wouldn't, he would surely have died. Why
the hell he was going on this crazy expedition? He hadn't a clue; he
wanted his head seeing to.

'When we get there, we will break into two teams: Campbell and
myself will guard the craft and keep an eye open for any mutants
and hope we will give you plenty of warning. You two will make the
actual search for the crystal but if, and when I call you, come straight
away, don't hang about. I've lost one hand and I don't want to make it
two.' The general handed a drawing of the inside of the enlarged cistern
to each of them.

'As you will see, there are quite a few different chambers. The red
cross is the last place Hydra's scout was seen alive so that will be your
starting point. Mind you, there is no guarantee that he is even in the
building.'

'Thank you for that vote of confidence, General, you've made our
day, but there is one thing we will have to remember when we get near
and while we are there: to put the ship in silent mode. If we go in very
low and very slow, we might stand a chance of avoiding the mutants.'
Malise felt there was another point he wanted to make but it had
slipped his mind. The door opened and shut. Father Selby waited for
an invitation to speak and the general waved him in.

'How are you young Selby?'

The priest looked uncomfortable: he had always been slightly afraid
of the general. 'I'm fine, sir . . . the cardinal would like to see all four of
you in her private chapel . . . if you please, sir . . . when you are ready
of course, sir, thank yo . . . uuu, sir.' A red-faced Selby closed the door
quietly behind him. He knew if he stayed any longer, his stutter would
get worse.

The general shook his head. 'I'll never understand that lad. Every
time I speak to him, he seems to fall apart.' Campbell smiled to himself,
he too knew the charisma of the general's presence.

'Right gentlemen, we could go over and over this but I think the

143

time is now. Chez, I think you can be spared the cardinal's farewells. Take this list to the armoury and then to the stores. Don't leave it to anyone else. Fill it yourself, then meet us at the ship, in fact, Campbell, go with him. You to the armoury and him to the stores and Campbell, make sure the rifles and the pistols are fully charged . . . understood?'

Campbell saluted the general's request but mumbled some obscurity under his breath as he left the room which made the general smile.

'You know, Malise, that young bastard reminds me so much of me . . . he's always got to have the last word.' They left the room laughing at Campbell's spunk.

They found the cardinal kneeling in front of her altar with her beautiful crucifix wrapped around her hands. She stood to greet them. On their entry, her eyes looked for the other members of the party. The general explained what he had done and she nodded her head in understanding.

'Have you decided, Sophronia?' Malise's voice sounded loud in the small chapel, she looked away for a second then met Malise's eyes square on.

'Yes, I have decided you can have your city . . . clean, as you put it.'

'How do you intend to do it, to be sure everyone is out?'

The cardinal smiled thinly at his question.

'The same way you have always thought: the church held power by deception, Malise, pure and simple deception. I think this time I will be forgiven . . . I will soon find out . . . yes?'

'Yes, Cardinal, we all will, but we, like you, are balancing on trust and Hydra on us most of all. If one of us doesn't get back with the crystal, what of all our futures?' The afterthought of his remark turned Malise cold. 'You still haven't told me how Sophronia.' She smiled at him in her condescending way.

'It's quite simple, Malise, I will gather all the religious sects together and ask their leaders to hold one last service outside the dome. You could call it the last rights. I will be the only one here with a key to switch on the electric carpet. This I will do at the end of the service, taking me and the whole population into the Umbra, so you tell me. We will await our further fate, which will be in your hands, yours and Hydra's. I am looking forward to meeting him.' She looked very calm and resolute. Her plan had been laid there was no going back . . . not now!

'You will need this, Sophronia, I've done what you asked. Only you will know these numbers.' Malise handed her the newly programmed controller for the electro carpet.

'I have one too. If . . . sorry, when, you switch on the carpet again I will know, mine is programmed to the same frequency. The vacuum will come on automatically and that will be it!' She looked long at the two men. Large tears welled up in her great brown eyes and slowly broke the dam of her resistance. She lent forward and touched Malise's face. She moved her lips but nothing came out for a moment, she tried again, clearing her throat. 'Yes, Malise . . . that *will* be it.'

'Come, Malise, the time is *now*.' The general's voice was strong and commanding, just what the situation needed. Malise felt things were getting a bit out of hand. Although she had changed beyond all recognition, she was still the cardinal. The general's wrist receiver crackled into life and its voice static was clear.

'General . . . sir.' The general raised his arm and spoke into the small microphone.

'Yes, Campbell.'

'The time is *now*, sir.' Both men looked at each other and broke into laughter.

Malise patted him on the back. 'General, he sounds more like you every day. He is even stealing your lines.'

The ship looked cold and grey as it lay in the shadows of the bay. As the two men approached, it burst into life, its various flashing lights fighting with the shadows. They were seeing themselves off this time, the cardinal had more than her share to cope with.

9

The Last Journey

The ship was quiet as it slipped through the mooring gates. Malise
stopped her and let her hover for a few seconds. He watched the
outer hatch slide quietly into place, keeping the world out and the people
in. But not for much longer, the airlocks' loud hiss could be heard
above the engines' quiet pulse. He pointed the preset infra-red controller
at the large panel close to the hatch: the electro carpet blacked out then
came on again proving at least that it worked. The cardinal should have
no trouble, he tried to keep his thoughts away from her terrible ordeal.
One press of a button and thousands of people would disintegrate
without a sound.

'All right, Campbell, put her on course for Cyprus. Don't forget we
approach the island from the east . . . let me know the first radar
contact . . . did you hear me, Campbell?'

'Sir!'

'Well, answer me immediately in future . . . this isn't a training
flight . . . got it?'

'*Sir!*' Campbell let it lie. He knew the strain Malise had to be under.
He had learned a lot about this strange man: he and the general were
very much alike and that was good enough for him.

Chez looked up from his blip in the belly of the craft. He could feel
the strain hang in the air, he was thankful that he really didn't know
what it was all about. All he was sure of was he wanted to be with

146

Malise for he was like the big brother he never had. He turned his head back and looked down into the yellow mist: the electro carpet was just left to the corner of his eye, the carpet his parents would be standing on soon, to go where? They had been good to him as an only child; he had been spoiled but he had never taken advantage of it and had always tried his best for them. His mother was the strength in the family. She was tall, blonde and blue-eyed; going back a few generations, she had French blood in her family. Whereas his father, a research engineer, was very quiet to the point of being absentminded for his work was everything to him. He could never stand stupidity: his reaction was always so predictable, his temper was like his red hair, violent in its colour but short and forgiving. When he had told them of his decision to ask Malise to take him they just smiled; they knew it was inevitable. His father had shaken his hand and wished him luck; his mother had held him close for that extra second that says so much and only a mother can do.

They watched their progress on a small computer screen: they were making sure this time, Malise had brought it with him. The world as it was was laid out before them: the different countries and states had their own colours and boundaries and there was a straight line drawn from the city in the Australian Simpson Desert to the east coast of Cyprus. Campbell followed it up: they had just passed over Christmas Island, where the rot had first started. The line passed through Southern Sri Lanka, the tip of India, Oman Saudi Arabia, the tip of Iraq, Syria, then into the long dead Mediterranean Sea and then Cyprus itself. There would be no mistake this time. With this new gadget they would know where they were all of the time, with its close phase it could bring the picture down to a mile and even show up local movement.

The general took a side glance at Malise: he was deep in thought; he would hate to be in his position for his military mind had no long-term imagination. Even when talking to Hydra, he couldn't accept the millions in terms of years. He wondered if Malise would have considered taking on the position of keeper if Shla hadn't been there for company, he doubted it very much and thanked god he hadn't been put in that position. He was quite happy with his role.

It seemed strange that in what seemed only a few days ago there was

147

no hope farther than they knew that they were going to die, so much had happened since. Hydra's last remark had puzzled him: it kept turning over in his mind ('you will find great joy before we meet again'). He still had no idea what it was but there was one thing. . . . he would soon find out.

Shla's beautiful face kept drifting into Malise's thoughts. Her smile was so real he knew she was aware of his decision to stay with her. If she couldn't go, there was no second thought, they had become almost one person. He would have so much to learn when they were eventually on their own. She had been well taught but only he had the choice that was the role of the keeper.

The general's reflection bounced back from the rear port – he was polishing his sword. He touched it as if it was a fragile child and loving care shone in his eyes. To him it was the epitome of beauty in the art of fighting, one man against another, the winner surviving by his raw courage and skill, each knowing that death would be inevitable. There is always one better than one's self, the art was in the knowing when to sheathe your sword, to be the teacher rather than the warrior; the art of knowing just when must have been micro thin. The thing that worried Malise was what side of the line the general stood. But what did it matter? He had chosen his destiny, he had no right to impose his thoughts on others.

'You're very far away, Malise?' The general's voice broke into his daydream. 'Having second thoughts?'

Malise mentally threw a bucket of water over himself to kick his brain into reality. 'About what?'

The general slowly slid his sword into the shining leather scabbard and looked at Malise.

'Everything . . . I feel sort of guilty in a way, if I hadn't spouted my mouth off a few . . . whatever it was . . . ago we would have never left the city in the first place. Most of all we would still be ignorant of our fate.'

'That's rubbish and you know damn well it is. It had nothing to do with you. Would you rather not have met Hydra?'

Malise watched the general's reactions. He ran his hand backwards and forwards along the sword's scabbard. 'Of course not.'

'Well, he's the one to blame if there is a blame, he sent Amy . . . I mean Shla. We didn't stand a chance right from the start . . . agreed?' The general slowly nodded his head.

'You can't blame yourself, sir!' Campbell's reassuring voice came out of the gloom.

The general smiled. 'For god's sake, shut up Campbell.'

'Sir!'

Malise laughed to himself, the shadow strikes again. 'Where are we Campbell?'

Campbell's voice came back immediately. 'Fifty-five degrees east of standard time zone, twenty degrees north of the equator, about to cross over the Tropic of Cancer.' The general's neck reddened as a warning to Campbell.

'Campbell, I didn't ask for a bloody map-reading exercise . . . *Where the bloody hell are we . . . without degrees?*'

'Oman, sir . . . we are two-thirds there.'

'Thank you, Campbell, a good soldier keeps his answers short and to the point . . . right?'

'Sir.' There was a further inaudible mumble that no one could catch and once again the general held back.

'I'm going to decrease altitude . . . can you see anything at all down there, Chez?' Malise knew he was asking the impossible.

'Not a thing Malise, just yellow mist. It's as thick as hell. I've caught sight of something now and again but nothing I could recognise . . . sorry!'

'Don't worry, I'll be bringing her right down soon. I want a long slow approach, the lower the better. If we see the terrain all to the good.'

'Where are we now Campbell?'

'Saudi Arabia, just west of Kuwait; we are drifting slightly we seemed to have picked a bit of a head wind; we're about eight degrees off and widening . . . can you correct it, sir.'

Malise checked his instruments he should have noticed it. 'I've got it . . . bringing her back into line now!' They felt a slight movement as the craft turned onto her true course.

149

'Sorry about that Campbell . . . glad you spotted it . . . good lad.' He could almost feel Campbell's smile; the general grunted.

'It's time to get into our suits. Don't bother with the masks yet but have them hanging around your necks for quick access. Chez and Campbell first . . . come on lads, move it!' The tone of the general's voice brought reality to the situation – it wouldn't be long now. The suits were hot to wear and smelt foul. The thick plastic creaked at the slightest movement. The general's voice broke the silence once more.

'Test your radios: call on these numbers – Myself, number one; Malise, number two; Campbell, number three and Chez, number four. Now remember, every time you call use your number. If the static gets too bad we may be able to distinguish who it is by the number if not the voice . . . sound off!' All radios were perfect and excessively loud in such a small space.

'I'm taking her down now to a few hundred feet and slowing down. Is that all right with you, General?'

'No problem, Malise . . . just make sure you know where we are at all times.' The craft tilted onto its slow descent. There was a slight buffeting as the power was reduced. Malise looked in Campbell's direction.

'We are still over the desert . . . Jerusalem a few miles to port if you are interested, Malise.' Campbell knew damn well he would be, it brought back memories to them both. 'Malise, look.' The controller, the red speech indicator, was flashing brightly in the dimness of the cabin.

'It has to be the cardinal . . . now, for Christ's sake, keep quiet. We have to be at the limit of its range . . . that's if we can pick anything at all up.'

They sat quietly, their ears straining for the slightest sound. Malise gently adjusted the fine tuning – it was faint but clear.

'I thank you all for your trust in me and for becoming one on this, our last meeting, in this place we have called home for so long. We send our collective thoughts to our comrades who are out there on our behalf . . . let us send them one last message from us all, let us pray!' The red light stopped beating, the green indicator light flared like a dying star and was gone. Silence descended on the cabin, no eye wanted to meet the others, it seemed to last for an eternity.

'That's it?'

'That's it, General . . . they have all gone . . . it took a great deal of courage to do what she did. I don't know if I could have done it.' Malise's throat felt thick; he coughed to clear it they all felt the same.

'Right, let's make it worthwhile . . . position Campbell.' The general gave them no time to think. They couldn't help them now. Anyway, who was better off?

'We are approaching Lebanon . . . ten minutes to the coast, next stop Cyprus.'

'I would like to take her down even further, General and have a slow glide in.'

'I'll leave it in your hands, Malise, just let us all hear what you are doing. The rest of you, check your equipment and arms.' The general rose and checked Chez, then moved on to Campbell, who was his usual immaculate self, or as much as he could be in a plastic suit. He was just about to return, when something caught his eye. He lent across Campbell. It was a small flash of gleaming silver that caught the light. He slid his hand behind the navigational panel and slowly pulled out the offending object. He held it in his hands for a moment, turning it over and over, admiring the scroll that ran its full length and the bright scarlet inlay.

'Does Hydra know?' Campbell shook his head.

'You just took it?' The general's voice was just above a whisper. 'Stole it?'

Campbell nodded.

'Why?' Campbell seemed to ignore the question. The general knew perfectly well why, he handed the young trooper the sword and placed his hand on his shoulder for reassurance.

'Claymore . . . very original, laddie.'

'Two thousand five hundred and descending.' Malise's eyes were glued to the instruments. He watched for the slightest ground variation.

'Two thousand . . . speed one eighty . . . anything yet, Chez?'

'No Malise I can't see a th—' The collision happened so quickly no one had the chance to move the general, who was watching Chez for

151

his reply and just saw the look of surprise as the blip was torn from the belly of the craft. The noise was horrendous a high-pitched whistle pierced their eardrums.

'Put your masks on for Christ's sake . . . slow this damn thing down, Malise, before it breaks up!' The general's voice screamed above the in-rushing air. Slowly and painfully, the craft came to a juddering halt, it hovering uncertainly. No one moved. All eyes were on the floor of the craft. One minute Chez had been there and the next . . . gone.

'What the hell was it . . . he was there a minute ago, it happened so fast.' The mask did little to hide the emotion in Campbell's voice. Malise climbed down and inspected the damage. He pulled various metal fragments from the gaping hole, some painted red with Chez's blood. The general lent over offering Malise his hand. Campbell sat astride the general, one hand holding his belt the other, a rung of the internal ladder.

'For god's sake be careful, Malise, we are still about a thousand feet up.' The general's voice crackled loudly in his ear, he could feel the sweat running freely down his back. His legs felt weak and awkward, the knuckles of his hands stood out pure white. He looked for the ground – nothing.

Poor Chez, he wouldn't have known what hit him, he would have died instantly . . . all he wanted was to be with his friend at the end, well that at least was true. Malise grimaced. He was thinking he would have to tell his parents, then remembered they had died just before Chez. The whole bloody thing was becoming ridiculous, how much more pain?

'What was it, Malise?' The general's voice seemed far away and unreal, he felt his companions turn him over, their masked faces looked down at him, alien and foreboding.

'Number two to number one . . . we've lost the poor bastard and then there was three!' The general patted Malise's shoulder in sympathy. There was nothing he could say, he had never been any good at handling emotion not since, well, not since a long time ago.

'What caused it Malise?'

'A radio tower by the look of it.' He put the debris on the cabin floor, it was old and well rusted.

'There were hundreds of them along this shoreline over a thousand years ago. I would have thought they would have all collapsed a long time ago . . . but obviously not.'

'What now, sir?' Campbell asked the question for them all.

'We go on, what the hell do you think . . . we have no option. Well Malise?' The general kicked the debris out through the gaping hole, they picked Malise up and sat him squarely in his seat.

'Well what, General?'

'Well Malise . . . is there anything we can do with that?' He pointed to the gaping hole, the yellow mist curling around the jagged edges.

'It will blow a gale if we pick up any speed, plus it will fill the cabin with this yellow muck.' Their suits had begun to feel slimy and the inside of the cabin filled with condensation. Malise tried to get his brain to deal with the situation but there were too many ifs. He had never been outside like this before, they couldn't make repairs in mid-air.

'I don't know, General, it would be different if we were on the ground in a service bay – it would be a piece of cake. The trouble is, what's down there?' He pointed his finger into the darkness and looked at the general.

'There is no choice . . . we're going down . . . *Now Malise!*'

'Now hang on a minute, General. Let's think this one out, I'll try anything but we don't know what's down there!' He turned and looked at Malise, his eyes hidden by the mask, but Malise knew that look mask or no mask.

'What do you suggest, Malise, I'm no wiser than you?'

'Where are we Campbell . . . as near as you can tell?' Malise knew he was asking a lot. They must have drifted well off course . . . again. Young Campbell studied the screen and tried the fine adjustment tuner, then shook his head.

'I'm not sure but, as near as I can tell, we are just off Beirut.' They couldn't ask more of Campbell he had so little to go on and it being night it made things worse. Malise turned to face his two companions.

'Has anyone any bright ideas?' All he could hear was his own breath in his ears. He looked around the cabin: the condensation had increased, the yellow stain was running freely down the walls; it could only be a matter of time before it affected the instruments. They looked a pathetic trio, his two companions had their eyes fixed on the damage below. It wasn't a case of giving up but what to do. Campbell turned and faced Malise, his voice slightly muffled over the intercom.

'Can I run this past you, Malise . . . I'm not saying it will work but.' The general grunted his disapproval; Malise ignored him.

'Go on Campbell . . . we can't be any worse off than we are now.'

'The radar of this ship can be localised, say to a spread of about five hundred yards, that is straight down . . . yes?'

'Yes . . . or even less if need be.'

'We have four very powerful searchlights on our belly and a metal detector mode that will cover the radar spread, right?'

'Right.' Malise was beginning to catch Campbell's idea.

'Malise, that's all we need at the moment. If we just keep ahead of the drift, we can use them as our eyes and ears. What we want is something off the ground to land on, metal preferably. What do you think?' There was a silence for a moment. The general's mask and Malise's looked at each other. Malise lifted his hand, indicating the general's right to reply. He in turn flicked his mike switch.

'Malise . . . what are we going to do with this lad?' The general lifted his hand to stop Campbell interrupting. 'It must be the Scot in you boy . . . you don't have a lot to say but when you do!' Campbell was still confused. He could never tell with the general so he turned to Malise, who patted him on the shoulder.

'You beat me Campbell. Let's try it, we'll read the instruments. You keep your eyes below, General. The joystick in front of you will move the lights independently. Let me know right away if your spot anything . . . ok?' The general nodded and wiped the front of his mask.

Malise adjusted the thrust to compensate for the drift. Their ground speed was about forty kilometers per hour, just enough to keep her moving without causing problems. The radar was blank, the metal detection unit silent. Malise spoke to himself rather than his companions.

'We must still be over the sea. There's nothing down there. I'm turning her ten degrees to starboard, that should bring her back towards the shore . . . keep your eyes open!' An hour went by with not a blip on the screen. The metal scanner screeched a couple of times but the object had to be very small, it could have been anything. Despondency was beginning to set in, when the first positive strong blip bounced from the panel. All eyes were on the radar screen. Irregular bright shapes fashioned themselves on the dark background, their metal density was very high.

'What do you think, Malise?' The general still had his eyes fixed on the gaping hole.

Malise spoke softly not really wanting to commit himself . . . it was too soon. 'I'm going to take her down slowly this time.' The screen was full of unrecognisable shapes but there was no doubt about it – they were metal. It was the regimentation of the layout that was strange. They were still over the sea and there seemed to be dozens of them.

'What are they, Malise?' Campbell was staring hard at the screen. He had never seen anything like it, they looked like long rows of old-fashioned coffins, there was so many of them.

'I'm descending to five hundred feet then slowing her right down, whatever they are we are right in amongst them. For god's sake keep your eyes open, General.'

They descended slowly, so slowly it felt for a while that they were not moving at all. The only indication was the increasing size of the blips; the lower they got the less uniform they became and the louder the metal mode screeched. Malise turned it off to everyone's relief.

'Anything yet, General?' The headshake answered Malise in the negative.

'Hang on a minute, there is something there . . . can you take her down just a bit more?' Malise turned and looked down the gaping hole. He could see something reflecting the lights but it wasn't clear.

'I'll try a bit more but we're getting too bloody low to be safe, another hundred feet and that's it.' Malise's mask was full of condensation from his body sweat. He opened the release valve and blew the offending gunge out, his visor cleared instantly.

'Well, bugger me, look at that.' The general's voice made them both turn, it was perfectly clear below the craft which was still drifting slightly.

'They're ships, by Christ!' The gentle drift took them over all shapes and sizes of floating memorabilia, each reflecting back its own distinctive silhouette.

'There must be dozens of them, but there's something about them

155

that's strange; look at the way they shine, they ought to be rot buckets by now. This acid shit's highly corrosive.'

Malise smiled to himself, the general had a way with words.

'Malise . . . look at this one . . . far corner of the screen.' Malise pushed Campbell's finger aside. The gloves made his hands twice the size.

'What's that one, Malise, it's twice or three times bigger than the rest, with very little superstructure. Malise compared the blips on the screen; he hadn't a clue about this sort of thing. The general's voice broke into their conversation in a very matter-of-fact way.

'It's a carrier.'

'A what?' Malise looked at Campbell, who shrugged.

'It's what they used to call an aircraft carrier. It did what its name implies . . . carried aircraft. Neither of you are very bright at history. They didn't have the fuel or the technology, so they had to take the aircraft to the wars, never mind that, have you seen the width of her deck?'

'Extend the landing legs, Campbell, let's try for a touchdown. Everybody hang on to something, there doesn't seem to be any obstruction, but you never know.' The loud hiss of the hydraulics could be heard quite distinctly, followed by a loud clunk as the gear locked into place. The deck was quite visible now, the lights flooded a hundred foot circumference, more than they needed to work by.

'Ok we're down . . . use the main hatch not the floor, some of these edges are like razors. Rip your suit and you've got problems. Campbell come with me. Malise stay and put her on standby, I'll give you a signal when we've checked things out . . . come on, Campbell.' It took both of them to crack the hatch. Malise made a mental note to check it when he got outside. Malise closed down everything except the main power unit: they might have to leave in a hurry.

'Ok, Malise, all clear, no immediate danger. Watch the ladder, it's as slippery as hell.' The outer lock had been slightly damaged, as Malise thought. It had either been struck by parts of the disintegrated blip or, god forbid, Chez's body. Malise shuddered at the thought. There was blood splattered all around the hatch, he couldn't have suffered, it had been too quick.

'Malise, come over here and look at this.' The general was poking about with his sword, the point disappeared into the deck about four inches. He turned and looked at Malise.

'That's why they reflected so well . . . the ships are all cocooned. That's also why they haven't rotted. Well, damn me, it must have been one hell of a job, they must have been done in dry dock and towed here . . . but why?' Malise and Campbell had followed most of the general's comments but not all. As he had said, history wasn't their strong point.

'It looks like some high-grade plastic. The only way they could have done this was to spray it, you would think it would be slippery but it's the opposite.' It felt good to be out of the craft even if they couldn't get air to their bodies. Just the movement got their blood flowing faster, their limbs had become cramped with sitting. Malise cleared the remains of the damaged blip while the general kept watch. Young Campbell went off on a tour of inspection. The general told him to keep his radio channel open and to shout at the first sign of trouble . . . but would he?

'Have a look at this Malise.' The general was still prodding the deck.

'Watch this!' He thrust his sword into the shining surface he cut a small square and lifted it from the deck. As the two men watched, the hole regenerated itself; in a matter of seconds, there was not a trace of a break on the deck's surface.

'Amazing stuff . . . self sealing . . . it feels almost alive, it's warm to the touch, these ships will never rust . . . but why?'

'I have no idea, Malise . . . let's get on with this.' They removed the steel backing of the large instrument panel and welded it to the underside of the craft with their lasers. It was a Heath Robinson repair but it did the job. Malise filled the cabin with pure oxygen, left it for ten minutes, then cracked the air lock. All the stale air rushed out into the night. They should be able to manage without their masks now.

'That's it, General. It's the best I can do. Let's get Campbell and make a move. I don't know why but I'm not very keen on this place.'

'I know what you mean, Malise, there's something abo—' Campbell's voice broke in; his tone did little to console them.

'Number three to number one, there's something strange here, General . . . I don't get it . . . it's weird.'

'Campbell, stop babbling. I've told you concise reports, what's bothering you laddie?'

'Number three to num—'

'For god's sake forget the numbers, Campbell; Malise and I are here, it can only be you at that end.'

'Yes sir . . . as you know we are surrounded by ships of all sizes . . . well, they seem to be joined together. I've done a complete check on all four sides of the carrier, the ships are definitely attached . . . but god knows why.'

'Hang on, Campbell, we'll come to you, switch on your homer beam and we'll find you, but stay still till we do.'

'Sir!' Malise made sure the craft was secure. He would rather have set off there and then, but the general's curiosity had been aroused. It was a strange feeling, making their way across the giant deck; there was hardly a drop of wind. They could feel the ship move under their feet the thousands of tons of metal bobbing like some great cork. They couldn't see, only feel, the ships around them as they bounced out of sync with the carrier and, as Campbell had said, why were they attached? They found Campbell standing next to the massive superstructure which towered high into the night sky.

'Have you found anything else Campbell?' The general's voice held little understanding. He wasn't in the mood to be compromised.

'Not really sir . . . but there is machinery working somewhere on this ship. It seems to kick in every quarter of an hour and is strongest where we are stood. It lasts for about a minute then cuts out again. If you kneel down and place your hands on the deck, you will feel the vibration; it's weak but it's there . . . it's due any time now?' The trio knelt on the deck, pressing their hands, or in the general's case hand, as flat as possible. The plastic was springy to the touch. If a machine could be felt through the thick covering, it had to be pretty powerful. It came and went with only a slight judder. The general looked at Malise.

'What do you think . . . I hardly felt anything. It could be caused by the surrounding ships rubbing against each other.'

'No, general, that was definitely a mechanical sound, the vibrations were constant, like a refrigerator turning itself on and off. Something on this ship is still in good working order.'

'Malise, have you any idea how old these ships are? We're talking over a thousand years old, and still working?'

'General, as you said these ships will never rot. Why they're still working I have no idea but let's find out.'

'Yes, let's do that, Campbell, have you found a way in?'

'There's plenty of ways in, sir, but we'll have to cut our way through the outer covering . . . it's pretty thick, sir, it seems to repair itself instantly.'

'Yes, we found that out Campbell . . . we'll use one of the smaller doors and batten it back or we'll never get back out again. That stuff, whatever it is, is really strong. As you said Malise, it was meant to last.'

Campbell drew his sword and traced around the door frame. Malise and the general pulled at the same time to stop the plastic reforming. The door was heavier than they thought and it took all three to hold it back. They locked it firmly back against the outer casing, making sure it couldn't close by mistake. If it did, the overlapping surround of the door would make it impossible to get back out once the plastic had re-formed. The inner door acted like an airlock keeping the acid atmosphere out.

They moved cautiously at first, not knowing what they would find. The outer corridors were warm and the air breathable, it was dim but adequately lit. The lights came on and switched themselves off automatically, on entering and leaving the cabins and corridors. They stopped for a moment as the slight vibration burst into life; once more then it was gone. Each cabin they entered was spotlessly clean, not even a sign of dust – they looked as if they had been regularly cleaned. They entered a funnel-shaped tunnel half-way down the carrier's hull which stretched across to the companion ship. As they entered the temperature dropped dramatically. The most amazing thing was the inside of the ship – it was gutted, only a floating shell. There were hundreds of tables, each about a foot above the ground. On each table was an animal. Every ship they entered was the same. There must have been thousands of different breeds and species.

'Who the hell would pack ships full of dead animals? It's crazy, what's the point?'

'They're not dead Campbell . . . look!' Malise slid open a small panel

159

at the edge of the table; red, white and green lights flickered in the half light.

'They're sprayed with the same stuff as the ship but only a fine layer . . . they're suspended in time like the ships; they are alive, Campbell.'

'Are you sure, Malise?' The general was prodding the carcass of a very large bull – it responded like a jelly, with no sign of life or movement.

'They're in suspended animation . . . and look at those shelves. There must be every seed man ever cultivated stored there.'

'What are these?' Campbell had walked into a large cold store. There were thousands of glass jars, each with a different label. Malise had never seen anything like it. He walked around picking up and inspecting dozens of jars.

'Do you know what they are?' The wonderment in Malise's voice was irrepressible. 'They're fish eggs of thousands of different species . . . they must have been collected over a thousand years ago, before the sea became sterile. I don't understand any of this unless it's another store built by Hydra. Did he say anything to you about it, General?' The general shook his head and carried on inspecting the contents of the store. Malise had had enough, he turned to his companions.

'Let's get back to the ship. We're not doing any good here and Hydra's bound to have the answer.' They made their way slowly back to the carrier, trying to find their way in the maze of corridors as the massive ship was like a beehive. Just as they thought they had found their starting point and they turned into the main lower flight deck, it seemed to stretch for ever, as huge as far as the eye could see. It too had tables but they were set in four great circles, their outer edges all but touching.

'Good god, look at that . . . so that's why!' The general unceremoniously pushed Malise to one side.

'What the hell is it now, your . . .' He stopped mid-sentence and glanced at Malise. His eyes hadn't moved from the scene.

'General?'

'I know, Campbell, I can see them but I don't believe it.'

The four great circles were made up of bodies . . . human bodies. There must have been at least six hundred. The outer rim of the circles were made up of males, the inner circles all females who all looked

160

about twenty years old and in excellent physical condition. They, like the animals, were suspended in time. All were completely naked with a thin coating of the now accustomed plastic. Campbell stood looking at a particularly beautiful girl. His body moved involuntarily and he thought to himself, a different place and a different time maybe. The general's voice barked in his ear.

'For Christ's sake Campbell, get your mind above your bloody navel or you'll go blind!'

Malise laughed at his reactions. 'Leave the poor lad alone, just because you're past it . . . he can't do any harm.'

The general mumbled under his breath. 'I wouldn't put it past him the young sod!'

They made their way to the far end of the flight hangar where they could see what looked like a shrine. At closer inspection, it was with a very strange layout. In front of it lay three separate tables raised higher than the others. On the table closest to the shrine lay the body of an older man in his sixties. He too was naked but adorned with a large medallion and a fine golden crown was placed on his head. In the centre of the medallion was a triangle encasing an open eye. Slightly forward, but flanking him, were two women of about the same age. They were not such a pretty sight and were obviously priestesses of some sort. Campbell kept well clear.

The general turned his attention to the altar which was a blaze of colour; the centrepiece was the most striking, it looked almost alive. It was a large goat-like creature with two black wings protruding from its back, which were half open. It sat crosslegged with what looked like half a gold disk in its lap portraying two intertwined serpents. It had full female breasts, its right hand was raised, pointing to a white crescent moon, its left hand pointed downward to a black crescent moon. Huge horns sprang from its large ugly head, a five-pointed star adorned its forehead and a long slender crownlike shape sat firmly on top of its head. A black matted beard fell almost to its waist, and it smelt foul. Above the effigy was a large two-headed eagle: the whole effect was grotesque. The creature sat upon a block of granite; inlaid on the front was yet another triangle with an open eye depicted in the centre. Two unlit candles lay each side of the cloven feet ready to shine on its glory. The

161

altar was flanked by two very large paintings: one was Jesus on the cross
with a Roman soldier plunging a spear deep into his side, the other was
of Jupiter seducing Cupid.

Campbell looked at Malise for some information but Malise shrugged
his shoulders. They both turned to the general.

'Are you sure Hydra or Shla didn't tell you anything about this,
Malise?'

'No. What does it all mean? Anyway how the hell was I to know
Chez was going to be killed and we would have to land here . . . answer
me that!'

The general shook his head. He had a good look round the artifacts
before answering, thumbing his way through a book left open on an
ornate rostrum.

'Hydra should have told you of this Malise, it could have altered your
decision to stay. Mind you that's if *he* knows, which I very much doubt.'

The whole place was beginning to get to Malise. Then he noticed
666 engraved in the granite.

The general looked around at the remaining artifacts. 'I would say,
without a doubt, it's your advisory of the future, Malise. The negative
to your positive. I saw you looking at the corner of that stone, the 666
as you probably know, it's a Satanic mark.'

'You mean they're Satanists?' Malise felt himself break into a sweat.

'It's not quite as easy as that . . . if I'm right they are a very special
order. Strangely enough, Malise, I happen to know quite a lot about
this cult. It used to be a hobby of mine when I was younger, that
hideous thing,' the general pointed to the goatlike creature, 'that is the
god, Baphomet, associated with the Gnostic Catholics or the Oriental
Templars. They practised, amongst other things, what they called sexual
magic. Their headquarters in the twentieth century was at the Abbey
of Thelema in Switzerland. This was when they split into two sections.
One was headed by the abbot of Thelema and, at that time, the other
by the English poet, Alaistair Crawley, who called himself 'the Beast'.
The press at that time called him the wickedest man in the world. They
were largely concerned with unorthodox occult interpretations of the
Masonic secrets. They were indoctrinated to different levels: the god
Baphomet was worshipped as the god representing sexual forces. The

sixth degree, the Knights Templar of the Order of Kadosch, was the most curious of them all, a grade of vengeance for the destruction of Christianity. I believe that is what they are here for, just waiting to be called.'

Malise and Campbell sat in silence, letting the general's words sink in. If all he said was true, this was indeed an evil place.

'Well, Malise?'

'Well, general, what can I say? If you are right, these people will be my future enemies. If they manage to wait out the time, one breakdown could finish the lot off.'

'Can't we finish them now?' Campbell looked at the general for approval. The general shook his head.

'We can't . . . just stop, and think for a minute. What if Hydra knows about this and it's all part of the overall plan?'

'Some plan, you could be talking about the Crusades all over again. So much for your quiet life, Malise.' Campbell was prodding the effigy with the point of his sword. By the look on his face he was expecting it to come alive any second.

The general answered his comment. 'I must admit, Malise, forgetting the timespan, everything seemed too pat. Life, love and energy have always had and needed their equal and opposites.'

Malise took a good look around him: this kind of opposite he didn't need but if it wasn't part of Hydra's plan it would give him something to think about till the awakening and to plan for. Malise insisted they stayed a bit longer. He spent his time browsing through the various books, gleaning as much information he could from their contents. If there was any flaw at all, he wanted to be aware of it. Eventually the general intervened.

'Come on, Malise, we've seen enough. You've read through that twice, all you'll do is read it and read it till you read it out of your mind. You can't absorb it all.'

Malise nodded. 'You're right but they write with such fanaticism. I have never read so much evil and hate . . . and yet a lot of it makes sense for it applies to both evil and good . . . the line is so fine. I've never had to think about it before, you have to reach inside yourself and ask your own maze so many personal questions to find out which side of the line *you're* on or do you stand in the middle taking no part?'

'You're not getting cold feet and changing your mind about being the keeper?' The general looked at Malise's face but it gave nothing away. He had moved across to the elderly man and stood looking down at him before answering the general's question. The large eye in the medallion stared back at him unblinking.'

'No, I haven't changed my mind . . . but I do believe in one thing that the Bible says . . . know thine enemy. In that respect, I'm luckier than him, I know of him if not about him and I can use that to my advantage.'

'General I'm sure we're being watched. I keep getting this strange feeling in the back of my neck.' Campbell slowly pivoted, looking as deep as he could into the shadows. The feeling that a dozen pair of eyes were watching him wouldn't leave him and he tightened the grip on the hilt of his sword.

'I have had the same feeling for some time, let's move!'

The general's tone left no room for argument. Malise took one last look around before he following his two companions from the large hangar. His last glance was for the presumably high priest. He was sure he would meet him again, under what type of circumstances he would have to wait and see.

After half a dozen wrong turns, they found a way out. A wind had sprung up and the deck was rising and falling as the sea threw her might at her giant hull. Their craft stood like a beacon as she lay bathed in her own bright light and it made them feel warm to see her.

'This door's been tampered with, General. Look at the handle – it was at right angles but it's been moved a few degrees.' The general tried to focus through his replaced mask but it kept fogging up. He blew through the valve to clear it. There was no doubt about it – it had been moved.

'And look at the deck . . . footprints. Look how small they are . . . they're like children's.' They all focused their light beams on the deck nearest to the hatch. They were footprints all right, prints of bare feet and, as Campbell had said, they looked like children's.

'Shut the hatch, there's nothing we can do here, whatever they are,

164

they know this ship inside out. We wouldn't get near them. At least we know now what's keeping the place clean. They have to be some type of mutant given shelter in return for services rendered.'

They battled their way to the craft, hanging on to each other for support. The wind was now blowing a gale and tried to pluck them from the deck. Only the tackiness of the surface kept them from being blown away. Malise pointed to the underside of the craft: the lights glared on the shiny surface, revealing dozens more footprints. They had been busy little creatures but they couldn't have entered without the code number. By the look of it they had tried. As the hatch closed behind them, they took a deep breath clearing their lungs of stale air. Malise gave the cabin a two-second burst of pure oxygen to give them a boost for, after the last couple of hours, they needed it.

'Look at this . . . there's a farewell!' They sat peering into the night. As Campbell raked the ship's superstructure with the strong beams of the searchlights, dozens of small gleaming eyes peered back at them, Malise whispered. 'I hope they are as pleased for us to go as we are.'

The engine hummed into life as they settled themselves into their positions, each wondering if anything else could happen. It all started off being so straight forward. Malise tried to keep his mind off Chez. It was funny, his face seemed hazy and he probably wouldn't remember it at all after a while. He wondered if that was life's way of healing the hurt.

'Do you have any idea where we are Campbell?' The generals voice was full of concern not for himself but for the young trooper.

'To be quite honest son I haven't a clue where we are. We've been blown all over the place, what about you, Malise, any idea?' Malise shook his head.

'Not for sure.' Campbell's eyes scanned the radar screen for any help. He placed an inlay map over the screen and made a few calculations.

'I think we're off the Syrian coast and with this change in wind direction it's pushing us towards Cyprus but where we'll break land I haven't a clue, I think we should go up to at least four thousand feet.'

'Why four thousand? We won't be able to see a thing at that height. Now the blips gone we've only the radar to rely on and I did say earlier that we would go in low.' The general's voice again held its edge. 'Don't you listen, Campbell?'

Campbell's look would have chilled an iceberg. 'Sir, I would be obliged if you would let me navigate the ship. Point one, sir, you don't know where we are. Point two, Malise has already said he doesn't. I have made a calculated guess which, in my opinion, can't be far off and you tell me I'm not listening. Sir, if we don't gain height and not knowing exactly where we are, we could crash into the Troodos Mountains. Is that what you require . . . sir?'

Malise looked from one to another. Both their necks were bright red. Campbell looked rigidly to the front, awaiting his next instruction. It was the most Malise had ever heard Campbell utter. He turned and shook his head at the general. There was an awful pregnant silence in which he could hear himself breath.

'I think we should take the navigator's advice, Malise, at least till we find the coastline, what do you think?'

Malise took a sideways look at Campbell: the red had begun to subside.

'I'm sure you're right, General . . . he seems to be capable!'

Malise took her up to four thousand and levelled her off. It was only a matter of time now, they couldn't be far off the coast. Campbell was still glued to the radar: he had every intention of being right. The general sat looking at the plate they had hurriedly welded over the hole; it was a poor job but effective. Poor Chez, it wasn't meant to be. If only he could let them know there was another side, if only they were running out of 'if onlys' but, strangely enough, he didn't particularly care. If only was yesterday, he was looking forward to tomorrow and the supposedly new life it would bring. That voice he had heard, it seemed a thousands years ago, it had belonged somewhere in his past, or was it his future, he wasn't sure of anything any more. Here they were three people given a task to save . . . to save what, he really didn't know that, not the world, at least not for him. Was it for all those souls waiting to be gathered? Would it really matter if they were gathered or not, and if it did who did it really matter to? What happened after the final gathering? Where were they to be taken to?..His eyes slowly shut and he gave way to sleep. Malise touched Campbell's arm and pointed to the general.

'It was bound to come, he's had one hell of a twenty-four hours. I don't know how he's stayed awake this long. He's one giant of a man . . . I hope I can do it when I'm his age.'

They looked at each other and laughed, what a stupid remark to make, at his age. One was due to die, the other to live thousands of years.

Another half-hour went by before the radar threw up the slightest blip, then it slowly filled the screen, so this was Cyprus, but where?'

'Any ideas?' Malise found himself whispering for there was no point in waking the general up yet. Malise stood and moved behind Campbell for a better view; the coastline stood out sharp and clear. Campbell looked across at Malise's panel for reassurance.

'Don't worry, it's on auto. I'll take her down when you're ready.'

Campbell pointed at the screen. 'See that large curve, that's Larnaca Bay. Larnaca to the left and Xylophagou to the right. If we start descending now, we can follow the coastline and there will be no mistakes. Wake the general up now, he'll play hell if he misses it.'

As Malise turned to waken the general, Campbell lent across and touched his arm.

'Just a minute, Malise, I want to ask you something before he wakes up. You might think this a bit bizarre, but what the hell.' Malise could see that Campbell was now visibly embarrassed.

'Spit it out Campbell . . . for god's sake!'

'Well, that elderly man we saw in the hangar . . . the one we thought would most likely be a high priest. I would think there is every chance you two will meet again . . . yes?'

'If what the general said is true and I have no reason to doubt him . . . yes . . . why?' Campbell still looked very uncomfortable.

'Do you remember his face . . . well, I mean?'

'Not really, I didn't think it important at the time.'

'There's one way you will recognise him if you should bump into him again.'

He wasn't making sense to Malise. 'How?'

Campbell smiled. 'He has only four fingers on his left hand.'

167

'I never noticed that.'

'You wouldn't.'

'Why?' Malise's patience was running short.

'Because I went back and cut one off after you left. I thought I might be able to give you an edge some time in the future.'

Malise shook his head in disbelief. 'You know, Campbell, I would never have thought of that, you never fail to amaze me.'

'What's he done now Malise?' The general's voice was thick from sleep as Malise handed him some water. He drank deeply before repeating the question.

'Nothing untoward, General. He has brought us almost dead on to where we want to be . . . that's what I call navigation.' He winked at Campbell: one good turn deserved another.

'Where exactly are we, Campbell?' The general rose and stood directly behind the young trooper. All three had their eyes glued to the radar; the coastline stood out bright and clear.

'That's Paralimni on our port side: it's about two kilometers from the coast.'

Malise moved back to his seat ready to take her down. This was it. He wondered what they would find, if anything.

'Take her in at about a thirty-degree glide, Malise, we will be at about a thousand feet as we approach Famagusta.' The general's knuckles turned white as he hung onto the back of Campbell's chair. The craft tilted in response to Malise's directions, held the glide for what seemed an eternity, then straightened out.

Campbell's voice was slow and deliberate. 'Throttle her back to fifty kph.' The small craft juddered slightly in response to the deceleration.

'Famagusta directly below, throttle back to thirty kph and try and keep her on the coastline; Salamis is only seven kilometers from Famagusta. General, will you go to the side ports and see if you can spot anything; if we can land without lights it would give us more of a chance.' The general did as he was asked and sat peering into the yellow mist hoping for a break.

Campbell licked his lips – his throat felt thick and dry: Famagusta Bay lay waiting for them below, one wrong move and they would be going for a swim.

'Right, we're just approaching Salamis . . . take her down slowly Malise . . . very slowly, I'll call out the height, ok?'

Malise nodded his head but didn't take his eyes off the instruments.

'Nine hundred . . . eight hundred . . . seven hundred, six, five, four, hold her there Malise. Can you see anything yet, General?'

The general was rubbing the port in front of him trying to keep it clear of condensation. 'I think so, Campbell . . . can you take her down very, very slowly but be ready to reverse and stop as soon as I tell you.'

Campbell and Malise exchanged glances. They were at a hell of a low and the strong wind was making it difficult to keep her stable, but they had to try.

'Going down, but for god's sake keep your eyes open, General, it will only take one mistake.' A deep growl was the only answer Campbell got.

'Three hundred . . . slower, Malise for Christ's sake . . . two fifty.' The small craft swayed as the updraft hit her belly.

'Landing gear down . . . two hundred.' Campbell's voice was getting higher in pitch the lower they got.

'Hold it . . . for Christ's sake, Malise, I can see something, try and hold her.' He pressed his face hard against the port to get a better wider view.

'Easy now . . . gently that's it . . . look out we're going, Christ, hang on!' There as an almighty bang as the high wind tipped the small craft onto her side and one of the three protruding legs snapped off half-way up, leaving her lying at a precarious angle. The engine groaned to an unsteady halt. The only thing they could hear was the whistling of the wind. Malise took stock of the cabin; it seemed to be pretty well intact but of the crew. Campbell lay unconscious, with his forehead gaping open and the blood pumping steadily onto the instrument panel. The general was just shaken.

'We are going to have to do something with this and quickly pass me the first-aid kit.' Malise found what he was looking for and stitched together the swollen flesh. He had just finished when Campbell came around. He groaned and wiped the blood from his eyes.

'Why the hell does it always have to be me?' Malise laughed and bandaged the oozing gash.

169

'It's because you heal quicker.'

'Thanks . . . what damage have we got?' Malise checked the circuitry: all seemed to be intact.

'I don't know about the external, I've been too busy sewing you up Campbell. We're at about a forty-five degree angle.'

'Will we be able to take off at that angle?' The general was trying to prize open the hatch with no success.

'I honestly don't know, General, but what we could do is plant a couple of small charges on the olio legs to go off just before we leave to bring us back level, it's worth a try!' The general didn't look very convinced. The hatch suddenly hissed open.

'Masks on, let's have a look at what we hit.' Luckily the hatch was facing towards the ground. They had to be careful not to fall out. It was still a good twenty feet to what ever it was below them. The general swung out onto the ladder.

'You two stay here and I'll have a quick look see, and if I tell you to get out . . . do it!' He quickly disappeared into the yellow mist.

'What do you say, Malise, do you really think we can get out of here?'

Malise shrugged and shook his head. 'We've got two choices.'

'Number one to number two, over.' Malise adjusted his set.

'Number two receiving you . . . come in General, over.' The general's voice sounded far away.

'You'll never believe it, Malise, we hit a bloody monastery, how's that for ironic?' The general's laughter filled the cabin and his two companions joined in.

'If I remember right it's called St Barnabas and it's not far from the cistern . . . there's not a sign of life down here but the visibility is really bad. The ground is as slippery as hell, god knows what it smells like. Have you got anything on the main detector screen?' Malise searched for any hidden life form but there was nothing. He tried for the crystal vibrations, still nothing. It could be they were too far away.

'There's nothing yet, general, is it ok for us to come out now . . . over.' The general begrudgingly gave his permission telling them to stay together when they hit the ground. Malise handed Campbell the mobile detector unit and slipped two charges for the legs into his jacket. The ladder was wet and slippery. Malise set the charges halfway down the remaining legs and joined Campbell. Under the ship was a pile of rubble obviously caused by the crash. They could only see about twenty feet in front of them, there was no sign of the general.

'Number two to number one, come in please . . . number two to number one, come in please. Where the hell are you, General?'

The static grew louder as they moved among the decaying buildings, Malise tried again to raise the general.

'Number two to numb . . .'

The general's voice broke in. 'Belt up Malise . . . there's movement out here. I don't think they've spotted me yet. Keep coming ahead but for god's sake keep off the air and be ready for them. Don't think twice, kill them!' Malise looked across at Campbell to make sure he understood, he answered by drawing his sword and nodding. They crept slowly through the yellow mist it made things worse by not being able to see the enemy. It was the enemies' terrain not theirs and they must know every inch, every hiding place, an ambush was on their side. Campbell took the lead which wasn't very reassuring as he kept disappearing every few yards as the thick swirling mist devoured him. This was not Malise's game and he didn't like it at all.

Malise felt the presence of the form before he saw it or rather stumbled over it. He bent on one knee to have a closer look . . . it had no head, at least not attached. It lay just to one side of the body, if you could call it that. It looked like one suppurating mass, pale green in colour and the whole body was covered in weeping sores. There was no sign of hair either on the body or the head, it was completely naked. The skin on the face was taught and clear; teeth were black stumps and the eyes deep set in the misshapen skull; in all it was a revolting sight. It had obviously met the general . . . Campbell was too close. He froze to the spot as something touched his shoulder: the steady pressure seemed to be trying to push him sideways. He let his hand travel slowly up his leg to his holster but the butt of his weapon was slippery to the touch and, as he tried to unbutton his holster, he froze. The pressure on his arm had increased and it was shaking him more and more violently. He heard a voice but it seemed so far away.

'For Christ's sake, Malise . . . move. Damn you or are you stuck to

171

the bloody spot . . . either move or I'll leave you here.' Campbell's sword glinted in front of his mask, he turned and looked at him and whispered quietly into his microphone.

'Campbell, one day somehow I'll get you for this, you nearly frightened the shit out of me, I thought it was one of them.' He pointed to the suppurating mess on the ground. Campbell flicked the head away with the point of his sword. Malise could see his broad smile through his fogged-up mask: the young bastard was enjoying it, he could have his share.

They came on the general crouching behind a ruined wall. Campbell had obviously caught up with him as he was using the portable detector unit. He had something, they crouched down behind him and looked over his shoulder. There were bodies moving about in front of them; they could pick up the slow movements. Not many but enough, the detector had also picked up the crystal, it was very faint but it was there.

'The entrance to the cistern is about two hundred yards away we'll move out together . . . have your weapons ready but don't use them unless you have to.' The general turned and looked at young Campbell and laid his gloved hand on his. He just sat for a moment saying nothing.

'Watch Malise, laddie . . . and don't turn your back on them.' They crawled on their bellies the last fifty yards stopping every few feet. They saw the creatures moving about, the noise they made was spine-chilling it was high pitched and easily penetrated their masks. It was a soulful sound similar to the cries they had heard in the Umbra, with the same startling effect. They had to clear the rubble from the entry hatch one stone at a time trying not to make the slightest sound. Malise's skills came into play as he dealt with the complicated combination. They surrounded the panel to stop the bright dancing lights stealing into the dim and dank surroundings . . . then they were in.

There was a rush of air as the panel cracked. They turned and looked at each other. The air purifier was still working – that meant they could discard their masks.

'Thank god for that, I could hardly see a thing out of it, could I Campbell?' The general looked at Campbell for an explanation, he in return only smiled at Malise.

'Leave your masks here, we can pick them up on the way back and

Malise, let Campbell and myself go first, we might need your expert brain to get us back out of here.'

'Suits me . . . ready when you are.' They made their way down into the depth of the old cistern. It was huge, broken into floors, rooms and companionways. There were statues everywhere they looked, richly carpeted from wall to wall but where were the people? There wasn't a sign of them but plenty of signs that they had been there. Partly eaten meals that had long since gone mouldy, glasses of drink of various kinds, clothes thrown carelessly onto a chair or bed, open doors and wardrobes. They made their way down into the depths of the cistern, floor by floor, till they came to a massive stainless steel air-tight door with the usual combination flickering its different colours to test the brain. The door was forty feet in height and this had to be a special place. Both his companions looked at Malise for an answer.

'We can only try it and see but what's behind it is anyone's guess. Mine is that it's the main assembly and control room for the whole complex and you know what that means.'

'No Malise, I don't, you tell us.'

'I think I know what Malise is getting at, sir.'

'You do Campbell . . . what?'

'We have found no one so far so they have to be in there!'

'Give that man a prize . . . there is nowhere else they can be. We haven't even found the trace of a body.' The detector screen was flickering wildly in both modes.

'At least we know where the crystal is.' The general's voice was no longer full of confidence. He too was now worried as to what was behind the great door.

'How's it going, Malise?' Campbell was hovering over his shoulder wanting to get in.

'I'm not sure, I've seen this once before but it was a long time ago.' He had taken the front plate off and was slowly manipulating the internal micro-switches, making sure he didn't cross one against the other, the last thing they needed now was a short circuit.

'How do you mean you have seen this before?' The general had moved in to watch him. Malise asked them both to move back a bit, his hands were running in sweat.

173

'As I said it was a long time ago. It was when we still had dogs in the city. One was taken very sick, in fact, it was rumoured that it was rabies. What they did was corner it in a room and lock it in, jumbling the combination so no one could get in or out. It was done on a time basis. I think that's what's been done here: they've locked themselves in from the other side and not just themselves, whatever was chasing them too, to stop them getting back out.'

'That's a bit far-fetched Malise, they wouldn't be that stupid.' Campbell stood shaking his head. The general said nothing. The creatures can make you do crazy things, he should know.

'Hang on a minute, I think I've got it, there'll be a few seconds' delay.' All three stood looking at the crack of the door, their eyes alert for the slightest movement.

'Have your weapons ready if it opens and stand still till I tell you to move.' The command was back in the general's voice. No one was going to argue . . . not this time. There was a slight movement then a judder. It grew louder as the door slowly opened. It opened unevenly as if it was pushing something out of the way, there was definitely something jamming it. Then it hit them: the smell, it rushed past them to fill the corridor and was swept on up to the higher levels seeking a way out and contaminating any clean air.

Malise felt his stomach heave. The vomit flew from his mouth in a great spray. If their masks had still been in place they would have drowned in their own sick. Never in Malise's wildest dreams had he smelt such foul-smelling emanation. Campbell was bent double, the general was hanging on to the face of the door for support. They each remained stock still for several minutes trying to get their constitutions under control.

'What the hell's happened to the lights, Malise?' The general's white, drawn face was running with tears of exertion. It was the first time Malise had noticed the deep lines under his eyes: he suddenly looked his age. Malise pressed his eyelids tightly shut to try and clear the nausea. His stomach's pumping action was slowing down and his muscles ached with the unaccustomed effort. He thought to himself, do we really want to see beyond the darkness? Whatever was making that smell had to be horrendous . . . little did he know . . . 'I might have cross-linked . . .

174

hang on a second.' He once more probed the micro switches nothing . . . then a spark, then a great blaze of light . . . then a plummet into hell.

The sight that met their eyes was so grotesque and on such a vast scale that their brains refused to react, only to look on in wonder and disbelief. There were bodies as far as the eye could see; some in great piles, as if harvested for future use; others with their limbs dislocated and broken even more, with their appendages torn roughly from their blood-spattered sockets. They all had one thing in common: the look of unspeakable fear, the look one sees on the face of a trapped animal when it is corned and knows it is about to die in a slow and savage way. Each walked his own course among the dead, his weapons ready for self defence or attack. God help anything that moved even if it was one of their own kind, their nerves were so raw they would never be able to stop themselves. Each body had a bloated look as the poison from the mutants' own immune system was breaking down, the once healthy bodies extracting every ounce of goodness.

Malise had to turn his head away to keep his emotions in check, a woman had been caught running with her child in her arms. She must have been thrown to the ground, her spine had been bitten through and she would have died instantly, but the child had died of suffocation through the weight of her mother's body crushing her tiny ribs and her eyes bulged with the internal pressure. The general knelt and took a young boy of about eight years old into his arms, his neck had been broken and his body flopped like a rag doll. He held his head steady and said something that Malise didn't quite hear, then bent and gently kissed the rosebud mouth. His tears washed the cheeks of the slender shell as he laid him on his chest to rest . . . for just a while.

Campbell's eyes darted into every shadow, his Claymore prodding its way to the fore. He was looking for the slightest excuse to use it, and it came when he least expected it. A body slipped from the middle gantry above him. He caught sight of it for a split second as it fell, he lunged with the reactions of lightning pinning the falling body to a large wooden door. The long sword had penetrated the chest of the dead woman, her bare breasts lay either side of the blade. There was no sign of blood for she was just a white rotting shell. His embarrassment became more acute as the body danced like a puppet as he tried to

175

withdraw his sword but it was stuck fast to the thick door. He placed his heavy boot on her body and pushed, there was a sharp crack as her crutch bone gave way, but his sword was free. He apologised under his breath and moved on. Nothing was alive in the chamber, at least nothing that resembled a human being. They had seen several mutants twitching but had not gone near. The three companions congregated at the far end of the chamber; they stood in silence for a moment each with his own thoughts. In all their lives they had seen nothing like this: it was even way out of the generals experience. Still, the world didn't end every day.

'One hell of a massacre.' The general's remark covered everything.

Young Campbell turned to Malise. 'Why have they changed colour, the mutants I mean and why have they died, I don't get it?'

Malise looked at the closest mutant – it was a pinkish colour instead of being the usual slimy green. The body sores that they were infested with had healed up and all that remained of them were white scars.

'It's only an educated guess . . . these creatures have lived for so long on next to nothing and even that had little or no nourishment that they have literally gorged themselves to death. The colour change I think came about with drinking the rich blood. The vitamins denied them so long have caused their bodies to react in such a way you have this pigment change and god knows what other biological changes and disturbances. In other words, the poor bastards don't know what's hit them, they seem to have become immobile.'

The smell had become manageable; it was strange how the human body coped even with mass carnage. Its acceptance level was enormous – it had the ability to shut out what it didn't want to know. Malise stood pointing the detector at different angles in the room, trying to find the strongest signal. The mass of electrical equipment did little to help. The false variation in the signal could be quite substantial in the huge chamber.

'If we fan out and go for the strongest signal it will be a start, Let's keep our eyes open and don't touch anything if you can help it. If any of us comes across it, shout for the others . . . don't try it on your own . . . got it?' The general and Campbell nodded. 'They fanned out, the general to the left of Malise, Campbell to his right, their eyes sweeping backwards and forwards for the slightest sign. On the third sweep, the detector was going haywire, the needle juddering on its pivot. Straight ahead of them was a great pile of bodies in various states of mutilation and decay. They stopped and searched the necks for any sign of the crystal; they just couldn't be sure for the bodies had been thrown onto the pile at all angles. Malise was just about to shout the others when Campbell's excited voice broke into his thoughts.

'Around the other side . . . it's here.' Malise and the general moved as fast as their protective clothing would allow. Campbell stood pointing his sword at some pathetic creature in front of him that made only the slightest move to protect itself or something . . . the something turned out to be a child, a mutant child. The general leant forward to have a better look: it was a female mutant. The body of a man lay beside her, it was obvious she had been feeding from it: great chunks of flesh had been torn from the naked torso, her long painfully thin arm lay across it as if to protect it from any other predator. Her other arm was clutching a very young child. It like its mother was pinkish in colour and it lay sucking on her now ample breast. The greyish liquid dribbled from its chin onto its belly, which looked as if it was about to burst, its large bulging eyes watched every movement the general made. The crystal lay in the well of the mother's neck, rising and falling with her shallow breathing. She was a poor and pathetic creature. The general thought to himself, there for the grace of god; his heart went out to them both knowing they would soon be free of their awful existence.

'What are you waiting for, sir? We can take it from her easily.' Campbell's cocksure voice rang in his ear, his sword appeared over his right shoulder on its way to the creature's neck. He pushed it to one side.

'For Christ's sake, Campbell, the poor bitch is defenceless look at her . . . that's not the way, every creature should be allowed some dignity.' Malise knelt down beside the general and watched the creature's reaction as the general spoke to her. Her large eyes were straining to watch all three at once, she was afraid but for her child more than for herself. As she pulled it closer, her nipple fell from its mouth. It panicked and lunged for her breast, its small sharp teeth sank into her swollen flesh, her involuntary start made the child lift its head revealing the punctures.

177

Pale red blood spurted into the air like small fountains, then subsided as the unnatural pressure was released. Her long slender right arm moved from her prize corpse and helped the child back to her breast which by now was red with blood. She turned her eyes once again on the three men, awaiting her fate, for it was surely in their hands. The loneliness of self-survival was etched in her large round eyes, their depth seemed to go on for ever.

'You know, general, I think it . . . she understands what we are saying, maybe not all of it but a good part, watch.' Malise moved a bit closer and the creature moved her head in his direction, watching his every movement. He tried her with a sequence of word suggestions: there was not the slightest hint of recognition, he tried signs still nothing.

'I'm afraid you're wrong Malise, this is getting us nowhere, the only way I can see without killing them is to take the child away from her, then take the crystal by force. Do you both agree?'

The creature's neck cracked as her head spun to face the general, both arms encircled the child and her eyes blazed.

Malise immediately twigged. 'Very clever, general, attack the enemies weakest point, yes?'

'Yes, Malise . . . if you like . . . but it worked.'

'Touché general . . . what now?' The general told them both to stand back so that he could move quickly if he had to. He handed Malise his sword and his laser, then held his hands above his head to show that he was unarmed, then he once again knelt down to face the female creature.

'We mean you no harm, we are not from this place, we are from far away, what has happened here was not all of your doing or all of your fault. All will be well soon for you and your child . . . but we need your help now!' She looked long at the general before replying. She slowly lifted one finger and inclined her large bulbous head in answer. The general looked over his shoulder at Malise in open triumph. He lifted his hand slowly so as not to frighten her and pointed to the crystal. It no longer shone brightly, its many colours now encased in one; the creature's blood had dulled its every facet.

'We have come a long, long way. It is needed for greater things than all of us, to make the world well again.' He sat for a moment letting his words be digested as well she could.

'To make you and your child well again, to walk in the sun without fear.' She looked down at the suckling child, her spidery fingers tried in vain to stroke the nodding head, her eyes welled and involuntary tears filled the corner of her mouth but there was no belief in her large wet eyes. The general moved closer putting his metal arm to the fore, he knew the consequences of being bitten.

'Will you give us the crystal . . . for all our sakes?' She looked at him for a long time. The general felt as if his soul was on trial. She answered him by the closing of her eyes and a slight shake of the head: it was in the negative.

'She must know we can take it if we want to.' Malise's voice was just above a whisper; the general replied in the same vein.

'Of course, she does that's what makes it more courageous. Would you sit there and do what she's doing?' Malise shook his head in reply. The general had only one other avenue and then, well, then there would be no other choice. At least he had tried and not just killed out of hand, in the very near future he wouldn't have that choice. He had never really been a religious man and with the religions of the world intertwining over the years it was hard to tell one from another. His family had, in the far distant past, been of Jewish stock and in that he had always felt a secret pride. She was still looking at him, he could see the fear in her eyes. He spoke softly to her, trying to gain her confidence.

'Do you remember God?' He looked upwards and raised his hands as if in prayer.

'The great one . . . up there.'

Malise grunted behind him. 'For Christ's sake, General, would you after being left like this.' The general spoke between clenched teeth. 'Look at her, Malise . . . look.'

The female creature was drawing something on her chest with a long ragged but sharply pointed fingernail. As she pulled her hand away, a contortion that could have been construed as a smile played on her grotesque feature. The two bright red weals stood out proud on her swollen flesh and all three men looked on in disbelief.

'It's a bloody cross . . . well, damn me.' The general pulled down the front zip of his suit and fumbled inside. Whatever he was after flashed in the light as he pulled it over his head. He looked at it for a moment

179

and offered it to the creature. Malise could see it plainly. It was a long, thick, gold chain with some sort of heavy misshapen pendant on the end; some sort of strange writing was cut deep into the shining metal. The general moved closer, offering it with his metal hand. Campbell gave a sudden gasp and disappeared from Malise's sight.

'I offer you this in exchange for the crystal. It is very special to me and is one of a pair of Mizpath pendants, it contains half of a Hebrew prayer. The other was given to the only woman I ever loved . . . or wanted, together they read! THE LORD WATCH BETWEEN ME AND THEE WHILE WE ARE ABSENT ONE FROM ANOTHER; I offer this precious thing to you.'

The creature's eyes once again ran with tears; it was obvious it was the first kind gesture she had ever encountered. The hand on the general's shoulder became more insistent. The hoarse voice of Campbell fell on his ear as he lent past him and put something shiny over his cold metal hand.

'She might as well have the pair . . . FATHER.'

The general leant forward and placed the two pendants together, the rich rose gold blended as one, the eccentric edges fitted exactly. He had had them made to his own design in what seemed an eternity ago. There were no others like them in the world. The strong grip on his shoulder tightened for a moment then relaxed, as if to point home that this was not a dream. Why now, why this moment, his head swam with images of the past and the present. He had felt that bond from the first, in the cardinal's chamber when he had defied him and levelled his laser at his chest and he would have used it too. He would have done the same when he was a young trooper and his head was full of principles, that had been his battle cry, the principle of the thing. He should have known by the smile alone and certain mannerisms. It all seemed to jell: he hadn't noticed what had been under his nose. He suddenly felt very old. His throat was sore and thick with restraint, he wanted to stand up and hold his new-found son to ask him a thousand questions, to search his face and form for likeness of himself and his beautiful Margo. He knew if he moved towards that goal he would be done for. General Zerta had to take command of the situation. He shook the tears of pain

180

from his eyes and cleared his throat, his lungs were almost bursting with restraint:

'One thing at a time boy, one thing at a time!'

Campbell removed his hand and stood back from the general, the look of disbelief on his face told of his rejection.

'Sorry, sir!'

Malise felt for both of them. The general looked as if he had been struck by a thunderbolt. If he wasn't careful he would lose control and for him that would be a disaster. His pride was like his compassion, strong and unwavering. The female creature had been watching the drama that had been unfolding before her. She was struggling to remove the chain of the crystal from around her neck. It was taking a tremendous effort. They were all willing her arm to reach the top of her head but it fell back in complete exhaustion. She lay with her eyes shut for a moment, she knew that death was not far away. Before either man could stop him, the general was at her side. She opened her eyes in alarm. The general sat very still for a moment then slowly placed one of the pendants around the child's neck; the female blinked and raised a finger in appreciation. She tried to lift her head but it was too much for her. The general slowly placed his hand around her back and supported her as he removed the crystal and replaced it with the shimmering pendant. The long fragile fingers wrapped themselves around the general's hand and pressed as hard as they could, then she was gone. He felt the life slowly drain from her body; the child's head fell forward as it followed its mother into a long-awaited peace. The general sat very still not knowing quite what to do.

'Help me up, Campbell, what the hell is your name anyway, your Christian name, I mean?' Campbell bent and helped the general to his feet. He could see the strain on his face; it wasn't easy for either of them.

'Aaron, sir, the same as yours . . . the Campbell was my grandmother's maiden name, they brought me up till I was old enough to join the military.'

Malise moved away it was now so obvious that they were Father and Son; it was one of those things that stare you in the face and you never

181

notice. He knew he wouldn't like to be in the general's shoes, or would he?

The general directed his son to a large bench and sat him down. He found it hard to look him in the eye.

'Did you know before a few moments ago, truthfully?'

Campbell had no inhibitions: he had found something he had been told didn't exist.

'No, sir, I had no idea but, like you, I had a feeling there was something more but what, I couldn't put my finger on.'

'Your mother is she . . .' Campbell's look stopped him.

'Dead, sir, she died when I was born.'

'How? A woman dying in childbirth has been unheard of for over a thousand years.'

'According to my grandmother, she just gave up, she said she didn't want a life without you. My grandmother tried to get my grandfather to change his mind and by the time he did, it was too late.'

'But why wasn't I told, they had no right.' His loud and self-righteous words rang hollow in his head, how hard had he tried after the first few years.

'You had no idea at all?'

'None sir, till a few moments ago, but I am very proud, sir.'

'Yes . . . yes but I'm not sure you should be, you don't really know me and I sure as hell don't know you!'

The general looked hard at the young man before him. He was taller than himself but very slim as he had been at his age. There was nothing he could do for him, it had all come too late. He had a lot of his mother in him, his calm eyes could have been hers, pride had overcome embarrassment and for the first time death was a frightening word. To have never known was one thing but to have found a son and to have death take him from you in such a short time was another.

'Aaron, it is difficult for me. I am used to commanding obedience. People see but one side of me. I have loved only once in my life and when I lost her I locked whatever feelings I had away.' The general felt the ache in his throat return as the look of confusion clouded the young man's eyes, but what could he do?

'Aaron, I just don't know how to handle it . . . the best thing to do is wait till we get back to Hydra then we can talk it out . . . all right?' He held out his hand to his son who took it gladly.

'Come on then, boy, let's make a move and get the hell out of this bloody place.' As Campbell bent to retrieve the two pendants, the general caught his arm and pulled him away.

'No lad . . . when you give your word, keep it, we don't need them any more we've got each other.' A large grin of satisfaction spread across Campbell's face: that was what he had wanted to hear.

'You're right, Father, let's get to hell out of here.' He made sure he was a few steps ahead of the general as they made their way through the maze of passages and eventually found Malise patiently awaiting them. He could tell by their expressions that some form of understanding had been formulated at least for now.

'What now, General?' Malise handed his two companions their masks.

'To the ship and clear off out of his damn place, but for god's sake be careful. We don't know what the hell is out there, check your weapons and your oxygen valve for clearance . . . ok?' They checked each other's backpacks and were ready. Campbell pushed his way to the front – he was even more determined to prove himself, now more than ever.

The only thing they could hear was a slight hiss as the heavy door slid back and the yellow haze was quick to enter. They left the door open, there was no point in shutting it, they wouldn't be going back and nobody down there would care that is for sure. Campbell pointed the way.

'The ship's over there . . . I'm sure, come on,' They were almost bent double as they entered a large open space. The ship was just visible, their breathing sounded loud and rasping in the confines of the sweltering masks. Malise was the first to spot them.

'Jesus, we're surrounded . . . the bastards are everywhere. What now, General, we don't stand a chance in hell, there's two of them.' The shadows moved against what light line there was: they could feel their presence rather than see them.

'Stand back to back and move slowly towards the ship, don't fire till I tell you, we might still have a chance.' They moved slowly across the square in a crablike fashion, their weapons at the ready.

'Malise!' The general's voice hissed through the earpiece of the masks.

'General.' Malise had never felt fear like it in all his life, it was fear of the unknown: they had seen at first hand what the creatures were able to do. They were completely incapable of pity: all they were interested in was survival; that meant food and they were the food.

'When I give you the word, Malise, make a break for the ship. If you can get her going, we will follow.'

Malise looked at the general in disbelief. The general nodded. 'Don't argue Malise . . . my boy and I will do our best to keep them off you.' Malise could almost see Campbell grow in stature. As far as he was concerned, there couldn't be a better way to die, standing back to back with his father. His clan war cry 'cruachan' screaming from his lips. His grandmother had always said he was a romantic, probably so. The ship grew larger as they slowly made their way across a rubble-strewn flat; they seemed to be moving out of their way.

'I don't get this, why don't they attack? They've got all the advantages . . . stop for a moment.' They knelt down but remained back to back.

The general's voice once more broke into their thoughts. 'There's something wrong . . . why have they let us get so close? See if you can see anything near the ship, Malise.'

Malise used the infra-red sight on the detector to get a better view of the terrain. He sat for a moment straining his eyes and his companions' nerves and finally handed the detector to the general and shook his head.

'Look underneath the ship, follow the outer ring.'

The general followed Malise's instructions. 'You know, Malise, I wouldn't have thought they would have the intelligence to do that.'

'Do what?' Campbell's voice was high with excitement. He was peering into the mist but could see nothing of any real significance.

'The bastards have plugged the engine intakes with rubble, no wonder they are not in a hurry. What the hell do we do now? Without the ship we go nowhere, or the crystal.'

They sat back to back, each trying to hatch a workable plan. Their suits were now beginning to take on the colour of the mist: they ran with yellow streaks, yellow droplets made patterns on their visors, like small rivers hustling and bustling their way to the sea or some great lake. Malise smiled to himself; he used to enjoy visiting the pleasure area in the dome. His favourite was the rain sector where you could go and walk for hours in the imitation fields and forests. He loved the noise of the rain as it sprayed his protective clothing. He loved the feel of it as it ran down his face and always found a crack in his collar, it was so clean even if it wasn't real.

'Malise . . . Malise!'

He grunted as the general's elbow crashed into his ribs. 'Are you all right, Malise?'

He turned and nodded. His thoughts were his own even at this late date.

'I know what it looks like and we might all be right but I've been thinking. We know one thing about these creatures: they are not very strong, so whatever they have packed into the intakes can't be very large or pushed in very far, do you get my drift, Malise?'

Malise nodded but didn't give it much of a chance of success.

The general continued. 'The plan more or less as before, we will get as close to the ship as we can. You, Malise, will try and clear both the intakes while the lad and I will do our best to protect you.'

As they moved closer to the ship, they could feel they were being watched. The general made his stand under the shadow of the outer edge of the craft and motioned Malise on.

'Get inside and put the floodlights on. They know we're here and we know they're there, so for Christ's sake let's have a look at them; I like to see what I'm fighting.'

Malise made his way to the hatch and punched in the entry number. The acceptance lights shone bright for a second then dimmed. The door was jammed but Malise gave it an almighty kick and it clicked open. The general's voice whispered in his ear:

'Very technical Malise . . . let's hope you are as lucky with the intakes; get the bloody lights on.'

Malise reached forward and flicked on all main lights. After his eyes became accustomed he wished to hell he hadn't. They were everywhere, they were completely surrounded. There had to be hundreds of them, their wet green bodies reflected back the bright lights. They looked like giant frogs as they moved slowly forward, tightening the ring. The general and Campbell came out from under the ship and stood back to back watching them approach. They both stood the same, laser in one hand and sword in the other, the general's voice blared in his ears.

'It's too late to clear the ducts, Malise, try and start her as she is, don't and I repeat don't come back outside . . . and Malise, if you have to go on your own, are you receiving me Malise . . . for Christ's sake, answer!' Malise tore off his mask and reached for the mike switch.

'Receiving you loud and clear, General, trying her now.'

He threw the four ignition switches. There was a low whine that became louder by the second then died he tried again with the same result. She was going nowhere with fouled intakes, what the hell now?

'She won't have it, General, I'll have to come out.'

'Stay where you are, Malise, there's no point, look.'

The two men were completely surrounded. Their lasers killing as fast as they could pull the triggers, they couldn't miss. Young Campbell tore off his mask and screamed 'cruachan' at the top of his voice. He lunged forward and cut a gaping wound in the nearest creature's side, then slashed again, taking an arm, then opened up another's chest. His claymore ran with blood as he cut down all before him. The general was taking his toll, there were bodies all around him but there were just too many for them. Young Campbell staggered and slipped, the nearest mutant sank its teeth into his upper arm leaving a large gaping wound from which the blood spurted in time with his pulse. The general waded his way through the bodies to his son's side, he knew the excruciating pain he must be in. Also it meant his certain death. Another creature bit into his other arm, causing him to drop his sword. He staggered to his feet, both his arms hanging uselessly by his side – he was completely defenceless. He turned and looked at his father, a look that only a son can give. He opened his mouth to shout 'sorry' but it never came. His father's samurai sword whistled through the air, cutting its target clean. The smile was still on young Campbell's face as his head left his body, his torso buckled at the knees and he was down.

'Malise, can you hear me . . . Malise, for the love of Christ, answer me . . .' Malise tried to answer but nothing came out. He wet his lips and coughed but nothing.

'Try using the crystal, Malise, it's your only chance . . . try and good
luck . . . tell Hydra I'll be waiting, goodbye friend.'

Malise watched in macabre fascination as the general spun round in
a circle forcing the creatures back from his son's body. He threw off his
mask and looked over his shoulder at the dead craft. Malise couldn't
quite make out his last words as his tears were almost blinding him. The
general lifted the beautiful sword and held it in front of him for a
moment then buried it deep in his chest. The blade passed through and
out the other side, glinting like a star in the bright lights. He knelt by
the body of his son, kissed his hand and was gone. The creatures stood
for a second, as if in reverence to two great warriors, then tore the
bodies apart.

Malise felt numb now he was alone but there was one thing: they
couldn't get into the craft but on the other hand he couldn't get out.
As much as he hated the ugly bastards he knew it wasn't their fault.
Their survival was a basic instinct. At least they wouldn't be forgotten
in the gathering, Hydra had promised that. Their souls were as pure as
any other. Their condition was a crime of man's choosing. He dug deep
into his pocket and retrieved the crystal. It was matted with blood. He
spat on the stone and wiped it clean. He removed his protective suit
and returned to the observation port where he could see nothing of the
bodies of his companions. The whole area was now covered with
the creatures: they knew that he was inside, all they had to do was wait.
He placed the crystal inside his cupped hands and thought of Shla . . .
his beautiful Shla.

10

The Gathering

He felt his body sink as the ground beneath him turned soft and warm. He kept his eyes shut as he lowered his hands and felt around him. If he hadn't travelled far, they would still be there, if death was to come, let it come fast and without acknowledgment. His senses slowly began to return, the smells of life played on his nostrils, the warm sand trickled slowly through his fingers, each grain a world on its own, sounds of living things filtered into his befuddled brain. Then the greater realisation . . . the smell of her.

His swollen eyes slowly unglued themselves, fought for their right to focus, then he saw her, unless it was a dream, he was back. She sat crosslegged, her hands open in front of her, her head bent as if looking at the crystal, shining brightly in her palm but her eyes were tightly shut, she was completely naked. Her beautiful body seemed to hang with age, her long black hair was matted with beads of dried sand, her eyes had sunk into her once beautiful face – she had aged a hundred years. He lent forward to touch her, she couldn't be dead, she had promised to wait.

'Leave her Malise . . . she will recover . . . she is truly yours, my friend. She started her vigil one hour after you left and has not moved since. You must have felt her, she has almost destroyed herself giving you protection and bringing you back to her. But she will survive, just leave her, she is stronger than you could ever imagine.' He bent and took the crystal from her hand and Malise surrendered his willingly.

'Come, Malise, let's go to my . . . sorry, our chambers. We have final arrangements to make.' Malise was finding it hard to cope with the physical change in Shla, she looked like a living shell and so vulnerable. Hydra encircled Malise's shoulders with his long slim arm and directed him towards the temple.

'I promise you, Malise, she will recover fully . . . but in her own time. There is nothing we can do here, come my friend.'

The two men spent the next few days in each other's company. Hydra showed Malise everything that he deemed important. He patiently answered the thousand and one questions Malise was to ask.

'I, too, have a question Malise, you still hold the last card in this grand game and I would like you to play it now. For you still have the choice, what is it to be, a new life among the stars, or the keeper of this bowl of dust till genesis comes again. The time has come my friend, your choice is my destiny, yours is in your hands.'

Malise sat back and closed his eyes. The choice was as though he was drowning: his life played before his eyes. Why should he stay? He could start all over again with his family, his wife, his mother, his father, Chez, everyone he had ever known and loved. Why stay? He had no real allegiance to this entity and he had already told him he had the choice a gift that this planet had been given.

'Malise . . . *Malise.*' He opened his eyes and she was there, gone was the creature he had seen on the beach. She stood as she had been, young and the most beautiful and desirable woman he had ever seen. Her red eyes flashed at him in defiance daring him to make the wrong choice. They all knew there was only one choice: it had been made for him a long, long, time ago.

He took her hand and kissed her gently. She melted into his every contour. She had nearly destroyed herself for him; there was only one answer. Hydra stood waiting with the patience of the ages.

'I am your new keeper Hydra . . . God help me.'

Hydra smiled and took his hand. He removed a large gold ring from the second finger of his left hand and placed it on Malise's what looked like a large diamond. It felt warm to the touch and its centre glowed as if on fire.

'That ring is the master key to the whole crystal bank only you have the power to use it. With this, you control all the twelve energies that will be stored there.'

Malise felt confused. 'Will be stored?'

Hydra smiled in reply. 'Yes Malise . . . will. Those stored now have served me for thousands of years. Surely you do not begrudge them their freedom to live a normal life again?' Malise wasn't quite sure what he felt.

'They will be replaced by the second orb, after, a long time after, it has laid its seeds, twelve will be chosen, each for their special gifts to help you rebuild your world. You will have an advantage that I never had; you will have the records of the first keeper to guide you. You also have all the time in the world to study them.'

'What of the group in the ships? Who the hell are they? You haven't mentioned them or come to that – the general and young Campbell.'

Hydra sat down heavily, he looked tired and drawn. 'Malise those on the ship, everything has an equal and an opposite well that will be yours. You will still be left with your choice for good or evil. As for my friend and his son, I knew their fate before they left and indicated as much to Aaron. He knew he would not be coming back, so he took his son with him. He wasn't going to let him go after just finding him under these circumstances, would you?'

Malise felt strange. A tingling sensation seemed to be reaching into every pore, the same sort of feeling he felt when he first met Hydra, as if he was being scanned. He could hear the blood pound in his ears and a surge of unusual energy filled his body – he felt strong and young again.

'What's happening to me Hydra, Hydra?' His body glowed with energy, his aurora spat all the colours of the spectrum into the scented air, then he was still. Hydra smiled and nodded his head in satisfaction.

'So, now it is complete. You are the keeper. You have the power and the knowledge of all mankind at your very fingertips. Use it well, my friend, and I thank you for my freedom.' The light had almost gone from his eyes. He looked very old and very tired. Shla knelt before him and bowed her head. He kissed her gently and stroked her long black hair.

'You are my only regret. You have served me long. I leave you my love and my body. I take only my soul to start again.'

'Hydra . . . Hydra?' A sudden panic struck Malise; did he know enough? What did he do now, how long, how long? His voice seemed to echo inside his skull.

'He's gone Malise.' Shla spoke quietly and calmly. 'Let's put his body to rest then see to the crystals.' They buried him on the far slope, among the young pine trees. It had been his favourite spot to sit and meditate. There were no words said, there was no point, he knew all there was to know.

The crystal bank shone brightly as they approached. Malise was sure he could hear the locked-in souls crying for their freedom, for they would serve only one master and he was waiting for them. Malise put both the halves of the crystal together and replaced them in their niche and the whole bank hummed with life. He bent to place the ring in the centre quadrant as Hydra had instructed him. Shla took his hand in hers and squeezed it tightly.

'When you place the ring in the quadrant, shut your eyes tightly . . . just do it, Malise!' She had already closed hers. He placed the ring in the designated spot, lowered his head and tightly shut his eyes. Nothing happened for a moment, then he felt the heat. It grew hotter and hotter until it was almost unbearable. Then the noise like a thousand cats screaming in the night, the pitch rose higher and higher till Malise thought his eardrums would burst. Then nothing for a few seconds. The quietness was almost as loud as the screaming.

'They've gone Malise . . . Malise, it's all right, it's all over, there's just you and me . . . and of course the animals. 'Her voice was high with excitement, it was a new start for both of them and she didn't have to be alone. The crystal bank looked dead, all the precious life that it had held had gone. The history remained but the life had gone; it would live again one day. They walked down onto the glistening white sands and walked along the water's edge, fingers entwined, each with their own thoughts until questions once again started to grow in Malise's busy mind.

'Shla, how do we cope with time, I mean the kind of time we will have to endure before the world is whole again, at least the land anyway?' She drew herself to him to give him what comfort she could, she knew it would never be easy for him. He had lived by clocks, by hours, days, weeks, years, he would have to adjust or it would drive him crazy. She had known both sides.

'Try to forget time as you have learned to know it. Here you can sleep as long or as short as you wish, a day, a week, a thousand years. You will grow no older Malise, for you and I time has stopped.' He looked down at her. She was indeed beautiful in form and in spirit, her strange red eyes held a look that would have haunted him for ever had he gone. He would have to take things as they came, she would teach him and he would learn in her time.

'What the hell is that, look!' Malise pointed to the sea. It was alive with jumping fish – the water looked as if it was boiling. The dolphins were skimming across the water, their tails thrashing desperately to keep them upright, their sonic screech ear splitting. Great flocks of birds filled the air, each intermingling with the other; their frenzy was one of utter panic. Animals darted in all directions, as if trying to hide from some invisible enemy. The panic spilled over to the two humans. They ran as fast as their legs would carry them closing the heavy temple door behind them. Malise looked at Shla, her chest was rising and falling at a painful rate as she gasped for breath. Fear was stamped on her beautiful face, Malise reached across and took her hand she clung to him for comfort.

'What the hell caused that?' They could still hear the uproar through the thick doors. Malise looked to Shla for an answer but he could see by her expression that it was new to her.

'I don't know, Malise, unless . . .'

Malise spun her round to face him. 'Unless what Shla, has this happened before?'

'No, never.'

'Then what do you think it is, for Christ's sake?'

'Let's go to the crystal bank just to be sure.'

'You can be an aggravating bitch Shla, what do you think it is?' She laughed and ran off. He followed close behind her. As they turned into the building that housed the crystal bank, they stopped short in their tracks. The crystals they had left only a short time before had come alive again. No, more than alive, the room was ablaze with colour, each was flashing, alternatively bouncing their multi-fractured flashes off all four walls and the effect was extraordinary. Malise found his heart beat adjusting to the flashes. He pulled Shla from the room. They both sat on the lush green grass and said nothing for what seemed an eternity. Malise finally gave way to his curiosity.

'If it's not asking too much, what do you think caused the panic?'

She smiled at his impatience. 'There is only one thing it can be, as I said it has never happened before not as long as I have been alive but . . .'

He stopped her in her tracks. 'Oh come on Shla, what the hell is it?' His temper was beginning to rise, she knew she had pushed him too far.

'It can only be one thing, Malise, with the animals reacting the way they did, it's got to be the ship, Fadar's ship. It's arrived and they know it. It must be sending out powerful signals that they can detect, well, just look at the crystals in there.'

Malise felt the hair slowly rise up on the back of his neck. It was one thing to talk about a greater being that controls the universe but to be confronted by him was another thing. He knew Shla had to be right but he didn't expect it to arrive so soon even now it was hard for him to take in. All of it from the word go had been like a dream. He wouldn't have been surprised if he woke up and found himself back in the domed city with Chez knocking on his door to get him up for work for the umpteenth time. He knew it was no dream. He had seen too much blood and lost too many friends for it to be anything but reality.

'What now Shla?' The question was as much to himself as to her. She sat staring straight to her front her unblinking eyes looked like marble.

'Shla..Shla?' He shook her shoulders till she blinked and looked up at him, she still looked strange as if she hadn't been listening to him at all.

'What's the matter Shla, what's happened?'

She looked at him and smiled. 'It was Hydra. He wants us to come to the ship now. The gathering has been done, we can stay for a short time but we must return.'

He looked at her and shook his head. 'That's an amazing gift. Will you teach me how to do it, and how pray are we to get to the ship?'

She threw her head back and laughed. Her long black hair fanned out and laid itself across her back.

'To the first part of your question, yes I will, to the second part, the same way as you got back the crystals, so he says. We have to use the crystal number one and crystal number twelve to make an even balance, you have to place your ring in the central quadrant and leave it there as a homer. We have to do it as quickly as possible, come on.'

Malise had no option. She pulled him into the crystal bank. The flashes almost blinded them as they reached for their respective crystals. They each took half and placed them about their necks. He took Shla's hand before inserting the ring. He only hoped she knew what they were doing because he hadn't the faintest idea. He lent forward and pressed the ring home. He shut his eyes as the nausea overtook him once again. There was no noise, nothing, he couldn't feel anything solid under his feet. He wanted to open his eyes but he had to admit to himself he was absolutely terrified. He felt Shla's hand press his to attract his attention. She had obviously opened her eyes, her squeeze became more and more insistent. He slowly parted his eyelids. His brain mentally vomitted. He was not in the ship, he was on it. They were hovering about a foot above the giant ship before they slowly came to rest on its surface.

'Why here, Shla, why not inside the damn thing? If I wasn't now immortal I would be bloody dead, from shock.'

'I wanted to see what it looked like and how big it was, you couldn't tell that from inside.'

Malise slowly turned full circle, not letting go of Shla's hand. It was big. Big wasn't the word for it. He couldn't think of one that would cover it. It stretched as far as the eye could see. Its shape was that of a cross and it was the largest thing he had ever seen. It had to be hundreds of miles long. Its very size was frightening. The moon looked uncomfortably close and he could see every crater and shadow.

'Look, Shla, moonbase.' It stood out proud and foreign, man's first step on another floating world. Faces flickered through his memory, faces of friends and colleagues he had served with on his three years of

194

service there. They had to be inside with the rest, hundreds of millions of people. It was way beyond the human concept and imagination.

'Shla, for god's sake, let's get inside the bloody thing, now!'

As they concentrated, they seemed to melt into the metal again. They felt nothing under their feet. It was only blackness that met their eyes, not the slightest chink of light. Malise tightened his grip on Shla. If he let her go he would never find her again. They stood in the darkness waiting for something to happen. Malise felt his heart racing in his chest. Shla squeezed his hand for comfort. She had no idea what to expect.

'Malise, what now?'

He grimaced at her in the dark. 'I haven't the foggiest idea.'

'You earth creatures are so pathetic and lacking in imagination. You have virtually learned nothing.'

A deep male voice filled their heads, followed by a higher female vocalism. 'They are only young, my love, this is their first gathering. Have patience, they are not to know.'

'Who are you?' Malise's voice sounded flat and unimpressive.

'We are the gatherers.' The blatantly simple reply stopped Malise in his tracks. Shla continued for him.

'Where are you, what are you, why don't you show yourselves?'

'We are what you want to see, we are whatever you want us to be, we are everything and nothing, we are your darkness or your light.' The pupils of their eyes felt as if they would burst with the suddenness of their contraction. The area had become flooded by a brilliant white light. They could still see nothing.

'Turn the damn light down before you blind us.'

'Turn it down yourself, you turned it on.'

Malise shouted into the brilliance that was bent on searing their eyes out. 'I don't understand, you'll have to help us we just don't know.' The female voice pacified the male counterpart and spoke to Malise in a soothing tone.

'It is easy to explain, when we said light, you thought light. Its intensity is due to the depth of the darkness you found yourself in, you over-compensated, that's all.' Malise thought of a dimmer switch in his minds eye and slowly turned it to the left. The light dimmed to a tolerable level and Shla squeezed his hand in appreciation. Malise smiled at her.

'As simple as that!'

'Yes, keeper, as simple as that. Now relate it to all things for the short time that you are here. For nothing has form as you know it. We are energy, unlike yourselves. You have substance and still have the need to see substance. All that were gathered have travelled well beyond such triviality.'

'We would like to see you, and the others who were our friends but how?'

'We are as close as your imagination, keeper, use it and we will be there for you.' Her gentle voice had a hypnotic quality that soothed the worst doubts in Malise's mind.

The scene formed before them: brown mosaic floors and great columns pointing to the sky; the sun played down on them through the roofless temple, white doves fluttered from one roost to another, the richness of the Roman architecture eased itself from Malise's memory. Two figures stood beside an ornate pool: a statue of Mercury, the messenger of the gods, stood in the centre, small golden fish played at his feet.

'What now keeper?' The man was tall and bronzed, his pure white toga was trimmed with scarlet to indicate his citizen stature. She was slim and wore a silk tunic decorated by a coloured shawl.

'As I said, you earth creatures have little imagination. You all have the same concept of life after death – everything must be white and clean, colours do not die with your body, the spectrum is the same everywhere.' Malise blinked and he was gone at least from sight. He turned to the female.

'I'm sorry.'

She smiled back at him. 'It is your prerogative, your friends await you but you haven't much time.'

Malise and Shla looked around them but could see nothing.

'We will release you when we are ready, there will be no warning, bring only those you want to see.'

'Malise . . . Malise.' The voice came from behind him and he spun around on his heel – it was the general and young Campbell. There was something about the general that seemed different. Then he realised he had both his hands. Gone was the metal glove and he looked so young. Their gold pendants shone in the sunlight. Malise pointed to them.

'How?'

The general laughed. 'She found us and returned them, don't ask me how anything is possible here. It's so beautiful Malise, everything and everybody you ever saw or knew, no pain, no suffering, and this is my Margo.' She was tall and slender. She looked more like Campbell's sister than his mother, no wonder the general had never forgotten her.

'Malise, Shla!' Hydra took Malise's hand and shook it warmly. Shla kissed him gently on the forehead and moved slightly behind Malise as if to point out that she was his woman now.

'Isn't it everything I promised Malise, there is no fear here, only harmony.'

Malise shook his head. 'To be honest Hydra I still have the awful feeling that this is all a dream. What will they do with you now?'

'Take us and plant us as seeds in another part of creation. Our energy will be used where it will do most good. It is all part of the experiment.'

'Experiment?'

'Yes, Malise, that's all we are all our planet was used for. We were grown as you would grow a culture and when the experiment had grown to its conclusion, it is harvested and planted elsewhere. We have no say in the matter. The only reward we have is rebirth somewhere, our planet is only one grain in the desert of the gathering, as he constantly reshuffles the universes.'

'He?' Malise tried to keep Hydra's eyes on his.

'No, Malise, that is even too much for me, he has to be obeyed not questioned.'

'Simeon.' The gentle voice that had haunted him all these years touched his brain. He had seen her smile a million times. She had even smiled as the carpet had taken her and his father's life. He felt as if he couldn't move. His legs were like lead, as he tried to run. His eyes blurred as tears of joy welled up inside him.

'Mother?' She looked younger than he remembered her. His father stood, as always, with his large protecting hand on her tiny shoulder. His smile always looked as if it had been painted on, as it never differed.

They stood not saying a word, their arms making a circle of love. The lavender his mother always used was strong in his nostrils. Tears of contentment washed each of their faces in turn.

There was no point in speaking. There was just too much to say and not enough time to say it. As he bent to kiss his mother, his stomach was thrown to the back of his spine and all went blank. When he opened his eyes, Shla was stroking his forehead, his head was resting on her lap. There wasn't a sound to be heard the water was calm and still.

'Gone?' The question could only have one connotation. She smiled and kissed him.

'Yes, my love, gone.' They hadn't given him time to see Ula. Maybe it was for the best. He looked at Shla's beautiful face and knew it was. The shining orb above him seemed to throb with life. He wondered how long it would be before it planted its seeds in fresh pure air. He knew one thing for sure, they would be ready for the next **GATHERING**.

THE END
OR
THE BEGINNING